knockout mouse

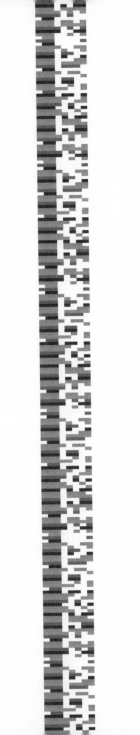

a bill damen silicon valley mystery

knockout mouse

james calder

CHRONICLE BOOKS
SAN FRANCISCO

acknowledgments I'm very grateful to my editor Jay Schaefer for his insight and guidance, and to Phil Cohen for sharing his time and expertise. Nurshen Bakir, Ted Conover, and Leslie Kogod were enormously helpful in reading early drafts. Many thanks also to Dr. Jeff Kishiyama for his expertise, and to Ralph King, Leslie Chao, Dr. Julia Gray, Suleyman Bahceci, Andy Black, Rita Roti, Lambert Meertens, Dr. Robert Leibold, Pam Strayer, Josh Crandall, KT Epstein, and Sasha for their generous help. Needless to say, any errors or shortcomings in this book are mine alone. —*James Calder*

Library of Congress Cataloging-in-Publication Data available.

ISBN: 0-8118-3499-9

Printed in the United States of America

Book and cover design by Benjamin Shaykin
Cover photo by Victor Cobo
Composition by Kristen Wurz
Typeset in Miller and Nillenium

Distributed in Canada by Raincoast Books
9050 Shaughnessy Street
Vancouver, British Columbia V6P 6E5

10 9 8 7 6 5 4 3 2 1

Chronicle Books LLC
85 Second Street
San Francisco, California 94105
www.chroniclebooks.com

For my parents

CHARLEY: You're pushing thirty, slugger, you know, it's time to think about getting some ambition.

TERRY: I always figured I'd live a little bit longer without it.

—*On the Waterfront*

1

I was not where I was supposed to be.
A crayon box of cartop colors glittered in the parking lot: Lexus
gold, Boxster blue, cyborg silver. The hood of my own car, a sun-
faded burnt orange, was propped open with an unbasketed ski
pole. I was unscrewing the air filter's wing nut when I saw the
SUV go round a second time.

I was supposed to be in the woods today, not stuck in the
Silicon Valley miasma. Wednesday rambles had become a ritual
since I'd left all this behind. But a friend had asked me to shoot
an industrial film for her, and I still needed to pay the rent, not
to mention some debts my alleged partners had stuck me with
from my last, truly last, venture in this neighborhood.

I lifted the air filter off and leaned in to examine the carbu-
retor. The choke was closed. I inhaled deeply. My engine had an
aroma all its own, rich in ancient oils, rubber, and steel. It was
the only smell with any real texture in this freshly planted parking lot, which served a complex of new tech office buildings.

The SUV came around again. I saw it from the corner of my
eye. A woodland green Lexus with smoke-gray windows. I might
not have noticed it, but by this point in my life I'd developed an
almost unconscious habit of playing cinematographer to my

day. I reflexively composed colors, patterns, shadows, and light into a frame. When I was here in the valley, it helped make order out of the disjointed landscape of freeways, corporate campuses, and commercial strips.

This was the third time the Lexus had entered the shot. I'd have felt better if I could see who was inside. I'd managed to make only one new enemy today, a small number on a job like this. Our client's marketing guy had attempted to educate me on what the look of the picture should be: handheld camera, desaturated color, that "gritty independent look." I told him he watched too much MTV.

Pressing down one side of the choke, I used an old cork to prop open the other side. As I straightened, I felt eyes on my back. The SUV was creeping down the row behind me. I turned to track it. My squint failed to penetrate the tinted windows. There were plenty of spaces in the lot, so why was he circling me like a cat on the prowl?

I tried the ignition again. The engine still wouldn't catch. I slumped into the seat. The dials were dead circles on the dash. My skin stuck to the seat back. There was no way I should be having this kind of trouble on a warm fall day.

A smudge of woodland green flashed in the rearview mirror. It was coming down my row again. I adjusted the mirror and watched it roll by. No security emblems, no company names on the doors. What did it want?

When it had passed, I got out and opened the tailgate. Behind my camera cases was a small cardboard box. Inside the box was a gas can and a hair dryer. I grabbed the can, took it 'round front, and slopped some gas into the choke. By the time I was back in the driver's seat, woodland-green was gliding down the row in front of me. I stared straight at him and cranked the ignition hard.

The starter huffed pitifully, a sign the battery was draining. I went back to the cardboard box. It contained one more option. As I unwrapped the blow dryer from its cloth, the SUV came 'round the corner and back down my row. I took a couple of steps into the lane and waited. The vehicle jolted to a stop, not quite blocking me in. Two doors opened.

The driver was young, yet stood with an air of casual author-ity, as if he'd pulled me over in a patrol car. But he was too stylish and smug to be a security guy. He wore a tight-fitting silk crew neck and creased pants. His hair was golden yellow, several shades lighter than mine, and cut more expensively than the scruffiness on my head. A little blond patch sprouted from his chin. Wraparounds shaded his eyes.

We stared at one another. At six foot two, he had a couple of inches on me. Maybe I did look a bit suspect among the sleek cars in this mint-new lot, stripped down to my ribbed under-shirt, tinkering with a battered old International Harvester Scout. But this would be the last car I'd pick to steal, and it was unlikely I was attempting a holdup with the blow dryer.

"Waiting for my parking space?" I asked him.

"Nah. There's one with my name on it over there. You look like you need some help."

I shrugged. "Ignition problems."

He glanced at the dryer. "Guess you've got them under con-trol."

"Is there something you want?"

The driver's stance remained casual. He steadied himself, as if on a sailboat, removed his glasses, and put out a hand. "Gregory

Alton. This is my partner, Ron." He pointed to the passenger, who stood stiffly and waved. Ron was stockier, with short brown hair. Apparently he didn't rate a last name. "We have a company called BioVerge."

Right, BioVerge: one of the occupants of the office park in whose lot I was stuck, along with Stellar Micro Devices, Campton Systems, and Kumar Biotechnics. Each company had its own four-story building, glass-skinned arrangements of cubes reflecting a liquid version of the checkerboard lot back into our eyes.

I stuck my grease-stained, gasoline-scented hand into Gregory's smooth palm. "Bill Damen."

"You met with Arun Kumar this afternoon," he said.

"That's right."

"Why?"

"To sign a nondisclosure agreement."

He gave a woofing sort of chuckle. "I guess I wouldn't want you to talk to strangers if you were working for me, either. You're doing a job for Arun. That's nice. He hires the best."

His gaze shifted to the dark bag in the back of my jeep. "You're the shooter. We tried to catch your boss—Rita, right?— but she took off. You guys are a good team."

I remained silent, waiting for him to come out with whatever he was nosing around for. He stumbled over that a minute, then said, "We want you to do some work for us."

"Oh yeah?" I stalled, debating whether I wanted to hear more. The guy's method of introducing himself had not endeared him to me. With the Scout acting up, I was already late for Jenny's dinner party. On the other hand, I knew I shouldn't let a business opportunity go by.

"You should talk to Rita," I said. "I'm just the camera operator."

He eyed the camera bag in my cargo space again. "What'd you shoot today?"

"Not much. The real shooting doesn't begin until next week."

"I just wanted to see a sample of your work. What kind of gear you got?"

I sighed. They always wanted to see the gear. I unzipped the bag and hefted out the camera. "It's a Sony 900 HD. Wide format, twenty-four frames per second, progressive scan."

Gregory whistled appreciatively. I didn't mention that it was rented. "Why not thirty frames, like most video?"

"That's the point. It looks more like film at twenty-four. I can also vary the frame rate to shoot in slo-mo."

"Sweet."

He was trying to pull me in. Generally, the best way to get rid of tourists like Gregory is to point the camera at them. I powered it up and put it in his face. "Gregory Alton, who are you and what is BioVerge's real mission?"

He grimaced for a moment, caught off guard. But then, just my luck, he proved himself a true member of the media generation by pulling a pose.

"As a matter of fact, Bill, we're about to roll out some proprietary software that's going to knock the sector on its ass. We'll bust an IPO a year from now, and in two years we'll be buying islands in the Caribbean and drinking daiquiris. You're invited."

He curled his lips into a smug grin. Smooth, no real information, ball back in my court. I zoomed in until the frame was filled with parallel lines of big, straight, white teeth. Rita would see it all on tape and be able to decide whether she wanted to call him back or not.

I lowered the camera. Ron-the-partner finally spoke up. "What kind of work are you doing with Kumar?"

"Nothing special. They've got a stockholder meeting coming up." I figured this was public information. To keep them from prying any more, I hoisted the camera back to my shoulder, pivoted, and began to shoot the lot and the BioVerge building behind it.

A woman walked into the frame from behind a black Range Rover. She had long, ringletted dark hair and a troubled face. Her right shoulder was weighed down by a bulky leather bag. When she saw us, her eyes went wide and she ducked behind a car. The next thing I knew, she was moving quickly in the opposite direction.

"Those were some guilty eyes," Ron said.

Gregory smirked. "Guilty or not, they rate a closeup."

I ignored him and packed away the camera. "If you want to give me your card, I'll pass it along to Rita."

Gregory gave me his card and said, "Hey, why not come up to my office? I've got a keg. The beer's always cold."

I stowed the camera bag and took the hair dryer in hand again. "Sorry. I've got to blow-dry my car."

He strode with me around to the front. "You don't understand. We *seriously* want to work with you. We'll double your fee. You and Rita are top guns. Your stuff is killer."

The bullshit was on full blast now. First of all, Rita and I weren't really a team. She was an old friend, and I liked to work with her, but we were no juggernaut. Nor were we widely known. Second, she only did tech industrials to support her real work. And third, every time I stepped foot into this world I was breaking a vow I'd made nine months ago. The catch was, my current financial situation didn't leave me much choice.

"Fine. I just can't talk to you right now. I'm late for a dinner party. I'll give Rita your card."

He frowned at me, then reached for the cell phone in his belt holster. The phone rang in his hand. He was delighted, as if he'd pulled off a magic trick.

"Gregory," he answered. He turned his back on us and retreated to the SUV.

I got back to work under the hood, prying the clips from the distributor cap. Ron peered through the driver's side window. "Look at that AM radio. A certifiable antique. You get anything on it?"

"My jeep does. Weather reports. Twenty percent chance of rain today. That means a 20 percent chance it's not going to start."

He laughed. I don't think he had any idea what I was talking about. He moved beside me, hands stuffed in his pockets, and craned his neck at the cirrus-strewn sky.

"I'd say the delta for rain is approaching zero."

"Yeah, but the Scout still heard this morning's forecast in San Francisco."

"Scout?"

"This thing," I said, smacking the bumper with the palm of my hand. "International Harvester stopped making them in 1980." I lifted the distributor cap, aimed the blow dryer at the points, and pulled the trigger. The batteries produced good heat and plenty of noise. I had to raise my voice. "Sometimes it just needs gas down the choke. If that doesn't work, it means moisture's the problem."

He nodded and stared at the inner workings as if perusing ancient technology in a museum. His eyebrows and lips had a kind of pleasing asymmetry. His nose took a small bend. Ron was the nerd half of the team, I decided. Probably the one who came up with whatever brilliant idea was behind BioVerge in the first place. Then Gregory moved in, fancied it up, got himself a big office, and would make a killing on the IPO. Ron would be out of a job within months.

After another minute, I put the hair dryer and gas can away. Ron was right, the jeep shouldn't be in a moisture pout in this weather. It was awfully delicate and temperamental for such a brute piece of machinery.

I turned the ignition. The engine erupted into its bone-rattling growl. Ron retreated a couple of steps. He flinched when I let the steel hood come down with a bang.

"Congratulations," he said.

"Thanks," I said, getting back behind the wheel. "See you later."

"Wait a minute—"

I threw the Scout into reverse and started to back out. But I had to jam on the brakes. Others were pulling out too, people who could actually go home, or to their cocktail meetings, at six o'clock. I saw by their dress they were marketing and management types. I also knew that back inside those buildings, the coders were just popping their first cans of Jolt, getting ready for a long night.

As I began to back out again, there was a banging on the side of my car. I slammed on the brakes once more. It was Gregory, still holding the open cell phone. He motioned for me to roll down my window.

"We've got to talk," he said. "Give me Rita's number."

"I already said I'll give her your card. That's enough."

The eyes narrowed. The lips pressed into a disapproving line. "Bill, I need a meeting tomorrow."

"Talk to Rita." I rolled up my window, but Gregory curled his fingers around the top and held it.

"Work with us. It'll be rewarding for you. Very rewarding."

How many times had I heard that promise in the last three years?

"I also know some things about Kumar that you need to know. Don't blow it, Bill." His tone was somewhere between that of a threat and a personal business advisor who would be very upset if I made the wrong decision. For a twenty-something with soft cheeks, he did a great job of impersonating a seasoned Bigfucker.

I gunned the engine. "I'm going now." How I loved its rumble.

"You're on my dashboard," Gregory said, looking me in the eye with calm certainty. "We'll see each other again."

He clamped the phone back to his ear and walked away.

I knew the limits of my vehicle, so normally I
didn't drive like everyone else trying to get across the valley,
racing to be first in line at the next stoplight, roaring up through
the gears, darting into open lanes. But this evening was different. I was annoyed by Gregory and his games, and even more
annoyed at myself for letting them go on for so long when I
was already late to my girlfriend's dinner party. Swerving into
the right lane, I gave an apologetic wave to a driver I'd just
cut off, let out a long breath, and tried to slow myself down.
Traffic was in its usual six o'clock clot. The freeway would have
been worse.

   Jenny's apartment was at the end of a curving subdivision
road. The enclave of three- and four-story redwood-shingled
garden apartments, dotted with eucalyptus trees, reached for a
feeling of rustic community and fell short. It wasn't bad, though,
once you figured out where in the parking maze you were allowed
to put your car. Silicon Valley housing could get a lot worse. The
back side of the apartments looked out over a fenced wafer fab,
a windowless block the size of a football field encasing a single
room. Chips were made in that room, a place so clean that the
human workers had to dress like aliens in space suits.

I buttoned my shirt back on, topped it with a jacket, and rang Jenny's doorbell.

As she opened the door, Jenny's pearl-blue gaze fell to my right hand. In it was a camera case, but not the bottle I'd promised to bring. "I'll go get some wine right now," I said. "Red okay? Something with a cork, right?"

She radiated one of her sunbeam smiles and pulled me inside. Her sleeveless blouse clung in all the right places. "Don't worry, Fay brought extra." She took me close and gave me a soft kiss that tasted like peppermint.

I set down the camera case and started to put my arms around her for another kiss, but stopped. "Let me wash my hands. The Scout got ornery. That's why I'm late."

Her hands went to her hips. "The Scout." She left it at that, shaking her head. I followed her down the hall. The overly plush carpet bounced under my feet.

"You look nice tonight," she said over her shoulder. She said this any time I put on a jacket.

Wes Garzen, my closest friend, sat on the living room couch. He was staring at his red wine as if afraid it was about to jump out of the glass onto the cream-colored fabric. I knew the feeling. The carpet and curtains were cream, too. The manager wouldn't let Jenny change them, so she went and got sofas to match.

"You're here early," I said on my way to the bathroom. Wes's head jerked at the sound of my voice. "You must be excited about meeting Jenny's friend."

Wes lifted a brow. "Friends," he corrected.

When I came back into the living room, I asked if he wanted a beer.

"Sure, if you've got one."

I went up two steps into a small dining room with a table and matching chairs Jenny had inherited from her grandmother. Flowers, candles, and a bowl of very realistic pears sat on a sideboard, along with several bottles of wine. Above the sideboard was a semi-abstract scene of a house and picket fence Jenny had painted.

Across from the painting was the door to the kitchen. I stuck my head through and said, "Ready for duty."

Jenny leaned slowly into me over the counter, a smudge of olive oil rimming her upper lip. She opened her mouth and gave me a long tongue-filled kiss. Dinner parties made her that way.

"We've got everything under control," she said, straightening and nodding to Fay, her friend and cohost.

"You sure you got all that oil off, Bill?" Fay remarked, turning to greet me. I smiled and opened the refrigerator, in search of an ice-cold can. Fay Ming was a graphic designer. A cascade of silky, jet black hair fell halfway down her back. She and Jenny were a knockout pair when they went to client meetings for Jenny's Web design business.

Hunt as I might, there were no ice-cold cans to be found in the fridge. Apparently I'd finished them off. Oh well, I thought on my way back to the sideboard in the dining room, Wes would have to stick to wine. And Jenny would be pleased to see me pouring a glass for myself. It was supposed to be that kind of party.

Jenny came out of the kitchen with a plate of cheese and crackers and slid into a dining room chair. I never got tired of watching her do that, especially when she was wearing Capri pants. She was lithe but strong, with delicate cheekbones, a little exclamation point of a nose, and a mouth perpetually puckering in amusement. She brightened any room, a talent I'd learned not to take for granted. I could see the effect on Wes, who peered in from the living room.

Cutting a sliver of Cambozola, Jenny asked about my meeting. I joined her at the table and said Kumar was fine. His company had had a very good year and wanted to show it off in twenty minutes of cinematic glory. The weird part of the day was at the end, with the Scout and Gregory Alton.

"Alton wants you to shoot a film for him? That's great!" Jenny said, a lilt in her voice. "See? All you have to do is put yourself out there. The work will come."

"It wasn't Rita and me, Jen. It was the fact we were working for Kumar."

"Maybe he's looking for a spy," Wes said, now hovering near the steps. "Or it might be even simpler. If Gregory and Kumar are competitors, Gregory probably wants you just because Kumar got you."

"Enough to pay double?" I said.

"That's the mentality," Wes said. "It's all about getting the other guy's toys. If you happen to spill a little data about Kumar on the way, so much the better." Wes was CTO of a startup that had defied the tech crash. He was flourishing.

"It scares me how well you understand these people, Wes."

"It still sounds like a good opportunity," Jenny said.

"Maybe I didn't make it clear how irritating Gregory was. Rita would never work with him."

Jenny's eyes gleamed. "That's perfect. Jump on it yourself, Bill. Make the leap to producer-director."

"I wouldn't cut Rita out like that."

Jenny gave me a smile that could charm a crocodile. "That's what I like about you, Bill. You're such a gentleman. Why don't you check with Rita, though. If she doesn't want the job, you can take it."

I returned her smile, but shook my head. "Gregory's a Bigfucker on training wheels."

Jenny's expression flattened into a mock pout. "Poor Bill. You're just mad you didn't get to go for your walk today. But we all have to work with people we don't like," she said sweetly. "Especially to get our first break."

I tried to think of a polite way to say, Never in a million years. Jenny was trying to help; I just wasn't sure whom. Her Web design business was taking off when we met seven months before, and the crash had dimmed none of her aggressiveness and enthusiasm. I saw, in those first few weeks, that my knowledge of the tech world turned her on, and I proceeded to make the mistake of talking about it like an old pro. I wasn't really, few were, but three years of being sucked into the Internet vortex and then spit out did leave me feeling *old*, even if I was only in my mid-thirties. As Jenny and I got to know each other, I tried to back off of my old pro status and explain how the dot-con had lured me away from the thing I'd actually meant do with my life: make films. I didn't yet know what was next for me, I was only resolved that it have little to do with the tech industry. She pretended to accept my resolution, all the while slipping me hints on how and why I should break it.

The shine faded from her eyes when I didn't answer. As I opened my mouth, the doorbell rang. Jenny put the lilt back in her voice. "Can you get that? I need to set the table."

I did a double take when I opened the front door. A small woman with long, dark ringletted hair looked up at me uncertainly. She didn't recognize me, but I'd seen her not long ago from behind a viewfinder. She was the one I'd caught on tape by accident in the parking lot. The one who had been so quick to hide from the lens.

"Is this Jenny Ingersoll's house?" she asked in a small, liquid voice.

"Yes," I said. "I'm Bill Damen, her doorman."

A slender row of fingers took my hand. "Sheila Harros." She handed me a paper bag. "These are tomatoes. For the appetizer."

"Thanks. I think we met about an hour ago."

She stopped in the middle of unwrapping a fine-woven scarf, threaded with glittering red and gold, from around her neck. "No, I don't believe so."

"In the BioVerge parking lot. Gregory Alton was there. I was behind a video camera."

Her eye twitched at Gregory's name, but she shook her head coolly. "You must have seen someone else."

It would have been easy to settle the matter. The camera was sitting right here. I knew I'd see the same scarf, the same dark curls framing a light olive face, the same almond brown eyes under long lashes. But my role here was not to make Jenny's guests feel uncomfortable.

She shrugged out of a linen jacket and came with me into the living room. As I opened the bedroom door, a meow came from inside. Jenny's cat Maggie poked her head through the crack.

"Oh!" Sheila said. "Please don't put my coat in there. I'm terribly allergic to cats."

"Sorry. I guess that's why closets were invented. Have a seat. I'll tell Jenny you're here."

Instead of sitting down, Sheila scanned Jenny's bookshelf. She clasped her hands behind her back, as if to resist some temptation. I turned for another look before I left the living room. In trim black pants and a subtle lapis blouse, she had an elegance to her. But she undermined it in small ways—her averted eyes, her nervous fingers. Maybe she was just tense around strangers.

Wes was in the kitchen with Jenny and Fay. I announced Sheila's arrival. Jenny sidled over and whispered conspiratorially, "Go talk to her, Wes."

Wes looked to me for a first impression. I hesitated. We'd known each other since college, but I'd gotten out of the business of setting him up with dates, at least not with women I wanted to remain friends with. Jenny had been glad to take over the job. He was quite the commodity: six foot one, dark hair sweeping across his forehead, sharp handsome features. He'd already cashed in his first set of options and had plenty still accumulating. Jenny was full of ideas for his social life.

I gave him a thumbs up, then tilted my thumb a bit. There was something unsettled about Sheila. Actually, she was probably more my type than Wes's.

"Who else is coming?" he asked.

I elbowed him. "Don't be greedy."

"Marion," Jenny said. "But you can't go out with both of them. They work together."

I poured Sheila a glass of wine. Wes grabbed it. "Allow me."

Wes always surprised me when he went into operator mode. In college, he'd been a stringy-haired physics major who'd had a hard time making eye contact with anyone, including me. And although his confidence had grown with success, he still would end a conversation abruptly if he started to feel nervous. He was a geek at heart, but some chemical kicked in around women.

I drifted into the dining room for a look. Sheila was telling Wes she got her doctorate in molecular biology. Wes gulped his wine.

The doorbell rang again. This time Fay got it. More people poured in. I put my facial muscles where they belonged, shook hands, and let names slip through my ears. Most of the guests were friends of Jenny and Fay, clients and potential clients. They were generally younger than me and sported the hip-nerd look: the correct era of retro haircut, the correct length sideburns, the occasional piercing. The more slickly dressed ones were probably lawyers or MBAs. A couple in shorts and sandals were likely engineers.

As I finished putting coats in the closet, Wes caught my eye. He held out his glass for a refill. I took it to the dining room, where Jenny was holding court. She was in her element here, keeping everyone entertained, dispensing drinks, and adding last minute touches to the table, all without skipping a beat. As I poured wine, she introduced me to a guy wearing a shirt in that blue that had swept the business world. He had a tie and an important busy look to match.

"I didn't catch what you do," he said.

What did I do? The number one question around here. The real questions behind it were, one, what can you do for me? And two, did you have the wherewithal to survive the deflation of the bubble?

"Film," I said.

"You must travel to LA a lot."

"I don't do features so much. Documentaries, and, if I'm forced to, industrials."

He nodded. His attention wandered to a tray of cheese. I didn't try to retrieve it. Jenny's friends did not inspire me to share confidences. Young and bright and good looking, they were all running in the same race. What brought them together was a sense of being career accelerators for one another. My friends had their quirks, but I knew I could count on them. Rita in particular—anywhere, anytime. Wes, usually, unless he was busy chasing some new capital or new romance.

I took Wes his wine. Sheila's back was to me. As I handed Wes the glass, she turned. Her elbow knocked the glass into my chest.

"Oh no," she apologized. "All over your white shirt. I'll get you some soda water."

Wes waved her off. "Bill's got a closet full of them. He wears the same thing whenever he goes out. White shirt and jeans."

I looked at the spot above my left breast. "Bad enough I have to drink the stuff," I murmured. "Now I've got to wear it."

"I'm jealous. You can't get away with wardrobe tricks like that when you're female," Sheila said.

"Nice meeting you," Wes said abruptly to her. He headed for a tall woman with large dangling earrings across the room.

I caught a *was it something I said?* glance from Sheila. I could only shrug and dab a napkin on the stain. "He's bad at good-byes," I told her. I didn't add that although I always told Wes he ought to go for a scientist, he insisted on being drawn to women who were fast-track lawyers, agents, marketing directors. He must have thought they had something he didn't.

Sheila was anything but fast. In spite of how nicely the black ringlets of hair framed her head, and the elegance of the single bracelet on her wrist, a sadness shadowed her face. She made a valiant effort to keep it tucked away, but it seeped from the corners of her eyes and the sides of her mouth. I wondered where it came from. Maybe she just worked too hard. But I couldn't stop thinking about how she ducked away from the camera in the parking lot, then refused to admit it. I was getting more and more curious about why.

3

Jenny called us to dinner. Sheila and I wound up together down at the end of the table. Across from us and over a seat, Wes was absorbed with the tall woman with the earrings. Marion, I heard someone call her, and remembered she was the other date Jenny had in mind for Wes. She had a strong jaw, pale skin, and long, flat blonde hair. Her height, mild European accent, and stylish glasses made her an imposing figure. She was regaling Wes with a story about mold colonies.

The talk at the rest of the table was of real estate, bandwidth, and the venture capital market. Sheila remained quiet. She ate methodically, using a fork and knife to neatly divide the appetizer of mozzarella, basil, and tomatoes. I noticed she was sniffling and her eyes were rimmed red. She kept rubbing them.

"Is the cat bothering you?" I asked.

"Cats. Trees. Grass. I'm pretty much allergic to life."

"This area is bad for pollen."

"It's getting worse. Cities and companies don't plant female trees anymore if the species is dioecious. Just the males. The females drop seeds, fruit, husks—litter people don't want to clean up. So we get the male trees, spewing pollen."

"It's always the males causing problems."

She flicked me a mischievous glance. "So I've heard."

"But let's face it, women *are* messy. Dropping eggs all over the place."

"It's tragic." She shook her head, deadpan. "Chemically driven to make the globe more crowded than it already is. Losing their minds when their biological clocks go off."

I laughed. "To be fair, it happens to men, too. Only with them I think it's more about ego than eggs."

"Or genes, the new superego. They demand to be propagated."

"So why is it that they make boys want one thing and girls another?"

"You mean the old, 'men want sports and women want shoes'? Nature is more clever than you think. We'd get bored with each other if we were too much alike."

Sheila returned everything I said with a little extra on it. I liked it. "So what I've heard is true. You're a molecular biologist."

"That's what my badge says. I work at a biotech company."

I pictured her in a lab, neatly dividing peptides the way she did her food. "Well, if you invented these tomatoes in the lab, you're doing good work."

She gave a doleful smile. "They're from a garden."

"What kind of genes are you splicing, then?"

"Gene transfer is old news. The new big thing in the field is proteomics."

"The study of proteins," I said. Kumar had mentioned it.

"They're the real building blocks of the body. DNA may spell out the recipes, but proteins do all the work. They're the big targets for control of disease. We might have thirty or sixty thousand genes in our genome, but hundreds of thousands of proteins are in the proteome. We have a long way to go to map them."

"I heard a bit about it this afternoon," I said, hoping to sneak back to the subject of the parking lot. "I've been shooting a project for a company called Kumar Biotechnics."

Sheila's expression betrayed nothing. I went at the question another way and asked who she worked for.

"LifeScience Molecules. I'm a junior scientist." She launched into a long explanation of target cells, hybridomas, and monoclonal antibodies. She was smart, articulate, and clearly passionate about her work. After a while I stopped listening and simply enjoyed watching her as she talked and made diagrams in the air. She was a beautiful woman.

It took me a minute to realize she'd stopped talking. I smiled at her to cover the fact that I'd been admiring her more than attending to what she said. The silence hung between us, a shared moment. One way or another, I wanted to see more of her, even if only as a friend.

Everyone had finished eating by now. Sheila nudged her leftover salmon, mashed potatoes, and salad with a fork, then started to tell me about how an experimental salmon without the urge to spawn was being created. Its chromosomes were engineered so that it had no desire to swim upstream. Salmon lost a lot of weight on those trips and would stay nice and fat if they didn't make them. Others were being fattened more directly by splicing a growth hormone into them.

"You do this, too?" I asked.

"No, no," she said quickly. "That's not *my* work."

From down the table, I caught a look from Jenny, which was followed by a smile with an extra little sparkle in it. I knew how to decode these smiles by now. On the surface it said she was thinking of me. The second layer said I shouldn't be monopolizing Sheila. And the third layer was telling me to cut out the flirting. But in my mind this wasn't so much about flirtation as about having an intelligent conversation for its own sake, a rarity tonight amidst all the infrared Palm Pilot mating.

Marion heard the talk of salmon. She looked at me and said, "Did you hear about the company in Syracuse that wants to produce a nonallergenic cat? They're planning to knock out Fel d 1, the gene linked to dander and saliva."

"Do you think animals will start to come with tags, like Beanie Babies?" Wes asked.

We were catching the attention of some of the other people at the table. "I'm more worried about the ones that *don't* come with tags," Fay said.

"That's small potatoes—" began Mr. Blue Shirt.

"Which are also being engineered," Marion put in.

"The real question," he went on, "is what happens when we start using the technology on ourselves."

"I'm not so sure—" Sheila began.

"If it can be done, it will be done," Blue Shirt declared. "Someone, somewhere, is mapping out their future child right now."

Fay gave him a dig. "If I know you, Chad, you'll just clone yourself. No improvements needed."

"I wouldn't recommend it," Sheila said. "Most attempts at nuclear transfer end in horror stories. It takes a kind of scientific voodoo to coax the embryonic cells to divide. Look at Dolly the sheep: she's obese, her telomeres are short, and there are signs she's aging too fast, possibly because her mother's DNA was old. The real action in biotech is treatment of disease."

"And plant research," Marion put in.

"I don't know anyone who wants to genetically program their child," Jenny said.

"Think about it," said Chad. "If other people start designing *their* kids' genes, are you going to let *your* kids be at a disadvantage?"

Jenny wrinkled her nose. "A genetic arms race?"

"And legs. And brains," Chad said. "You don't want to be left behind."

"I mean, your kids are your kids," Jenny said. "You just want them to be happy."

"How happy are they going to be if they're the shortest kid in the class? The ugliest? The dumbest?"

"I'd rather be short than have short telomeres," Sheila said. "And what you're talking about is still more science fiction than science."

Marion's pale eyes were fixed on Chad. "Is that your definition of happiness?" she demanded. "The boy with the most marbles?"

"Darwin said it, right?" he answered. "Evolution doesn't care who's polite and picks up litter. It cares whose genes get passed along."

I considered asking him if he planned to pass the arrogance gene on to his children, but decided to stay out of it.

"Evolution doesn't care how we feel at all," Sheila said. "In fact, maybe if we were built to be more naturally content, we'd be less inclined to reproduce. There must be some explanation for why it's so hard for us to be happy in our lives."

This brought an uneasy silence. The table stared at Sheila as if she'd admitted an embarrassing hygiene problem. These go-getters weren't about to admit any such weakness. Weakness made you—and your genes—an undesirable commodity.

Sheila's shoulders hunched. She wound a ringlet of hair around her finger, tighter and tighter, and looked down at her plate. The tangy voice I'd heard earlier had disappeared. I was amazed at how quickly her demeanor changed. She withdrew as I watched.

The conversation veered back to the subject of where to raise one's children, a hypothetical prospect for everyone there. Their faces were clear and unfurrowed. I didn't pay much attention. I was watching Sheila. She didn't look well. Her eyes were watery, her face was puffy, her neck red. She kept scratching the back of her hand.

"Are you all right?" I asked.

"I'm fine," she said, squeezing her temples. She attempted a smile. "Just allergies. Excuse me."

She disappeared into the bathroom. Other people moved into the living room. After helping Jenny clear the table and make coffee, I passed around a tray of coffee cups, while Jenny offered milk.

I wedged myself into a corner and watched Jenny keep her contacts warm. She chatted with each person about everything and nothing. It came naturally to her, which was good, because her business depended on it.

I wasn't much of a mingler, and no one chose me as a networking target. After a while I went into the dining room, where Marion and Wes were cocooned in a private conversation.

"Have you seen Sheila?" I asked. "She wasn't feeling well."

"Sheila went home," Marion said.

"Was she all right?"

"Should be. Just some overactive mast cells."

Wes found this funny. "That's a relief. I thought she was crying because Fay said something to her. It was kind of weird. Fay was irate."

"When was this?"

"Just as Sheila was leaving," Wes said. "She and Fay were by the door to the closet. Marion was telling me about mutated fruit flies that had their eyes in their asses." He laughed again.

I walked through the kitchen and out a door that led to a small back porch. In between the branches of the eucalyptus trees, stars twinkled feebly in the Silicon Valley haze. I thought about the guests in the living room. Was I just getting old? Everyone in there was close to Jenny's age, thirty. Only a handful of years separated me from them, but it felt like a chasm. Except for Sheila, they all seemed so sure of themselves, so entitled, so on the make. But then, I'd been out of step with the world around me for months. I wondered if I was beginning to fall out of step with Jenny, too.

I closed the door and went back into the living room. It was almost eleven. Some people had left already, others were saying their goodbyes. A few were going back to work, I suspected, and others out to clubs. Bed sounded good to me, though. I was glad I wouldn't be spending an hour on the freeway back to my flat in San Francisco.

Marion and Wes were the last guests to leave. Marion was not shy about giving him her card and planting a kiss on his mouth. As soon as I closed the door, Jenny and Fay commenced a review of who was there, how much funding this one's venture was getting, how soon that one's startup would crumble. The dinner party was judged to be a success. They were particularly pleased by the sparks flying between Wes and Marion.

"I'm glad he latched on to Marion," Fay said. "She's much better for him than Sheila."

"What's wrong with Sheila?" I asked.

"She's just kind of . . . flimsy." Fay pursed her lips. "Flimsy and stubborn."

I was too tired to pursue it. Who cared what Fay, or Wes, or the rest, thought of Sheila? She was the most interesting person at the party, and the one I most hoped to see again.

It wasn't until the next morning that we learned she was dead.

4

When the phone rang, I was still in the bathrobe that Jenny kept for me. I was collecting stray wine glasses, coffee cups, and cracker bits hidden around her apartment from the night before. She was in a soft cotton nightie that ended just below her hips. I was enjoying the way her polished toe scratched her calf as she cradled the receiver.

Then her face went pale. Her hand shook. Maybe a client was reporting some server meltdown.

"Yes, she was here . . . No, no, we didn't . . ." Her mouth gaped. "That's impossible . . . But we knew . . ."

I sat on a sofa. Jenny's gaze was fixed in a line that ended at a point on the wall. "I guess so . . . Yes, I'll be there in half an hour."

She stared at the phone for a good ten seconds before remembering to click it off. She didn't look at me, but sat down mechanically. Her whole body was trembling. "Sheila's dead. They found her in her car out on Page Mill Road last night."

I blurted the first word that came into my mind. "Suicide?"

Jenny's eyes filled with tears. "No, it was something else. Anaphylactic shock." I put my arm around her and held her to my chest while she cried. "They said it was probably caused by a food allergy."

"Food?"

"That's what they said." Suddenly Jenny straightened and flung the phone to the floor. Her fists clenched and her arms quivered. "Bill, that means it could have been something she ate here last night!"

I took her to my shoulder and tried to soothe her. "I know she had hay fever. But did you know of any food allergies?"

"Yes!" Jenny shrieked. "She was allergic to shellfish. Fay and I were so careful. We asked her about the salmon. Sheila said it was fine."

"Maybe they're wrong about the cause of death. Who was it that called?"

"It was the hospital. They want me to come and"—she broke into tears again—"confirm her identity. They called her parents in Massachusetts but got a machine. It said they're out of the country. They found my number in her organizer. They know she was here last night."

I pictured Sheila lying on a gurney. Her black curls against the white sheet. Her olive skin, now waxen. Her wrist empty of the bracelet. Then I thought of Jenny having to look at her. "I'll go with you to make the identification," I offered. "Do you want me to do that?"

"M-m-maybe," she sobbed. She drew in a breath. "Thanks, Bill. I better get ready. They're waiting for us."

She dragged the heel of her palm down her wet face and went to her room. I stared at the fingerprint-smudged wine glasses, dark with sediment, still on the coffee table. I remembered Sheila's troubled look after the meal, her retreat to the bathroom. Should I have realized what was happening? She seemed in control of her condition. She was a biologist and would have known how to handle it. Marion saw her, too, just before she left.

If there was something seriously wrong, Marion would have spotted it.

We drove to the county hospital in the Scout. The building was a well-funded postmodern arrangement of cubes, cylinders, trapezoids, and cantilevers. The lobby felt more like a corporate office than a hospital. On the one hand, I didn't miss the aura of illness. On the other, it made me wonder what the bottom line was.

The morgue was in the basement. Jenny walked to the elevator with her back straight and shoulders square, her flats clopping softly on the polished floor.

At the entrance to the morgue was a small office. A man named Perkins said he was the one who'd talked to Jenny on the phone. I told him I'd be making the identification, then looked to Jenny. She nodded. The official took down my information and led me through double doors.

The formaldehyde hit me like a punch. There were three empty gurneys and two with occupants.

He lifted the corner of the sheet on the far gurney. "Is this Sheila Harros?"

I hadn't prepared myself for the moment. I felt instantly transported out of my body, as if floating, watching a film of myself. There she was, lips parted just a fraction, deep well under the collarbone. But inert, like some object, speechless, drained, stony, as if she could care less what we thought of her now.

"Yes," I said.

"Thank you."

We went back to the office. Jenny watched my face. I gave her a small nod and signed the form.

"Thank you," Perkins said again. "Now, we need instructions on removal of the remains. You should do everything you can to help us find her parents. Otherwise, we'll have to send her to the county undertaker."

"Removal . . . of . . . the . . . remains . . ." Jenny repeated.

"Yes. To a mortuary, or—"

"We're not the ones who should be doing this," I said.

"We tried her parents, as I mentioned," the official replied. "We'll keep trying them, of course. Do you know of any other family?"

Jenny shook her head.

"No? Well, you're the closest party we have for the time being. There was a mention in her organizer of meeting a Karen yesterday afternoon, but no last name. You were probably the last to see her alive."

"What about her work?" I asked.

"We called LifeScience Molecules before we talked to you. No one was available to come down."

"Not even Marion?"

"I didn't speak to anyone by that name. I'm terribly sorry. I know this is difficult. But we can only keep the corpse refrigerated for twenty-four hours."

Jenny straightened abruptly. "I'd like to talk to the doctor who saw her. I want to know what happened."

Perkins cocked his head. "I don't think that's possible."

"Look, our friend is dead," I broke in. "The least you can do is let us speak to the doctor."

He uncocked his head, made a call, and then told us to go to the ER desk and ask for Dr. Curran.

We stood and thanked him. "What about her car?" I asked.

"The police have it," he said, getting up to see us out.

"Are they investigating her death?"

"Not at the moment. The coroner has accepted Dr. Curran's determination for the time being."

"There'll be an autopsy, won't there?"

"If the coroner orders it or the family requests it."

"Because I don't think a food allergy was the cause of her death," I said. "At least not food she ate last night."

He gave a neutral shrug, then put out his hand. "Please let us know if you find a way to reach the parents. Or any next of kin."

The emergency room was on the first floor. We collapsed into some soft chairs and waited for the doctor to become available. Five minutes later he greeted us. Dr. Curran was young. He had short red hair with a curl or two on his forehead and wire frame glasses. We followed him into a small examining room to talk.

"Sheila was brought in by ambulance," he told us. "She was not breathing when the police found her. We tried everything. Oxygen, intubation, adrenaline, dopamine, IV Benadryl, CPR, you name it. It was just too late. She had no vital signs."

"So she died from—?" I asked.

"Anaphylactic shock. A severe allergic reaction."

"And you're sure about that?"

"The skin welts, hypotension, angio-edema, and broncho-constriction were clear."

"Isn't it just incredibly rare for this to happen?" Jenny asked.

"The hospital gets several cases a year. Most of them aren't fatal, but I wouldn't call it rare. Usually it happens to children. I'm afraid your friend was just unlucky. I'm sorry."

Jenny gazed at his badge. "Are you a full doctor?"

"I'm a third-year resident. The indications were not hard to spot."

"She knew she had allergies. She would have been prepared and taken an antihistamine or something," I said.

"An oral antihistamine wouldn't do the job. But yes, she was prepared. She'd administered epinephrine with a device called an Epi-Pen. Unfortunately, the solution had gone bad."

"Gone bad how?"

"We found the Epi-Pen in her bag. Traces of fluid in the injector were brown. It had probably been exposed to heat, which would have spoiled it."

"So who's got the bag now? And the rest of her stuff?" Jenny asked.

"The morgue. It'll be handed over to the family."

Jenny lowered her eyes. I saw her brace herself for the next question. "And what—what do you think caused Sheila's allergic reaction?"

The doctor adjusted his glasses. "We inspected the body for insect bites. There were none. We found a card telling us she had no drug allergies. Her tongue and gut were swollen. She'd vomited. That indicates a substance she ingested."

"Like food."

"That's the likely pathway. We'd have to do some more tests to nail it down. For my money, it was something she had for dinner last night. The reaction comes on quickly."

Jenny's face melted into tears.

"I'm sorry about your friend," Curran said, momentarily lowering his eyes. "But I'm afraid I have other patients waiting."

He turned, then hesitated. "You can call me," he said to Jenny as he scribbled his number on a small pad. He tore off the sheet and handed it to me. "If either of you have more questions."

5

"**It was me, Bill.** Something from my kitchen killed Sheila."

Jenny was sunk into her couch, arms folded in a tight knot. I had not expected her to face the issue so directly, and I welcomed it. To me, the need to respond was clear. That moment in the morgue, gazing down at Sheila's corpse, had frozen in me. It required some kind of action or explanation to thaw it. A life in motion had stopped abruptly. Whatever moaning I'd done about my own life being in a state of suspension now sounded trivial.

I remembered our last bit of dinner conversation, how Sheila hung her head under the gaze of the guests. How she pressed her fingers to her temples as the allergic reaction came on. She was starting to feel the constriction in her throat. Her body was coiling for an overwhelming, self-strangling counterattack on some seemingly harmless bite of food. She excused herself to the bathroom, hoping the symptoms would pass, then rushed to her car, where perhaps she had left the Epi-Pen. Maybe she'd realized the epinephrine had gone bad and was racing home for more.

And the rest of us oblivious all the while. If only we hadn't been so clumsy, so self-absorbed . . .

It was this idea—the fear of her own negligence—that Jenny focused on. I told her that whatever caused the reaction couldn't have been something she cooked last night. Jenny knew Sheila was allergic to shellfish and had specifically checked with her to make sure the entire menu was safe.

The phone rang. It was Fay. Jenny told her the news. Fay said she'd be right over.

When Fay arrived, she and Jenny threw their arms around each other. After some tearful commiseration, they sat down in the living room to review what might have gone wrong at the dinner party. I went into Jenny's room, where the computer was. I wanted to learn more about anaphylaxis on the Internet.

"Listen to this," I called a few minutes later, moving to the doorway. "Apparently just a few particles can cause an attack. On an airplane, people with the allergy can get sick just from other passengers opening their peanut bags. Diners with fish allergies can have problems from residue left over in restaurant woks."

"That's right, blame the Chinese," Fay said in her melodic voice, then smiled. She was an unusual combination of playful and intimidating, ambitious and coy.

Jenny bit her thumb. "Maybe I had shellfish here this week. Wait, no—I'm sure I didn't. I ate out every night. Anyway, a little residue couldn't kill her, could it?"

"Who knows?" Fay said. "She was so sensitive. She had those small bones. Simon said she was sick for an entire vacation once because a shred of crab got into her omelet."

"But she lived," Jenny said.

"Wait a minute—Simon?" I asked. He was Fay's boyfriend.

"Sheila used to date Simon," Fay explained. "Poor Sheila. She was actually convinced he wanted to get back together with her."

"Is that what you were arguing about last night?"

Fay stretched her neck and rolled her shoulders. "I was just trying to help her move on with her life. Simon sent her a few letters while he's on his trip to Australia. She took them the wrong way. He's English, he was trying to be polite."

Fay spread her fingers and regarded her nails, a deep shade of blue. "Jenny, you know what we should do? Tear apart your kitchen from top to bottom. We'll find out for sure what's in there. You'll be able to stop worrying about it."

Jenny's face lit up. She popped to her feet. The two of them rushed to the kitchen. Pretty soon they were flinging open cabinets, emptying drawers, and inspecting labels.

I followed them and asked Fay if she had any idea how to find Sheila's parents. She didn't, but said that Sheila had a brother named Abe, a doctor who lived in Europe.

She checked her watch. "I'll call Simon. He might know. This will really upset him. He always felt some kind of duty to protect Sheila."

I went back to the computer. A search for Abe Harros turned up nothing. While I was online, I checked my email. Rita had sent a message, all in capitals. Rita never used capitals. It was considered bad form, unless you meant to shout at someone.

WHAT IS WITH THIS GREGORY GUY??? HE'S BEEN CALLING ME EVERY HOUR. I HOPE YOU DIDN'T GIVE HIM MY NUMBER.

No, I hadn't given him her number, I emailed back. I explained who he was and that he was offering a lot of money for our services. But I'd call him and tell him to lay off. I added that I'd stay another night at Jenny's, then come up to San Francisco for the prep meeting Rita and I had scheduled tomorrow morning.

"Bill," Jenny sang from the kitchen. "Come look!"

Laid out on the floor were primary-color plates, champagne glasses, diet milkshake powder, four kinds of granola, and what was perhaps Silicon Valley's largest collection of animal-shaped salt and pepper shakers. The stove and counters and cabinets were spotless.

"Not a smidgen of shellfish," Jenny announced. "Just some clam chowder, safely inside the can."

Fay held up a small closed tin. "And Cajun seasoning, with authentic fake crawfish flavor."

"And these." Jenny had a pair of crab-claw crunchers hidden behind her back. She snapped them at my nose. I frowned at her. It didn't seem like the time to play around.

"Plus, I talked to Simon," Fay said. "Abe works for Médecins Sans Frontières. He's based somewhere in Europe or Africa."

"Thanks," I said. "I'll tell Perkins at the hospital."

Fay gave a catlike smile. "I've got a quicker way to find Abe. Simon told me where Sheila keeps a set of keys to her apartment."

>> >> >> >> >>

Sheila's apartment complex resembled a motel. We navigated down an alley of covered parking spaces behind the complex to the number that corresponded to Sheila's unit. The space was empty, of course, and I put the Scout in. Fay looked under a filament-encrusted flowerpot in the corner. The keys were there.

We walked around to the complex's back gate, unlocked it, and entered a long courtyard. A small, plain swimming pool with a concrete deck shimmered to our right on the other side of a low chain-link fence. An older woman was fishing debris out of the pool with a net. She stared at the three of us as we walked by. Jenny smiled at her and waved hello.

It didn't work. The woman came to the fence. The manager, I figured. Her hair was falling out of its bun, her cheeks ruddy. She looked ready to use the net on us.

"Who are you?" she demanded.

"We're friends of Sheila's," Jenny answered.

"Sheila's dead," the woman said bluntly.

Jenny recoiled. "We know that," I said quietly. "The hospital asked us to come and look up a phone number for her family." At least, I imagined Perkins might have, if I'd reached him instead of his voicemail before we had left Jenny's place.

"Someone's already been here." The manager's voice was flat.

"Who? The police?"

"No. Someone from her job. Guy with short dark hair. He was a high-up, showed me his card."

I looked at Jenny and Fay. It seemed odd that LifeScience would come here but send no one to the hospital. I reminded myself that we needed to call Marion.

"Did you let him into her apartment?" I asked.

"He said there was some kind of work product they needed right away," the manager said. "Some presentation. Even though it was a time of grief, et cetera, they had to have this info."

"Well, we're just here to locate her family," I said. "As you can see, she gave us her keys."

The manager nodded reluctantly. "Don't be long. I had to chase that other fella out. I didn't think it was right, him poking around for a whole hour."

We proceeded down the courtyard, which was lined on either side by a double-deck row of apartments. The center was a strip of trampled lawn with some plastic furniture, charcoal grills, and a palm here and there. Jenny jiggled Sheila's door open. The apartment consisted of three rooms plus a kitchen, basic boxes with low ceilings, but Sheila had fixed it up nicely. The living room furniture was low to the ground, which made the room seem bigger. There were two upholstered, semicircular chairs, a divan, and a collection of brocade pillows for lounging. She had hung fabric on the walls, intricate patterns in earth tones. A large rug, also intricately patterned, covered the worn carpeting. The biggest things in the room were the two bookcases, which were crammed with books on science as well as novels and biographies. A whole shelf was given to Sufi poetry.

"What a cozy place," Jenny said. "I didn't think she'd be one to put so much effort into decorating."

"Feels like an opium den," Fay whispered.

None of the lights was very bright. I meandered into the kitchen. There was something uncanny about knowing the occupant would never return, would never again brew tea in the blue-tendrilled pot on the stove, would never wash the cup in the sink, would never eat the dried lentils, beans, rice, bulgur, almonds, and mint rowed neatly in jars.

The bedroom was simple. A low bed platform faced a sliding door closet. Next to the bed was a little table, on which sat a lamp and a small book bound in black hardcover. A piece of sheer fabric billowed from the ceiling to soften an overhead light. Curtains of the same material covered a back window.

"This is beautiful," Jenny gushed. She had picked up a scarf draped over a chair in front of a vanity. A handful of bottles of perfume, lotion, and almond oil sat on its shelf. She shook the scarf into a square to admire the pattern.

Then, as if it was crawling with bugs, she dropped it. "Let's get what we came for. I don't feel right being here."

"Besides, we don't want that manager giving us a hard time," said Fay, sliding open a closet door. She did a double take. "So this is where Sheila threw all her clutter!"

We left Fay in the bedroom and went back through the living room to the small den. It was strewn with books, journals, and file folders. A computer desk was piled with documents. I sat down and turned on the computer. Nothing happened. It sat there dead for a minute before I wriggled under the desk to take a look at the CPU. The cover was loose and a hole in the tower gaped at me.

I called to Jenny, then dragged the tower out a little and turned it to show her. "Someone removed Sheila's hard drive. The LifeScience guy. Had to be."

"He said he needed a presentation. It must have been on her hard drive."

"Maybe. But I'd like to have it explained." I had a growing feeling that Sheila's place had been raked over. But why?

"Don't forget why we're here, Bill." Jenny opened a drawer in the desk. Almost immediately she plucked a red address book from the top drawer. She turned to H.

"Here we go." She jotted down Sheila's parents' numbers. I looked through the rest of the H's with her. No sign of Abe.

"I know," Jenny said. She turned to A. There it was.

"Of course," I said. "That was probably why Perkins didn't find it in her organizer, either."

Jenny wrote down Abe's information. "He's based in Cairo now."

"Look for one more number," I requested. "The name of Sheila's doctor. Her allergist, in particular."

Jenny sat in the rocker and leafed through the address book. In the meantime, I checked the drawers for disks. Either she didn't have any or they'd been cleaned out. A zip drive sat on the desk, so the former seemed unlikely.

I sifted through the items strewn on the table and floor. A lot of them were professional journals with articles on transgenic animals, immunology, and bioinformatics. There were also a number of reprints about subjects like interleukins, apoptosis, and laboratory mice, with sections highlighted in yellow.

I got up and looked through the bookshelf. A knock came at the front door.

"The manager," I said.

"I found Sheila's allergist," Jenny said. She took down a number, put the address book back in the desk, and went out. I told her I'd be right there.

I pulled books off the shelves in bunches. Nothing. Then, opening a carved box that sat on the shelf as a bookend, I found what I wanted. Three zip disks. I stuffed them into my pocket.

Fay and Jenny were standing by the apartment door. The manager was sniffing around to see if we'd done any damage. I nodded at the pile of books on the dining table, which we hadn't gone through yet. "Shouldn't we clean those up?"

"Don't worry about it," she said.

I started back toward the bedroom. "Time to go!" she growled.

"Just turning out the lights," I called.

I entered the bedroom, turned on the light, took one last glance around the room, and turned off the light.

The manager was closing the front door behind us when I asked, "Did you notice if the man from Sheila's work took anything away with him?"

"He had a briefcase," she said as she escorted us to the gate. "I wouldn't know what was in it."

We walked down the alley to the Scout. I was glad Jenny insisted on climbing into the backseat so Fay could take the front. Instead of aiming the Scout toward the street, I drove back to the apartment gate. "Fay," I said, "we should find out the manager's name. Could you?"

"I'll do it," Jenny said.

"That's all right," Fay said. "I'm in front."

Once she'd left, I leaned over and rifled through her handbag.

"Bill!" Jenny protested.

I held the black book up for her to see. "Sheila's journal."

I slid it under my seat, then straightened to wait for Fay. In the rearview mirror, I could see Jenny staring at the gate, her face as stunned and blank as a vacant window.

6

Jenny kept her eyes glued to the landscape of strip malls, upscale car dealerships, and corporate campuses as we drove east across the valley, toward the bay. Biotech companies tended to grow in bunches, and several were nestled down there. LifeScience was about half a mile south of BioVerge.

Jenny and I wanted to talk to Marion in person. I waited for Jenny to say something about Fay, or the diary. We'd dropped Fay off at her apartment. Jenny had stared silently at her the whole way over. Fay seemed unaware that the trust had suddenly drained from their partnership.

"The manager's name is Jennifer Poloni," Fay had said when she got back into the jeep. "Looks like you're not the only Jennifer on the scene."

Jenny just wrinkled her nose. I knew the expression was aimed at Fay, not the manager.

After we crossed under Highway 101, the neighborhood turned industrial. We passed generic business hotels, bulldozed lots, and nameless aluminum sheds on our way to a more landscaped area near the water. LifeScience sat by itself at the end of a sinuous drive. The bay beyond had the thick, greenish look of antifreeze.

The LifeScience complex consisted of two four-story wings in front, bisected by an atrium, and a new addition in back. At the fulcrum of the three structures was a central tower. All were built of lightweight greenish-silver materials. A thin colonnade encircled the building.

Jenny paused at the main entrance. Her shoulders sagged. I touched her arm. Her skin, always soft and milky, felt vulnerable under my fingers. "Are you up for this?"

She gathered herself and we went in. The atrium soared above us. Sunlight streamed in, feeding a cluster of tall bamboo. The walls were flagstone, wood panelling, and glass; the floors were polished stone. None of it was overdone, not the way certain tech firms were. Not a bad place to shoot a film, I thought; at least the set would look good.

A long granite counter blocked further entry. Behind it was a wall of frosted glass etched with LifeScience Molecules. The receptionist, a pony-tailed twenty-something, smiled at us.

"We're here to see Marion Roos," I said.

He punched a button, listened, and said, "I'm sorry. She's not picking up."

"Ah." I leaned over the counter and noticed his thin fingers and clean white nails. Was he the only security in the place? "We're here about Sheila Harros."

His face remained placid. "Would you like me to try her?"

"No, we need to go to her desk to give her something."

"You can leave it here. I'll make sure she gets it."

His switchboard bleated. He held up a finger for us to wait while he answered. "No, I'm sorry, Dr. McKinnon is in a meeting . . . Yes, with investors . . . I'm sorry, I can't tell you that . . ."

He looked up at us. Jenny put on her platinum-melting smile. But the phone interrupted again. The receptionist went through a virtually identical conversation with this caller.

"Your company is popular," I commented.

He blew out some air. "Especially today. I can't even get up to use the bathroom."

Jenny put her smile back on. "About Sheila—it's just *really* personal."

He returned the smile, but the corners of his mouth stayed firm. Pressing a button under the desk, he said, "Someone will escort you."

A man in a blue suit appeared so quickly it startled us. His sober features and by-the-book hair left little doubt about his job. "Why do you want to see Ms. Harros?"

"It's kind of private," Jenny said, wielding her smile.

It bounced right off. He turned, walked a few feet away, and spoke into a handheld computer. Over his shoulder I glimpsed bamboo on the handheld's screen. He was getting a video feed of the lobby. I glanced up: the cameras were mounted above the front desk, each with a small shotgun mike pointed down at us. Mr. Security had been watching the whole time.

"Come with me," he said.

"Badge them?" the receptionist asked.

The security man waved him off. We followed him around the frosted glass, under the bamboo, and across the polished floor. At the far end was a curtain wall. Through it, the bay winked in the afternoon sun.

I was disappointed when we took a right into a conference room. I'd been hoping to get upstairs into the offices, maybe the labs. A moment after we sat down, three men entered the room.

"Don't get up," said the first and tallest. He bent to shake Jenny's hand, then mine, which prevented us from standing. He was probably six foot three, around fifty, athletic and tan. His golden brown hair was swept back, revealing a high forehead and a congenial face with a strong triangle of a nose. He wore a tawny wool suit and a sky blue tie that matched his eyes.

"I'm Dr. Frederick McKinnon," he said. "This is Doug Englehart."

The one behind him came forward. Englehart was all elbows and knees. He was younger than McKinnon, with a mustache, a narrow jaw, and a bulbous skull, across which a few lonesome strands of brown hair crawled. He gave the impression of being choked by his tie.

The third man did not give his name. His clipped dark brown hair made a crisp square line around his ears and across the back of his neck. He stayed by the door and in turn was joined by Mr. Security.

McKinnon did not sit but leaned toward us from the head of the table. "Now, about Sheila . . ." He stared at his hands for a moment. They were large, the fingers elegant, wrinkled at the knuckles, a thick gold wedding band on the fourth. A small quiver came into his voice. "I'm afraid I have some bad news—"

"Actually, we know about Sheila," I said. "We came to see Marion."

"We feel just terrible, as you can imagine," Dr. McKinnon said. "Today of all days. We're hosting some critical investors. I haven't had time to process the . . . losing her."

"You had to make presentations, I imagine."

Doug Englehart spoke up. "Yes. The hospital called for help identifying Sheila. I was obligated to show the investors around the lab. Otherwise I would have gone."

"Jenny and I did it. Were you her supervisor?"

"I'm the group leader," he answered with a sidelong look at McKinnon. "I'm executing the program."

"I direct the research," McKinnon said. He shook his head with regret. "It's been painful to pretend nothing happened. We feel the loss keenly. On behalf of all of us, accept our condolences."

Suspicious as I was, I saw no signs McKinnon was faking it. His voice was authoritative and precise. His blue eyes were fierce but had human warmth in them.

"We're all in shock," Jenny said softly.

The room was silent. Even McKinnon, for all his presence, seemed at a momentary loss. Still, I sensed tension coming from somewhere. It was the dark-haired man. He had that implacable alpha look, as if the entire conversation was taking place only at his pleasure. He stood stock still but brimmed with testosterone, a solid two hundred pounds, but not dumb. His eyes picked up everything.

"So, about Marion—" I said.

Alpha Man spoke up in a clear, hard voice. "She has a vendor meeting."

McKinnon turned to him in surprise. "Today?"

"Yes." The man rocked forward on the balls of his feet, but didn't elaborate.

After another silence, McKinnon glanced behind him, in the direction, I supposed, of where his investors were waiting, then at his watch. "Well. I'm terribly sorry, but I have to go."

"Do you think—" Jenny began, waiting for his attention. "We'd like to see Sheila's workspace."

Doug Englehart cleared his throat. "It's, ah, all packed up."

"Too painful to see her things there, I imagine," McKinnon said.

"Perhaps we should take them for you," I suggested.

Before Doug could object, Alpha Man spoke. "We'll release them to next of kin."

"We're in touch with the family," I said. The apartment manager had stimulated my misinformation faculties, though it was true we'd called Perkins at the hospital to give him the phone number for Abe, Sheila's brother. "They won't be here for a few days. They asked us to take care of her effects. We have the key to Sheila's apartment."

I watched the man carefully. His thick brows rose slightly. "Next of kin only. Thank you for your concern." He crossed his arms in a way that said he wasn't thanking me at all.

McKinnon looked at his watch again. We stood to shake his hand. "I'd like to talk to you some more," I said.

"Of course," he agreed. "When time permits."

The dark-haired man frowned. "You'll need to clear that first, doctor."

McKinnon whirled just before exiting the door. "I'll speak to whomever I like, Neil."

Doug Englehart glared at the man named Neil, and followed McKinnon out. We started to leave as well, but Neil blocked the door. "You said you had something to give Sheila—which strikes me as strange, since you already knew she was dead. Nevertheless, I'll be glad to handle it."

I wanted to see how he'd react if I mentioned the journal. He could well have been the one who'd been in Sheila's apartment. If Jenny was right and their reasons for taking the hard drive were purely work-related, the diary wouldn't concern him. But it was also possible that whoever was snooping had been interrupted by the manager and hadn't seen the black book in the bedroom. In that case, he might want it.

Curiosity got the better of me, as it usually did. First I asked, "I'm sorry, Neil, what was your last name?"

"I'm an officer of the company."

I waited for him to go on. He didn't. So I dropped my little bomb.

"We have Sheila's diary."

His eyes flicked up and down in a quick inspection of our persons. He settled on a straw bag Jenny was carrying. "We'll keep it with the rest of her effects."

"That's all right," I said. "We'll give it to the family ourselves. I'm sure they'll also want Sheila's hard drive, when the police find out who stole it."

My comment about the hard drive was rewarded with a visible tightening of his facial muscles. He said nothing, but edged over to fill the door frame.

I stepped toward him. "We'd like to see Sheila's workspace."

"Impossible, I'm afraid." He remained still, his features frozen.

I said, "Let's go, Jenny."

The man didn't budge. His smile grew, which only made it more menacing. "Why did you bring her diary? You must have intended for us to have it."

"I'd hoped to cooperate with you in finding the cause of her death. I can see that's not going to happen."

"Your definition of cooperation is rather self-centered. Leave the diary with people who know what they're doing."

"We're done here." I advanced on the door. Jenny cinched the bag to her shoulder and followed.

I didn't stop when we got to the door. Neil and Mr. Security turned aside at the last second, allowing just enough space for us to squeeze through. The bag brushed against him. We strode across the lobby to the door.

Jenny waited until I'd pulled the Scout out of the LifeScience lot to turn on me. Her face was red. "Bill, you are so *dim* sometimes. I can't believe you told him about the diary. What if he tried to get it?"

"The diary's safe under my seat. It was the only way to break through his mask. Now we know he's serious about getting it. I want to know why."

7

I joined the stutter of Friday morning traffic the next day as I made my way toward 280, the freeway that would take me to San Francisco. Maple, oak, and sycamore flared gold and red in the morning sun. To drive through Silicon Valley was to jump abruptly from one era to another. One moment you were in a shaded postwar suburb of ranch houses, car washes, and drive-ins; the next you were passing by the expansive green campus of a big tech firm, complete with swimming pool, gym, and gourmet cafeteria. The recreational facilities were set right out front, too, for potential employees to see how good they'd have it.

Interstate 280's eight spacious lanes undulated through pastures in the shadow of the coastal range. It bracketed the west side of the valley, a mud flat that ran alongside the bay. Before its transformation, the flat had been a checkerboard of orchards and sunny towns, protected from the Pacific's cold fog by the coastal chain. When silicon and software replaced apples and apricots, the string of sleepy, pleasant communities—Palo Alto, Mountain View, Sunnyvale, Cupertino—melted together into something that, viewed from above, resembled an etched transistor. On the east side of the valley was Highway 101, the main artery along the bay, forty miles of noise barriers and auto body shops.

I whizzed along without much problem. The commute had reversed its direction during the tech revolution, which to me was something like water flowing uphill. The heavy morning traffic now headed south from San Francisco to what were once suburbs.

Whizzed was a relative term for the Scout. I kept to the right-most lane. The car was in a good mood and had started right up this morning. Some day I'd get to the bottom of what made it sulk in the moisture. Jenny said I was just stubborn. She didn't understand how much the Scout had gotten me through.

The jeep had loomed mighty in my mind as a child. I insisted on being the one to turn the hub locks on the front wheels, and savored the sound when my father ground the secondary gear-shift into four-wheel drive. When I was in high school, after my parents split up, the Scout came into my hands. I couldn't imag-ine turning it over to some stranger, even as the paint faded and I had to replace one original part after another. It was an anchor for me through the high-tech whirlwind. Some people under-stood its charm, but most saw it the way Jenny did: a prehistoric box whose bucket seats were about as comfortable as a school bus and whose truck suspension allowed you to feel every pebble on the road. While new cars were designed to look slippery as a suppository, the Scout was all straight lines. The windshield was a flat piece of glass. The original black license plate with yellow letters, now beaten and bent, was still fixed to the bumper.

I was on my way to a meeting with Rita. Jenny had wanted me to stay another day with her in Palo Alto, but Rita and I had to prep for the Kumar shoot, which began on Monday.

Last night, after LifeScience, Jenny and I had ended up at a pizza joint for dinner. She could barely stand the thought of food, much less cooking, and just picked at her slice. She couldn't stop imagining Sheila's last minutes. I didn't want to tell her the details of what I'd learned about anaphylaxis.

Sheila probably first felt it as a tingle in her teeth, an itch on the roof of her mouth. Not suspecting food caused it, she might have blamed it on the cat. As the antigen was absorbed into her stomach, Sheila's immune system would have misidentified it as a threat. Mast cells were dispatched from various locations in her body, in search of the antigen. Histamine exploded like grenades out of the mast cells as they degranulated. Her stomach cramped. Capillaries enlarged and filled with fluid, which leaked into other tissues. Her gut, throat, hands, and feet swelled. Her skin started to feel hot and prickly. Welts spread over it. Her blood pressure dropped and she became dizzy from the onset of hypotensive shock. By now she must have known what was happening. A sense of doom overcame her. She tried the adrenaline injection in the bathroom, or maybe in her car. It should have relieved the other dangerous effect of the histamine, which was to cause her muscles to constrict, especially muscles in her bronchial tubes. But the solution was spoiled. Slowly her breathing apparatus closed up. She fought for oxygen. It could get neither in nor out. She suffocated with two hyperinflated lungs, like balloons full of air.

I got off 280 at San Jose Avenue and went straight to Rita's. She lived in a backyard bungalow, built around 1910, in the Mission. She'd bought it in the early nineties, when prices were low. Low for San Francisco, that is: at the time, her down payment seemed a small fortune. Rita had been smart in all the ways I hadn't. She'd stuck with filmmaking. A steady income from industrials had allowed her to make one independent documentary and begin research for a second.

Rita arched her brows as soon as I entered the house. The living room was an obstacle course of film gear. I left my camera there and we went into the kitchen, a large room with windows on two walls. A breakfast table sat in the middle. A couch was in the corner. I dropped into it and Rita stuck a cup of coffee in my hand.

"Two nights in a row with Jenny," Rita said. "I smell a matrimonial mishap." Her bright, throaty voice undercut itself with a low current of irony.

I frowned. "I haven't told you the reason yet."

I related the whole Sheila story. Rita's expression sobered. "I can see why Jenny's upset," she said. "But I don't see why she feels responsible. She took all the right precautions."

"The doctor was sure it was something Sheila ate. The reaction comes on pretty fast. Where else would the toxin have come from but dinner?"

"Something in her car?"

I shook my head. "Sheila was careful."

Rita gave a sympathetic shrug. "Just one of those terrible, inexplicable things, I guess. You may never know the real cause."

I looked at her without answering. She was nearly my height, with light sandstone hair that fell to her shoulders in waves. Her round face and fine features reminded me of a Botticelli painting. We had been a couple for two years, but that seemed ages ago, before the Internet bubble swelled big enough to separate us. While I got sucked into it, she stuck with film. We'd been a good team. I could shoot and she could direct, or vice-versa. On the kind of films I shot now—documentaries, industrials, independent narrative, most with small crews—half the directors didn't know how to compose a frame. Rita knew cinematography. We agreed about the process, and I didn't have to put up a fight to make the picture look good.

We sipped coffee for a minute and stared out the window. Her little house was set back from the street. A neighbor was hanging laundry on the line that stretched from her porch to Rita's roof.

Rita got up and tossed a script into my lap. She'd written it with someone from Kumar's marketing department. The first shoot would last five days, all next week. We began to plot out each day's work, each setup, each piece of gear. This afternoon I'd go and rent the specialized equipment we'd need.

It was a bioinformatics industrial, meant to show off the company's tech to the stockholders. There'd be lots of shots of computer screens. Not much challenge, except to use Clearscan to make sure no bars went rolling up the screen. We also came up with ideas for showing some of the micro world that underlay all that computation. That would be more interesting to shoot.

"We can get inside with the snorkel lens we used on our last microchip job," I said. "Put a one-and-a-half-inch probe lens on it, use a ninety-degree rotating periscope to get different angles on the circuitry. They don't want to use film, do they?"

"No, HD. Everyone's on a budget these days."

"I did some establishing shots of the building on Wednesday." That reminded me of the parking lot. "Hey, Gregory hasn't bothered you again, has he?"

Rita rolled her eyes. "Only six times yesterday. He doesn't leave messages, but I see his number on caller ID."

"I told him to lay off. You want to see what he looks like? I've got the tape in my camera bag. You're not going to believe this guy."

"Not necessary. I won't be working with him."

"I got footage of Sheila, too. She was in the same parking lot. The camera spooked her. I wonder what she was up to."

"You said she worked in biotech. People in the industry know each other, right? Maybe her company was doing business with Kumar."

"Why would she hide, though? There are so many weird things going on. The missing hard drive. Mr. Alpha Male at

LifeScience. Why did he want Sheila's journal? And Fay, stealing it in the first place."

Rita tsked. "Those are the kind of friends Jenny has."

"Come on now, you can blame Jenny for a lot of things, but not what happened to Sheila."

"Well, what's in Sheila's diary?"

"I don't know yet. I opened it last night, but . . ." It had been bad enough to see Sheila laid out in the morgue; I hadn't been ready to see her heart laid bare. The journal had gone into my glove compartment this morning. "I'll read it tonight. See what's in there about her allergies. LifeScience. Fay."

Rita's green eyes held me for several long seconds. They were aloof, like an oracle. "Why are you getting so caught up in this?"

"You know me, Rita. I like to get to the bottom of things."

She gave me a scolding smile. "The curious cat. Always chasing after things he can't quite catch. Pretty soon one of those things will jump up and bite you."

"I bite back, don't forget."

"Yes. One of the few men whose bite is worse than his bark." She smiled.

"Thanks for the upgrade to dog status. But look, I was dragged into this. I'm the one who identified the body. Jenny may get blamed for her death. And Sheila was—I don't know, something just clicked. You don't often meet people like her. You would have liked her, Rita."

"I'm sorry, Bill. I'm sorry she died."

"The guy at LifeScience was such a prick about it. He's covering something, I'm sure. It pisses me off, you know? The things people get away with."

Rita slowly exhaled. "Nothing surprises me anymore. I've been doing a lot of work in biotech lately. I see what's going on. The money osmosed to it after VCs came to their senses about the Net rush. Sequencing the human genome was supposed to open a new gold mine. But it's an industry like any other. A young one. Only a handful of these companies show any profit right now. Most of them are hot air, or years from a return on investment. Think of all the money that went into the dot-bombs: the startup costs of a biotech company are even greater."

"At least biotech makes an actual product."

"The lead time to results still can be long. And the shenanigans of the Web run-up are going on in biotech, too, with higher stakes in some cases. So, yes, there could be shenanigans at LifeScience, but they're probably nothing more than the usual."

"Except Sheila's dead."

"She had a medical condition. What, you think someone *tried* to kill her? Bad business strategy."

"Only if you get caught. And not if she was screwing up someone's plans while she was alive."

Rita leaned over and gave me a little punch on my bicep. "It's Jenny, isn't it? You're sweet to be so concerned. You're taking good care of her. Just don't let her run your whole life."

"Jenny is completely upset. She doesn't scheme nearly as much as you think she does. But this is as much for me as for Jenny."

Rita sat back. "I've seen it a thousand times," she said, nodding in the wise, wry way she had. "Death does it to people. It brings them together—or it splits them apart. One of the two. Rarely in between."

She tilted her chin up and added, "You've been on the fence about Jenny. Mark my words, you're going to fall one way or another before this is all over."

8

After I'd rented the film gear, I had just enough time to drop in at Dr. Jill Nikano's office. It was in the Sunset district, near Golden Gate Park and the University of California Medical Center. The nurse at the front desk was just putting on her coat to leave. I asked if Dr. Nikano was in her office. Yes, but she was done seeing patients for the day. I said it was a personal matter. The nurse buzzed her and then pointed me down a hallway.

The doctor waited outside her door with her arms folded. She was a sturdy woman with veins of gray in her short hair. A pair of trapezoidal glasses sat on her nose like a piece of furniture. Telling her I was a friend of Sheila's got me invited into the doctor's office.

"I got a call from Dr. Curran at the hospital this morning," Dr. Nikano said, sitting at a cluttered desk. Behind her was an image of lungs blossoming with bronchioles. "I feel terrible about Sheila. Made me wonder if I'd missed something at her last visit."

"That's just it. It's so rare for this to happen, isn't it?"

"Yes and no . . ." She hesitated. "A study was done a few years ago that found elevated levels of mast cell tryptase in a significant number of unexplained deaths. It may happen more frequently than we think."

"Well, I want to find out what caused such a severe reaction."

"The spoiled epinephrine didn't help. That surprised the jelly out of me. Sheila was as prepared as any patient I've known."

"Could she really have been taken down by a little speck of shellfish?"

"The long answer is that a number of scenarios could have brought on the anaphylactic reaction. People have severe allergies to nuts, milk, eggs, latex, even sperm. There's a disease called mastocytosis in which your body can induce the reaction on its own. But Sheila didn't have it, nor any of these allergies. So the short answer is, yes. A little bit of crustacean could be responsible."

I shook my head. "How can that happen?"

"Don't underestimate the speck. It triggers the whole arsenal of the immune system, a powerful thing. With allergic rhinitis, the allergen is pollen or dust and the reaction localized to the nasal cavity. In food allergy, it's usually a protein. The reaction is far more extreme when sensitivity has developed in the intestinal tract. There are several crustacean proteins people are allergic to, some of which allow the animal to survive in cold water. Sheila's immune system mistook them for a barbarian horde. We don't know why, exactly. Some doctors theorize our society has become too clean. Our immune system doesn't have as many germs to fight, so it turns its weapons on innocent allergens—or our own cells, in the case of autoimmune disease. People in developing countries have a lower rate of allergy and asthma, presumably because their histamines and eosinophils are kept busy with other things."

"How can we be sure it was a crustacean protein? We know she didn't eat any that night." I told her about the dinner party. "We're also certain there was no shellfish residue in the kitchen."

"Even if there was a bit of residue, it should only have made her sick. Not killed her."

I waited a moment before going on. "Right. So we're thinking about other sources. What about where she works—LifeScience?"

Dr. Nikano tilted her head. "You mean a biochemical hazard? I doubt it. They're super careful in those companies. What Dr. Curran told me points to anaphylactic shock, not some other type of poisoning. The protein hits fast and it hits hard. If she got it at the lab, she wouldn't have made it to your dinner party."

"What about after she left the party, then? She only felt a little bit ill at dinner. Maybe someone gave her the allergen afterward."

"Gave her?"

"It seems unlikely, I know—if someone wanted to kill her, why not just do it the old fashioned way?"

Dr. Nikano looked perplexed, almost hurt by the idea. She folded her hands. Lines runnelled her forehead.

"So this doesn't make any more sense to you than it does to us," I said.

"Nope."

On the wall I saw that she had an MD from UCSF, one of the best research medical schools in the country. "Can you find out what happened? Do some more tests?"

"Oh, I intend to. This one's got my neck hairs up. I'll request samples from Dr. Curran. If an autopsy has been done, I'll get the report."

I took a leap. "Her parents are on their way, but it may take a day or two. They've asked that everything possible be done."

"I'll call the hospital right away."

"Thank you, Dr. Nikano. We really appreciate it."

"Jill," she corrected. She gave me a small smile. "Here's my card. Call me as soon as you find out more."

I started out the door. Papers shuffled on the desk. Jill's voice called from behind me. "Sheila was . . . special. Life should have been kinder to her."

>> >> >> >> >>

I drove over Twin Peaks on the way home, just to get the view. The road carved a figure eight between the hills, and the city scrolled before my eyes, water on three sides. The line of the coast to the west was smudged by ocean haze. The towers of downtown sprouted to the northeast. Telegraph Hill and the Marina stood green to their left, the warehouses of South of Market, former home of the Web frenzy, to their right. To the east, beyond the flatlands of the Mission, a bump rose beside the bay. It was Potrero Hill, lit by the last of the day's sunlight. My flat was on the far side, the top floor of a peeling two-story Edwardian.

It took me fifteen minutes to cross the Mission and get home. As I clomped up the stairs, lugging the rented film gear, Jenny's voice called from above, "Bill, I'm here."

She met me on the landing and buried her face in my shoulder. A long sigh left her body. "I called to say I was coming. But your machine kept answering. I just—I didn't want to be alone."

"It's all right." I kissed her, held her some more, and put aside my reservations. Under normal circumstances I wouldn't be thrilled about Jenny letting herself into my flat without checking with me first. We had different ideas about boundaries— I thought they existed. But this was different. I had to admit it felt good to have her waiting here and pressing into me so hard.

I stroked her hair, kissed her again, and agreed that a beer was just what we needed.

My apartment was a railroad flat, four rooms off of a corridor of wide-planked floors and chipped moldings. I went into a small middle room that served as my office and pressed the play button on my answering machine. Between Jenny's messages was one from my new friend Gregory. Apparently he felt he hadn't come on strong enough the first time.

"Bill-boy, we need to talk. Rita's not returning my calls. There's something you need to know. I wanted to tell you in person, but—you're at serious legal risk if you proceed with the Kumar shoot. Call me back immediately. For your own benefit. You're on my dashboard and the light is blinking."

Jenny stood with a beer in one hand and a glass of wine in the other. She tugged at my belt loop. "Don't call him back right now."

"Don't worry."

We went to the living room at the front of the flat. A sofa just fit inside the cove of a bay window. Shelves with too much camera gear and too many books took up two walls.

Jenny and I sat on the sofa. She said Perkins had called to tell her that he expected to reach Sheila's parents soon. They were travelling in northern Africa. At noon she had met Marion for lunch near the small office Jenny leased in downtown Palo Alto.

"She'd already heard about Sheila," Jenny said. "She seemed, I don't know, kind of distracted, until I told her about going into Sheila's apartment. Suddenly she was all over me. She tried to get me to tell her where the keys were."

"Why?"

"She didn't say. I told her about the hard drive, too. That really set her off."

"I imagine Fay was snooping around because of Simon—but why Marion?"

"I don't know." Jenny's voice was soft and sleepy. Her head rested on my shoulder. Her finger traced a wandering pattern on my shirt. "You have the diary, right?"

"It's with the film gear. I'll get it."

She pulled me back. "Not yet."

"Did you talk to Fay?" I asked, staying put.

Jenny's head went back to my shoulder. She answered absently. "She called, asked about Sheila's parents . . ." Her hand strayed over my buttons, undid one, then went under the shirt. "Acted like nothing was wrong."

"I don't really like the idea, but we ought to read the diary. It might explain some things."

Her other hand slid under the back of my shirt, then down into my pants. "Let's forget about it for a minute."

I didn't object. Her head rose and she pressed her mouth into mine. Her fingers kept working the buttons. When she got the shirt off, she went for the belt. Pretty soon she was doing things to me that she hadn't done since we first got together.

She shed her clothes and pulled me on top of her. One long leg draped over the back of the couch and the other rested on the coffee table. With her musky wine breath hot on my face and her slender hips pushing up to meet me, everything else melted away.

As we lay entwined on the sofa, darkness crept over us through the bay window. Jenny stroked the back of my head. Her face glowed gently.

"Bill, I'm so happy to be here."

"Me, too." The statement felt true in both big and small ways. I was happy to have my limbs entangled here on the couch with hers. But I was even more happy to be here in my house, here on this planet. To have the fabric of an old sofa scraping my skin. To wiggle my toes. The keenness of the feeling was a little disturbing, given that I'd been gazing at Sheila's cold corpse just yesterday. It seemed wrong for us to revel so carnally.

"I feel so alive," she said.

"Alive," I agreed, "and a little guilty."

"We have to carry on, Bill. Celebrate life." Jenny rolled over on top of me and cupped my cheeks. Her eyes were full, a swirl of pearly blue at each center. "Let's have a baby."

A thrill fluttered through my stomach, as if the universe was focused on us at this moment with just that in mind: creating a new life. But an imp of rationality still scratched in the corner of my brain. Jenny and I were reacting to the stress of a death. The impulse to procreate right now was the most natural thing in the world. But we should wait and see what other emotions followed this one.

I just smiled at her and said, "Do you want something to eat?"

Disappointment clouded her face. "You don't have to feel bad about Sheila all the time. We're still here."

I stood, and Jenny started to get up with me.

"Stay," I said. "I'll whip up something for dinner." I wanted to be alone for a minute.

I started some water boiling and some oil heating in the kitchen. After taking Jenny a new glass of wine, I went back to the stove. There were three or four dishes in my repertoire. I had some shrimp in the freezer. I sautéed them with some red peppers and chili flakes, and put them on noodles.

We sat on the couch without talking, still naked, in the dark. Passing headlights slid up and away through the blinds. Now and then a car door slammed outside. The freeway hummed faintly in the distance. Before me, on the coffee table, was a bowl of shrimp that I knew would taste good. Jenny certainly seemed to be enjoying hers. I speared a shrimp on my fork, but couldn't bring it to my lips. Instead I just stared at it. This could have killed Sheila, I kept thinking. One little shrimp. It didn't, and yet Sheila was still dead, without having eaten a single bite.

9

If Potrero Hill had a center, it was Scoby's Cafe on 18th Street. After sleeping in the next day, Jenny and I walked up three blocks to the cafe. I brought Sheila's diary with me.

You could see the strata of history in the clientele. The newest stratum was the laid-off dot-com kids, in fleece and sandals, drinking coffee to no point, itemizing their severance deals and the hardship of living on unemployment. Just below that layer were the ones still plugged in by various gadgets on their belts, gulping coffee to propel them through a day of coding, milestones, delivery of deliverables, and the general job of monetizing the Internet. Then there were the artists, ambitiously scruffy in drab browns and greens. I'd moved in seven years ago during an earlier artist phase, just before the high-tech invasion, when rents were still sane. Actually, artist types had been moving to the neighborhood since the sixties and the days of the hippies. A few of them remained, too, hair turned the color of ash. Some Hell's Angels still lurked down in Dogpatch, and increasingly the hill was subject to the legions of cutthroat mothers aiming strollers of Jacobs and Madisons at your knees, as they did in the more affluent Noe Valley.

Now and then you'd see the guys with lunch pails stop in for a coffee to go: men who worked in the machine shops, warehouses, and piers at the base of the hill, a reminder of the days when the neighborhood was all about longshoremen and light industry. Before that, it had been a pasture called Goat Hill, with a great view and plenty of salmon in a creek long paved over.

Jenny and I got our coffee and some banana bread and squeezed into a table in the corner. A big storefront window was behind us, and we could see the dogs and smokers who loitered on the benches outside.

The black cover of the diary stared up at us from the little square of faux-marble. I turned the book over. "Let's start at the end."

I flipped through unfilled pages to the last page of writing. Sheila's tiny, neat script had a slight backward slant, as if braving a strong wind. I scanned for something—I didn't yet know what—that would help us figure out what had happened. Acronyms jumped out—MC124, Fc, FAb, HAMA—along with a slew of scientific terms. The page was dotted with small drawings as well, many of a Y-shaped figure that looked as though it were reaching to the sky like a Joshua tree.

"Maybe it's a work notebook," I said. That reminded me of the zip disks. I'd transferred them to a pocket in the case of my camera, which I'd left at Rita's for the Monday shoot.

"No . . ." Jenny was peeking at the previous page. "Listen to this: *Another letter from Simon. He wants a decision. I feel I'm in a tightening vise. How can I explain to him the decision is not mine, but was written generations ago?*"

Jenny hit the page with her fist. "How do you like that? She was fucking Simon after all!"

"How could she be fucking Simon if he's in Australia? But this does tell us that Sheila still had some interest in him, which might also explain why Fay stole the diary."

Jenny flipped through the pages. "I don't know. I don't see how anyone could be threatened by this girl. Look at these." She held up a page of inky self-portraits. The mouth was a thin, wavering line, the hair anguished wriggles, the eyes downcast dots. It made me think of how, in the medical literature I'd read, almost everyone who had experienced anaphylactic shock described a sense of impending doom as it came on.

We got some more coffee and kept scanning. Some pages were dense with writing, some contained only a few brief, melancholy entries. Drawings were sprinkled throughout. Some were strange figures that had appeared in her dreams. One was a mouse, surrounded by more of those Y shapes, and various calculations. I got the feeling she was trying to work out a scientific puzzle.

"I knew Sheila was shy," Jenny said. "I didn't realize she was so . . . sad."

"She was just struggling, Jenny."

"She had no self-esteem. Look at this business with Simon. Let's say, for a minute, it's true that he wanted to hook up with her again. It seems like she wanted to, too—but she couldn't. Or wouldn't. Or wouldn't decide. Or whatever."

"There's something else."

Jenny waited, but I couldn't explain it to her yet. I'd seen something at the dinner party, a pungent wit and an inquisitive mind. I saw it in the journal, too. Her hesitations came, in part, from being open minded, wanting to inspect things from every angle. The journal entries read like a series of investigations, even when she was analyzing the dark clouds of her own psyche.

No, something else had her in a twist. She appeared to be in a crisis about work. She described being transferred out of her group two weeks ago and being stuck with tedious titration tasks in the new post. It made her question her future at LifeScience and her sense of purpose in general. One of the last entries mentioned that she was going to talk with Karen about it—the same Karen, almost certainly, that Perkins had mentioned at the hospital. Sheila was very nervous about having set up that meeting, though she didn't spell out why.

But there was more to it than work. Something else between the lines—I took the diary from Jenny and looked for an entry that might unlock it. "Here," I said, "read this."

Called Mother tonight. Hard to tell if she understood me. Could barely make out her words. At first her responses seemed non sequiturs, but then I began to feel she had something incredibly wise and insightful to tell me, something just on the edge of my understanding, if only I could make that one last leap of logic with her. A leap beyond my scientific mind.

Father says she is fine, no change, no need to worry. But each time I call I feel she has drifted a little farther from my reach. The calls are painful. Why do I live so far away from her? I know the answer. It's not to do with her at all. I feel so bad for her—maybe because I fear seeing myself in her. I wonder if I'm just fleeing from my own fate? Not the one I have the illusion of shaping, but the one written in my DNA. Maybe what it comes down to is that I am afraid to face up to my own future. Mother's helplessness, our shared destiny.

We humans owe our existence to our genes, yet they will betray us for the smallest selective advantage. We're built for reproduction, and once that is done, our genes could care less what happens to us as an organism. Does the world really need more babies? No, it's our genes that do. They code for chemicals that make us want to propagate. From the gene's point of view we're just temporary vessels in which to ride until passed to the next vessel. The vast majority of mutations are disasters for individuals, but for genes they're the engine of immortality. One comes along every so often that happens to improve the species' survival and genes are all over it, like investors in a new technology. Most of the candidates are losers, but the winners win big.

Of course, genes don't think or plan. Like all life, they plunge ahead blindly. Their self-seeking nature is theoretical. Who's to say the theory is "right"? It's a choice, a glass through which to view the world. I never bought into the idea until I saw it in action here, but technology does have a logic and force of its own. Look at how the people in Silicon Valley drive themselves. Eighty-hour weeks, and that's when no deadline looms. Half of them barely exist in their bodies: their real lives take place on a screen. The other half tone and polish their bodies like sports cars.

I suppose my own work is a way of wrenching unwanted destinies away from nature. Taking them into our own hands, refusing to be cast as one of the losers. Yet even as I do this, I see how it can be twisted by others, turned to their own purposes. I see how unpredictable the effects of my actions are, as unpredictable as the effects of engineering a new molecule into an organism. As unpredictable as people are, even the ones who came into our field with the best intentions.

I know I'm only sabotaging myself, and yet I can't stop identifying with Smidge and her lonely fate. Mine may well be the same. By the time it comes, my mother, the only one who would understand, will be long gone.

"Jeez," Jenny said. "She really is kind of morose, don't you think?"

"Do you know who Smidge is?" I asked.

"No, she never mentioned her. Do you have any idea what she's talking about with this destiny stuff?"

I leaned back against the window and took a sip of coffee. "She's trying to recast her role, rewrite her script."

Jenny only shook her head.

Closing the book, I said, "Well, I don't see any obvious answer to what happened to Sheila. Unless it's in a language we don't understand yet. I do want to find this Karen. She might be able to tell us what is really going on at LifeScience."

>> >> >> >> >>

The walk back to my flat reminded me of why I live in San Francisco. There had been a few wisps of fog in the morning, but they were gone now. The sky was brilliant autumn blue, the bay a luminous mirror. A red and white container ship slid up the Oakland channel.

As soon as we got to the top of the stairs in my flat, Jenny turned to me in alarm. "Bill, where's my handbag? I know I didn't take it to the cafe with me."

"It was on the chair by the door, where you always leave it."

We began a hunt for it, starting in the bedroom, under the tossed clothes and unread newspapers. It wasn't in the living room, either. The camera cases by the bookshelves looked out of order. A panic hit me. I knelt and unzipped them. No, the Aaton, the lenses, the DV, the DAT recorder, all were safely in their bags. But something had changed. The side pockets were open.

I thought for a minute. The front door had been locked. I went to the kitchen in back. The window was partially open. I was pretty sure I hadn't left it that way. I stuck my head out. A sliding ladder leaned against the wall. The top rung rested just a couple of feet below the window sill.

"Jenny," I called over my shoulder, "someone broke in!"

I clambered out the window and down the ladder. No one was hiding in the weedy postage stamp of a backyard. No one in the garage either. I did a pull-up on the fences on each side of the yard. No sign of the intruders. I went back up the ladder, two rungs at a time, and called the cops.

10

The police didn't stay long. They were not impressed with the extent of our loss. Yes, I admitted, the expensive camera equipment was intact. My insurance company would be spared. The only things missing were some videotapes and Jenny's handbag. Luckily, she'd taken her wallet and cell phone with her. The cops wrote it up and told us they would be in touch. They also suggested I put the ladder away.

That much was true. Mrs. Debler, the owner, had some roof work done two years ago. The ladder had been leaning against the back fence ever since. I collapsed the ladder and stowed it in the garage. I also checked the yard again, more slowly, and this time found a few boot prints. I went back up to get a camera.

"This makes me so mad," Jenny said. She was looking around for what else might have been taken. "All this really valuable stuff, and what do they pick? My bag."

"You think they should have taken my livelihood—my cameras—instead?"

"You know I don't mean it that way. It's just that I had some personal stuff—some really good skin lotions I just bought."

"They weren't looking for money. This is all about Sheila. They were looking for specific items relating to her. My videocassettes, which probably are blank. They may have thought the diary was in your handbag."

Jenny's eyes widened. "You don't think it was Fay?"

"Could be. Or the guy from LifeScience. Or Marion. They all knew about it. I'll ask the neighbors if they saw anyone."

The sound of the phone ringing startled us. I picked it up in my office. Jenny followed, hand covering her mouth.

"Hi, Wes," I said. "Glad it's you."

Jenny exhaled with relief, then paced in the hall while I told Wes about the break-in. She came back into the room and said, "I'm going to look around the neighborhood. Maybe whoever took my bag tossed it in the bushes."

I told her I'd come find her.

Wes knew about Sheila, it turned out. Marion had told him. Apparently the two of them had been burning up cell phone minutes. Wes was seeing her tonight and expected cellular communication of another kind to occur.

I asked if she'd said anything more about Sheila. "Not to me. You had to go down and identify the body, huh? That must have been weird."

"It's only gotten weirder." I filled him in about LifeScience, Fay, and the diary, and wondered which one of them was connected to the theft.

"I don't know, Billy," he said. "Is it really worth getting involved in this?"

"I've been looking for something to do for nine months. This isn't what I had in mind, but I can't stop thinking about what happened to Sheila. My flat getting robbed means I'm already involved."

Wes's call-annoyance feature interrupted the conversation.

He said he had to take it, so we signed off. I went downstairs to photograph the footprints in the garden.

I was back inside when the doorbell rang. I assumed it was Jenny. But when I opened the door, there stood Gregory Alton. "You're here," he said. "Good. We can talk now."

Slamming the door in his face would have been enjoyable. But if I did, he'd just stand out there until Jenny came back. So I joined him on the porch. "Hey Gregory, how do you get the dot-commer off your doorstep?"

He looked over his shoulder, as if I was talking to someone else. I answered my own question. "Pay him for the pizza."

Gregory managed to crack a smile. Then he made a show of removing his sunglasses and looking me directly in the eye. "Bill, I hope you got my message."

"What's this bullshit about legal risk?"

He took a deep breath and started to make chopping gestures with his glasses. "Kumar's jumping our technology. We've got a way to model—well, never mind, the point is, Kumar's filched the key step in the process. We've filed suit, but by the time we get a decision we'll be broke."

"I'm sorry to hear that. What does it have to do with us?"

"Let me see the footage you got at Kumar's. I'll show you what I mean."

"Footage isn't here, Gregory. How long have you been in the neighborhood? Since, maybe, nine this morning?"

"Bill, the life of my company is at stake. Literally. You'd do whatever you had to do to protect your business, wouldn't you?"

"I wouldn't break into other people's houses."

Gregory skipped right over this. "You've got to help me. What's he's doing is totally bogus."

"Someone just climbed a ladder and broke in through my back window. They took my girlfriend's purse and my video-tapes. That's what I call bogus."

This stopped him, but only for a moment. "Buddy, that's a drag. But you don't think *I'd*—no way, Bill. Not me. Maybe it was Kumar. Seriously, he is scum."

"I've dealt with the guy. Nothing came off on my hands. Besides, he has no reason to break in. The footage is his."

Gregory answered with a slow head shake. "See, you just don't know how smooth he is. He's pulled some fast ones. Slimy, slippery fast ones."

I stared at Gregory. Kumar had not pulled any fast ones on us. Nor, for that matter, had Gregory shown any guilt when I mentioned the break-in. But what he was saying about Kumar could as easily be true of himself. I'd seen young CEOs operate. How they could be exhausted, discouraged, sullen—then turn on a dime for an interview, rev up the charm, roll out the company myth, and pronounce with utter sincerity the precise opposite of what they'd just said in private.

"Gregory, you are going about this in such the wrong way."

"All right, so I get a little . . . *enthusiastic* sometimes. But BioVerge, it's my passion, it's my life. What would you do?"

He looked a bit ridiculous, standing there with his shoulders cocked, wearing a yellow-print Hawaiian shirt and, incredibly, a yellow scarf round his neck. His hair was a peculiar—and it now occurred to me artificial—shade of yellow. With the little nub of blond turf on his chin and the pleading look in his eyes, he was starting to resemble a golden retriever.

"What was that bullshit about having us shoot a film for you?" I said.

"Absolutely real, buddy. We want you to do one up. If Kumar doesn't ruin us, I'll pay you like I said."

"I'll dashboard it, Gregory," I said, mimicking his expression. "But don't call us. We'll call you."

"I don't have that kind of time. A contract is coming up. Huge. We're bidding against Kumar. Whoever gets the LifeScience deal—"

Gregory caught the change in my face right away. His confidence came galloping back. "So you know LifeScience. Players, dude. About to bust out with a product that will turn the monoclonal world upside down. A big pharma is already courting them. We're bidding to partner up on their next project. We'll be riding their comet trail. You should get in on this action, Bill. Help me stop Kumar."

"What *exactly* is it that you want from me, Gregory?"

"Let me see the footage. It might have the evidence I need to derail his bid."

My phone rang upstairs. "Okay, I *will* discuss this with Rita, and I *will* call you as soon as possible."

"Thanks, buddy. Look, can I take you to lunch? To a ball game—the company's got—"

I shut the door and took the stairs two at a time. It was Jenny, on her cell phone. She'd wandered down to the waterfront and was ready to be picked up. I said I'd be there in a minute. Then I started thinking about what exactly I'd have to give up to get more information out of Gregory about LifeScience Molecules.

11

"No!" Jenny shrieked into the phone the next morning. "How can you say that? You bastard!"

She slammed the phone down. We were in my kitchen, the Sunday paper spread before us. "Who was *that?*" I asked.

Her face had turned the color of bleached wood. "My machine. Mr. Harros—Sheila's father—said I stole Sheila's diary and he wants it back right now. He didn't even say hello first—or thank us—or anything."

"How did he found out we have the diary?"

Jenny's eyes grew hard and determined. She punched some numbers into the phone. "Fay," she demanded, "*what* did you tell Mr. Harros?"

I watched Jenny's expression change from angry to outraged then back to ashen.

"The autopsy's being done Monday—tomorrow," Jenny told me after she hung up. Her eyes were blank. "Sheila's family holds me responsible for Sheila's death, unless the autopsy report—"

The rest came out between choked sobs. "They're going to have the police scour my apartment. If they find any matching—whatever—they'll file charges."

I cradled her head. "Don't worry. That's not going to happen."

"It was Fay who told them about the diary! '*You're* the one who took it,' I said. 'Sure,' she goes, 'to give it to her parents. I didn't want someone else to get it. Why did *you* take it?' She's blaming the whole thing on *me!*"

"How did she know the parents were here?"

"She must have talked to Perkins at the hospital. There was a message on my machine from him saying the family would arrive Saturday night. Then a couple messages later, there's Mr. Harros, accusing me of things. It's Fay they should accuse—she was the one having the fit about Simon. And now that I think about it, she wanted to have shrimp for dinner that night! I had to remind her Sheila couldn't eat it."

"Fay has her reasons for not liking Sheila, but I don't think she'd go that far."

"I don't know what to think anymore." Jenny stood with sudden resolution. "I've got to go down there. I've got to find out where the Harroses are staying and talk to them. I'll give them the diary."

"Not until after I've photocopied it. Let them cool down a bit. And let the autopsy happen. Until they get the report, they'll be filling in the blanks with their own assumptions."

"Fay's poisoned them against me. I can't believe her!"

"Let's go back to Sheila's apartment. See what else we can find, if the parents haven't already taken possession. If—"

"If Fay hasn't beaten us to it! Oh my God, I'd like to catch her there. Do you think she'd plant some kind of evidence on me?"

"I don't think she'd do a very good job of planting evidence even if she tried. But she might try to cover her tracks."

The image of Fay in the apartment got us moving quickly. Jenny drove her Miata down the Peninsula and I followed in the Scout. We dropped my jeep at her apartment and sped over to Sheila's complex. The keys under the flowerpot were gone.

"Time to talk to the manager," I said.

I brought the diary with me. I didn't intend to let it out of my sight. The manager, Jennifer Poloni, was watching a football game in her apartment. She talked to us in the doorway, wearing a 49ers cap and a red and gold jersey. She wasn't pleased about the interruption.

"Nobody else is going into that apartment," she growled. "You people treat it like a motel room, tromping in and out. Enough. Show the girl some respect."

"Who all's been in there since you last saw us?" I asked.

She waved her arms in the air. "The whole caboodle! That fellow Dugan from her office. I don't like him. Claimed her work product was the property of his company. I didn't let him in; told him he could just wait until the estate was settled. Then I caught another one right inside. Don't know how she got in, but she was having a good sniff around. Tall, sorta blonde—from the lab, too, she said when I stopped her. At least she was nicer."

"Marion," Jenny murmured. "Did you see anyone else?"

"That Chinese girl was here. Your friend. I didn't let her in."

"She didn't have the key?"

"She said you took it. You better give it back now."

Jenny looked at me, then at Poloni's outstretched hand. "We don't have it. Honest. We thought Fay did."

A roar came from the TV. Poloni ran to catch the replay. "Goddammit!" she yelled.

We turned and headed back down the walk. "Hey!" she called from the doorway. "I'm watching Sheila's place, you can bet on that!"

"Marion found the key," I said as we walked back to the car. "And Dugan must be the Alpha Male from LifeScience."

"What was Marion doing in Sheila's apartment?"

"I don't know. The same thing as Dugan, maybe. Then again—they can't be working together, or she'd have let him in."

"Dugan scares me."

"I've run into guys like him before. Business is war to them. They fight dirty, but they try to stay just this side of legal. I'd like to know what Sheila had that he wants so badly."

Jenny gave a little shiver as she pulled out of the parking space. "Let's stay away from him, all right?"

"I'm afraid the feeling won't be mutual. Not as long as we have the diary. Let's get to a copy shop. We'll make two copies. I'll lock away one as a backup."

An unexpected smile crossed Jenny's lips. "Mister Thorough."

I started to say something about my camera operator training, until I realized she meant it appreciatively. I smiled back. She stopped before pulling out of the alley and leaned into me. "Thank you, Bill, for being here for me through all this. I didn't know if you would."

Her golden razor-cut hair swung in front of her face in a way that I found utterly engaging. I could have jumped on top of her right there.

» » » » »

We'd just pulled into a mall anchored by a large office store when I noticed the maroon car behind us. It had taken a left with us into the lot. The car was a generic American sedan, but the color stayed in my mind. It had come into the frame near Sheila's apartment complex. Nothing was special about it— a lackluster maroon wearing a patina of dust—except its recurrence. I watched through my side window as the car tracked us.

Jenny wheeled into a parking space. I put my hand on her arm. "Let's just sit here for a minute."

She cut me a look and moved over for a kiss. I obliged, keeping an eye out the back window. "Check out this maroon car," I said as we separated.

With a gentle swat to my head, Jenny sank back into her seat. "What about it?"

The sedan took a slot a few spaces down from us. The Miata was low, though, and once the other car pulled in, I couldn't see it. I gave Jenny the diary, got out, and took a couple of steps to the front of our car. As I stretched my arms, I turned and got a look at the maroon sedan. Two men were inside. I waited. They didn't get out.

"Let's go," I said to Jenny. "Walk to the store with me. Fast."

She wanted to know what was going on, of course. I said I was just being safe.

The copy machines had their own little carpeted area in the front of the office store. The clerk assigned us a machine. I asked Jenny to photocopy the diary. There were about eighty pages, but we could fit two to a legal-sized sheet. The machine collated our pair of copies for us. I kept an eye out for the guys from the parking lot.

About ninety seconds later a guy as nondescript as the maroon car came in. He had bland light hair, poorly cut, and was wearing shorts and a polo shirt. A couple of inches of belly flopped over his belt. He could have been an engineer out for a Sunday visit to the mall. Nice cover.

He gave the floor a quick scan. He didn't linger, but his eye caught us. I knew, because it was the same fleeting glance an actor gives the camera if they're not sure where it is. First rule of acting: Never stare at the camera.

"Bill," Jenny said, "some of the pages have been torn out."

I put my finger to my lips and nodded toward the guy. He was perusing the cell phones, which were across the center aisle from us. "Just try to remember where they are."

When Jenny was done, I took the copies and the diary to the cashier. I kept them close to my body, hidden from the guy at the cell phones. I was wondering how to make our exit when the clerk slid our copies into a plastic bag.

"Can I also get fifty sheets of blank paper, legal-size?" I asked.

The clerk measured out a stack from below the counter. I asked for another bag, continuing to position myself between our watcher and our purchase. I taped shut the bag with the diary and copies, and did the same with the bag containing the blank paper.

"I'll carry them," I murmured to Jenny.

"Is he—?"

I gave her a small nod. I could be wrong about the guy. But I had to assume I wasn't. With my back to the door, I tucked the bag with the diary under my shirt, the bottom half of it cinched under the waist of my jeans. It took me back to my teenage years, when I occasionally borrowed expensive film magazines from stores.

As we headed for the door, the guy moved so very casually and yet briskly to meet us, reminding me of the time I'd been caught. But instead of the hand on the shoulder, he followed us out the door. That sealed off any chance of getting help from inside the store.

I picked up my pace. Jenny was right beside me. "Get out your car keys," I said.

She dug into her pocket. Her hands were shaking when she brought out the keys. "What's happening, Bill?"

"Don't worry. You're doing great."

The guy pulled even with us when we were still an aisle away from the car. "You've got something that's not yours. Why don't you give it to me."

His voice was smooth and calm. Like there was no question he'd get what he wanted. "Who are you?" I said. I didn't stop.

"We represent the rightful owners. Please. Make this easy."

The top was down on the Miata. I had thought we'd be able to jump in, until I saw the second guy waiting by Jenny's car. He was pretty much a replica of the first, but taller and chunkier. The main question in my mind was whether they were willing to get physical. There were enough people in the parking lot, potential witnesses, that I figured not. I *hoped* not.

I said to Jenny, "Can I use your phone?"

Jenny handed me her cell phone. We were at the Miata now. The big one blocked the path to the driver's side door. I said to him, "Would you please let her by so she can get in the car?"

He made a little bow and stepped aside. "I'll do the same for you, sir. Just as soon as you turn over the document."

"You're going to have to tell me who you represent first." With the bag lazily squeezed between my side and my elbow, I flipped open the phone. I made sure they could see the numbers I dialed. 911.

The first guy made his lunge. He took the bag from me cleanly. "Got it!" he announced triumphantly. They took off.

I shook my fist after them. "Hey! Hey! I'm calling the cops!"

"Tell them hello," the big guy said over his shoulder.

I dashed to the Miata's door. Jenny had turned the ignition. I pushed her over to the passenger seat. "Let me drive."

I released the brake and jerked the car into reverse, looking over my shoulder for the maroon sedan. It had already pulled out and was heading for an exit behind us.

"They should be untaping the bag just about now and finding those blank pages," I said. I peeled out in the other direction, praying there was an exit from the lot on the far side of the mall. There was. I made a rather reckless left turn and sped away.

12

I'd never thought of myself as being subject to the psychology of wanting something just because someone else wants it, too. But I have to admit to a little extra spur when I confirmed that Dugan from LifeScience was burning to get his hands on Sheila's journal.

After our escape at the copy shop, we'd decided to get the diary off our hands. We wrangled from Fay the name of the hotel where the Harroses were staying—one of those faceless corporate jobs near the airport. I left the original at the desk with strict instructions to give it to no one but Mr. Harros.

The message from the LifeScience man was waiting for us back on Jenny's machine. The caller identified himself as Neil Dugan, chief operating officer. The "notebook" we had contained intellectual property owned by the company, he said, and we were obliged to turn it over.

Now I really wanted to know what Sheila had on him. Obviously it was enough to make him hire two guys to follow us and commit a felony to get it, and maybe to commit another felony of burgling my flat. How far up the ladder of felonies was he willing to go?

Dugan probably failed to realize that his threats had the opposite effect of what he intended. I did not like having those guys in our face in the parking lot, nor having the Harros family blame Jenny for her friend's death. I hated seeing the dread in her eyes when the phone rang, or when we approached the door to her place. Her effervescence was gone.

But there was more at stake than Jenny's peace of mind and my itch to get back at Dugan. There was Sheila herself. The moment I opened the door for her at the dinner party, I was drawn to her. I felt that buzz of connection you get so rarely. We shared a kindred feeling of curiosity for its own sake. I admired her willingness to expose a bit of herself, show what she really believed, instead of keeping it superficial. She didn't stay alive long enough for us to know if there was more to the attraction. But I felt a strange intimacy with her now, having gazed down on her at the morgue, walked through her silent apartment, and read her diary. It was not right for her to be dead.

Jenny and I ate a quiet, tense dinner at her apartment. Afterward, I settled down with the copy of Sheila's diary. Reading it backward in pieces, quickly, hadn't turned up the answers I wanted. I'd seen Dugan's name once, when he and a new CEO had come in to take charge of the company. She mentioned her family only a few times. I got the feeling they were out of touch with her.

I started again at the beginning. She didn't write regularly, so the entries were spread out over a couple of years. At first she sounded optimistic. She had just started at LifeScience. She did, as time went on, have her bad moments. Maybe she even got morose, as Jenny put it. Her voice came across as being crowded by competing forces on all sides, yet alone. Still, she had an honest, penetrating way of examining herself.

The new job is everything I'd hoped for. The staff is inspired by Dr. McKinnon, and there's a sense of collegiality. Strange that to find this I had to leave the university. The work there can be more exciting, but you don't always get the satisfaction of seeing its immediate benefit. So many people are more concerned about where the next grant comes from, whose paper will be published first. Of course, people scare up money here, too, but they're on the business side, that's their job. Those of us at the bench are focused on a problem and are provided with the tools we need to solve it. Not that we're free of hierarchy, but it's quite clear, set down in the company bible. And yet the staff meetings are very open. Dr. McKinnon wants to hear ideas from everyone. If you go off in the wrong direction, he corrects you right away—not to put you down, but to save everyone time. We're all on the same team.

I have to admit there's also something nice about being compensated well. Payment in academia comes in the form of recognition. You'll get it, in the long run, if your work is good, but you get it a lot faster if you're good at the publicity game. Are the ones who thrive the ones most talented at gaining recognition, or the ones gifted at grasping the structure of a molecule, designing an elegant experiment, reading results insightfully? Here, all of us on the team are pulling in the same direction: nailing this target, curing cancer, and, by the way, cashing in on those stock options.

Found out today that this program is McKinnon's baby, from back when he first got into the field. Big risk, big payoff. We started off with a fairly specific target, but the

candidate seems to work on almost everything we throw
at it. It looks like we might have something huge! And here
I am right in the middle of it. It's like a dream come true.

It would take some studying to decode just what she was
working on, but I got the feeling Sheila was quite good in her
field. She clearly loved what she did.

Call from Abe, just back from Sierra Leone. His group
was held for three days by teenage soldiers. Abe speaks of
it the way anyone else might an airport delay.

And then look at me. Living in this apartment.
Waking up to drink my precious tea in my little den.
Following all the other tech rats in our shiny metal shells
down the dotted yellow line to another cage. Pressing the
right buttons and going down the right corridors to my
little station and my little reward. Moaning about the fact
that Simon wants me and it's making my life compli-
cated. Coming home late, alone most of the time, to nibble
on my anchovies and greens.

A waste of time to think too hard about this, Abe would
say. When you choose what you are going to do, choose it
strongly. Yes, this is what I've chosen. Yes, the reasons are
selfish. I love to find the telltale spots of multiplication in
a cell culture. To put that 138th try at gene transfer under
the scope and see we've hit upon the growth factor. To zoom
in on the mass spectrometer peaks and nail the molecular
weight of my protein. To be alone at the bench, coaxing
a cell line along as the clock ticks a late hour. Even the
smell of the acetone and methanol warms my heart. A
born lab rat.

Abe's work must give him the same pleasure. He was always so directed, so serious about helping humanity. But doing good is also a measure of achievement, a road to recognition, and an unassailable one.

Who knows if my work will ever make a difference to anyone. It's nice to imagine a future woman who finds, say, a lump in her breast, being able to go into her doctor and treat it with a simple course of pills or injections. Even still, if that day comes, people will say we were just in it for the money.

Simon rated only a mention or two as Sheila's relationship with him heated up. But he got more attention as things started to go wrong.

Simon is slipping away. I "forget" to return his calls. It's just because I don't know what to say to him. He thinks I'm sloughing him off. We plan a weekend outing, and I realize I have to be in the lab. My work day goes later and later, and he comes to meet me at night in the lab, only to find us whooping it up, doing a dance around the ELISA plate so it will give us the results we want. A couple of wine bottles waiting to be opened if the assay is a success. Simon must think we're in some goofy cult. How can I explain to him that he just happened to arrive after hours of mind-numbingly repetitious work and we are punchy from the tedium, the fluorescent lights, Doug's constant pressure? I don't want to make excuses, excuses are boring, and I'm sick of all mine. No one outside the lab would understand. So I just smile and hope he'll join in.

Simon can be so passionate, trying so hard to spark my own. He sees I'm holding back. It's not because of you, I say in various ways. He only tries harder. Men do love a challenge. But that's not the game I'm playing. There's no game at all, just my mind folded in on itself.

I've noticed his eyes wandering over in Fay's direction. She's certainly been trying to catch them. I can see how Fay would be more appealing. She has those playful black eyes, that beautiful glossy hair, that figure. She's fun and lively and a guy would be crazy not to find her sexy. Next to her I feel dry and mousy. Simon thinks "curing cancer" is noble and so on, but he can't follow the labyrinth involved in actually doing it. His eyes glaze over when I try to explain. I don't blame him. But it's my life, it's what makes my neurons snap crackle and pop.

Maybe I should just come out with my secret. Open the door for him to walk away. But what if he doesn't? I could see my condition making him feel sorry for me. We'll fall a little farther into each other's lives. Then when it starts to get serious it will slowly dawn on him what he's really getting into, and he'll begin to back out. Even if he didn't, I'm not sure I can bring a child into the world, knowing what I know. And I'm sure he's got kids on his agenda.

Maybe, for me, my work will be my child. My legacy, my regeneration—whatever it is that makes people crave offspring—will be my research, however small the contribution. Better that than to have my life run by genes nagging REPRODUCE ME, REPRODUCE ME.

They say childbirth is the essence of being human. Yes and no. It's the essence of bacteria, yeast, fungi, and every other form of life. But unless you want to say we're no different than snails, the essence of being human must lie elsewhere. Like in choosing our own destiny.

The phone rang. We were on Jenny's bed, pillows behind our heads. Jenny was watching a movie. When she hesitated, I gestured for her to hand the phone across to me.

It was Marion. She said a few polite words, but didn't waste time getting to the point. Wes had told her about the diary, and she wanted to see it. I asked her why.

"Let's just say that Sheila got herself in some hot water. I assume you're a friend—were a friend—and you care about her reputation. First of all, don't mention this diary to anyone else in the company—"

"Neil Dugan already knows about it."

This brought a moment of silence. "That's not good. He's the last person who should see it. Please make sure he doesn't."

"He won't get it from me. We don't have the diary anymore, anyway. Sheila's parents do."

"Can you help me get a look at it?"

"I'll see what I can do," I said noncommittally. "I have a question for you, Marion. Did you go inside Sheila's apartment?"

Another silence. "I did. You have to believe me, I'm trying to protect Sheila. These are complicated scientific matters that, really, are internal to our company."

"Complicated and scientific, huh? If I'm not bright enough to understand them, then I'm not going to be much help, am I?"

"Honestly Bill, I wish I could say more. The last thing I want to see right now is a smear on her name. If you help me, I'll do everything I can to prevent that."

"We can get together and compare notes," I allowed.

We left it at that, neither of us quite forthcoming or satisfied. I did ask her if there was to be a funeral, and she said it would be Wednesday, in Colma. Apparently Sheila's mother was from the area.

I related the conversation to Jenny, but she'd turned her brain off for the evening. She just wanted to watch her movie. I was restless. I got up and went into the living room to call Wes. After chiding him for giving away the existence of the diary, I asked what he thought of Marion.

"Marion's a gas. Kept me up most of the night, and drank me under the table besides. First thing in the morning she was back in action. I'm not sure she's a carbon-based life form."

"Sounds like you've found your soul mate, Wes."

"Are you kidding? I can't go on like this for more than a week."

"A week is a long time. Did she say anything about Sheila? Trouble she was in at work?"

"Yeah, something about Sheila putting her nose where it shouldn't have been. That's all I know."

"Wes, do you think I can trust Marion?"

He snorted. "Trust her? Sure, as long as she's in short sleeves and you can see both her hands."

"Do me a favor, then. Don't pass any more information to her unless I ask you to."

I called Rita next. I was going to be out for the funeral on Wednesday, I said, and might miss some more days after that if the Sheila business continued.

Rita was not happy. She'd have to bring a new director of photography up to speed on the project. Plus, the look of the film would change from day to day, depending on who was shooting. "I might have to drop you, Bill, if you're not sure what days you'll be there. Maybe I should just go with the new DP the rest of the way."

"I understand. You know I wouldn't do this if it wasn't absolutely, totally, completely necessary."

She let out a loud sigh. "I do, Billy. That's the problem. Now I can't even be mad at you. Wait a minute." She paused, as if checking. "It turns out I can be mad, after all. This sucks."

"I'm really sorry, Rita. Will you forgive me someday?"

"What a stupid question."

"You're the best."

Next I called the hotel and confirmed that the diary had been given to Mr. Harros. Yes, the clerk was sure.

That left just one more call to make. Dugan. I punched in the number he'd left. I was and wasn't looking forward to this.

He recognized my voice before I finished introducing myself. "I hope you've got good news for me."

I made myself take a slow breath. "Yes, as a matter of fact. Sheila's diary is in the proper hands. Her parents have it."

"It's not a diary. It's a notebook. If you've stolen our work product, we'll prosecute."

"This was not a company email account. It was a private diary. Her family owns it. If it was so important, why didn't you take it while you were removing her hard drive?"

A slight delay let me know I'd gotten him. "I hope you have a very good lawyer," he said.

"You, too. You've got a couple of felonies to deal with. One, when your agents stole my personal property in the parking lot. Two, when they broke into my house."

There was another hesitation. His answer had some pleasure in it, and I wasn't sure why. "I'd like to see you file charges.

I'd like it very much. In the meantime, I think everyone will be interested in the fact you photocopied the notebook. Twice, if the cashier is correct."

He had me there. My first thought, which I kept to myself, was that I needed to make yet another copy in complete secrecy. I told Dugan, "The copies are for the police. They'll want to look into the circumstances of Sheila's death."

"I'm sure they will. I'm sure they'll want to take a close look at your girlfriend's apartment and everyone who was there."

"We have no problem with that. I'm sure they'll also want to look at Sheila's place of work."

"I'll be assisting them in every way."

A drop of sweat trickled down my spine as I hung up the phone. I'd had an answer for everything Dugan had thrown at me. So why did I feel like I'd lost?

Maybe I was in over my head. If we got into a battle of lawyers, he had me outgunned. So what did I have on my side? Information. The journal. I'd yet to find any keys in it, but maybe that was a matter of correctly understanding the lock. I needed an interpreter, a data miner. Marion came to mind, if only she could be trusted. She did work for Dugan. There was also Karen, the woman Sheila was going to meet before our dinner party.

It could be, though, that Dugan's strength was also his weakness. Yes, he had the company arsenal behind him, but he also had a lot to lose if damaging news came out about LifeScience. Me, I didn't have much to lose. Not much in the way of assets except my cameras. And a couple of little things like life and limb.

13

Work with Rita at Kumar Biotechnics kept me fully occupied on Monday and Tuesday. Sheila's funeral took place on Wednesday at the Mount of Repose mortuary in Colma, south of San Francisco. Colma had once been the terminus of the coffin railroad, which ran from the funeral homes in San Francisco down to the cemeteries here. Three-quarters of the town consisted of green hills and white headstones. Someone had to do it—San Francisco didn't have room for dead people. In recent years the Lucky Chances casino had enlivened Colma's commercial base.

Mount of Repose had a neoclassical theme. A grand pediment and four columns framed a generous veranda. A few knots of people milled outside. I was glad I'd dusted off the only suit I owned, and glad it was a somber color. Jenny was stylish but subdued in a deep blue cashmere sweater and long skirt.

A group of guys stood on the steps in khakis, blazers, and dark shoes. The one woman among them wore a skirt that no longer fit. She fingered a wrap as if unsure what to do with her hands. The men all had theirs in their pockets. Engineers, I speculated.

They glanced at us as we paused on the steps. I nodded to the one closest to me. He'd made an effort to slick his hair back, but a few strands flew solo. His tie looked like a gift from an aunt. His head nodded in my direction, though his eyes wouldn't quite meet mine.

I set down the small briefcase I was carrying. Inside was a mini-DV camera, a DAT recorder, and a small shotgun mike. I wasn't sure I'd use the gear, but having it around made me feel better. A few years in the documentary world had helped me lose any inhibitions about walking up to people and posing questions.

"Hello," I said, stepping forward with my hand on Jenny's waist. "How did you all know Sheila?"

The guy with the bad tie scratched under his chin. "We worked together."

"I remember how excited she was when she started at LifeScience. Did you work with her before or after she got transferred?"

Glances were exchanged, then most of them gazed at their shoes. Finally the woman spoke up. "None of us were happy to have her go. She was really into the program."

"She told me about the monoclonal antibody. It's going to do some good things, I hear."

Their mouths remained closed. Jenny gave one of her candy-apple smiles, which loosened up the group. "It's all right," she said. "We're not in the industry."

"It'll be big," the guy next to me allowed, but went no further.

"Sheila had a real intuitive understanding," the woman added. "She always seemed like a favorite of Dr. McKinnon."

"That's why it was so strange that she got moved. Seems like the kind of thing Dugan would do, huh?" I tried to sound casual yet certain about my conjectures.

The group shifted uncomfortably. No one seemed to want to respond. The guys kept turning their heads, like pond ducks checking a dog on the bank. I followed their glances to the veranda and saw a man, medium height, in a plaid jacket. When he turned his head, I realized it was Doug Englehart, the balding leader of their group. Then another man stepped from behind a pillar. I saw only the back of his head, but the short hair and crisp, hard neckline of Neil Dugan were unmistakable.

"Dugan's pretty new," I said. "You guys get along all right with him?"

I felt like a teacher who'd just asked the class to explain the meaning of *Moby-Dick*. Finally one guy said, "What was your name?"

I shifted the briefcase and stuck out my hand. Only a couple of hands came out to shake it. "Bill Damen. And this is Jenny Ingersoll."

Jenny, about to move forward to offer her hand, froze at the cold looks she got. Her eye began to twitch. I took the issue head on.

"You guys are scientists. What could cause the kind of allergic reaction Sheila had? It wasn't anything she ate at our dinner party. Could it have been something from the lab?"

"Are you kidding?" one man said. "Regulations are so tight, you couldn't catch a cold in there."

Everyone was studiously avoiding our eyes now. We'd get no further with this group. I put an arm back around Jenny's waist and said, "Nice meeting you."

"I feel like a leper," she whispered as we mounted the steps.

"Someone's been spreading the news."

"Geeks," she muttered.

We crossed the stone porch behind Dugan. If he took note of us, he didn't let on. But Englehart gave us a nod of recognition. I reintroduced myself and Jenny. His voice was strained, as if stifled by his shirt and tie. A rash ran up the side of his neck.

Between his unease and the proximity of Dugan, I didn't expect to get much from him either. I murmured a condolence and moved inside with Jenny.

We entered a large anteroom with the usual urns and flowers. Some couches that looked too soft lined the walls. Ensconced in one of them was Fay.

Jenny gave a weak wave and went to join her. I would have liked to have heard Fay's excuses. But the sight of Frederick McKinnon through a big archway drew me into the next room.

The casket was here. Closed. I gazed at it and its swallowed secrets from a distance. An image flashed through my mind of Sheila being taken apart for the autopsy. What did the tissues tell?

Discreet organ music piped through hidden speakers wrapped us in a mild dolor. Grouped loosely around the casket were men, mostly, in dark suits. McKinnon's lanky figure was front and center, with his shock of golden hair and those translucent eyes. His suit was navy blue and his hands were clasped behind his back. He was speaking to a broad-shouldered man with streaks of steel through thick black hair. I couldn't see the second man's face. He wore a double-breasted suit. His broad hands rested lightly on the handles of a wheelchair.

I lingered in the background and listened. McKinnon must have just arrived. He was speaking: ". . . such a tragic accident. You don't know how sorry I am. Sheila was a natural scientist, exceptionally bright. Her work was first rate. I can only imagine how you feel—"

The broad-shouldered man hardly moved. His straight-ahead stare didn't waver as he interrupted McKinnon. "Of course, you won't object to a full investigation of the lab. Responsibility for Sheila's death will be determined."

McKinnon seemed like a man who was never at a loss. But this threw him. He recovered enough to say, "Naturally. Our doors are open."

"I've spoken to Mr. Dugan. He'll coordinate with our attorneys."

McKinnon's fingers tugged at one another. "I'll do all I can. Speaking as a scientist, the likely source of the allergen is a dinner party she attended that night."

Harros turned. His profile made me think of a grim Caesar about to pass sentence on a traitor. "Thank you. We'll be looking very hard at that party. I received the autopsy report yesterday."

"It confirms food allergy?"

Harros gave a curt nod. McKinnon appeared miffed that he didn't elaborate, but leaned over the wheelchair to check on its occupant, a woman I took to be Sheila's mother. She appeared far older than her husband.

I felt a tug on my briefcase. I turned to face a man about my age. Certain aspects of the face were familiar: the olive skin, the strong straight nose, the wavy black hair. Others weren't—a thrust in the jaw, a sense of its own rightness.

"Can I put this away for you?" he asked, reaching again for the briefcase.

I gripped it tighter. "Thanks, but I'm all right. You must be Abe Harros. Sheila talked about you."

"I don't know you."

"I'm a friend of Sheila's from the city." I went on to offer the proper condolences, working my way around to asking about the cause of her death.

He gave me a bald stare. I wondered if everyone got the same searching inspection. "The autopsy's been done. We have a good idea what happened."

His words sent a small bolt through me. I stepped closer. "What was it?"

His appraising look said he knew all, but wasn't going to tell me. Before I could press him, there was a stir at the entryway. A scent of musk and roses swept into the room. It was Marion, managing to look sorrowful and at the same time utterly sensual in a black ribbed sweater and flowered silk shawl. Her hair was up in a French twist. She went straight to Mr. Harros, who was powerless to resist a consoling embrace. The woman in the wheelchair got the same treatment, as did Dr. McKinnon and another couple who apparently were Sheila's aunt and uncle. Marion told them all that she was a very close colleague of Sheila's and went on about how she was devastated by the unexpected event.

The room was in the process of settling down when men with carnations in their lapels started touching people on the elbow and directing everyone out to the chapel. The service would start soon. Abe Harros remained next to me as people funnelled through the doors. Leaning toward him, I said in a low voice, "Watch out for Neil Dugan. I hear he's been trying to get his hands on your sister's diary."

It was a clumsy attempt to establish some kind of connection with him and take some of the heat off of Jenny and myself. Abe's eyes shifted left. Neil Dugan had silently slipped into the room. He stood with folded arms, tie knotted hard at his neck, staring at Marion. I wondered how long he had been there and what he had heard.

I looked straight at him. A smile that said nothing crept across his face, but he never returned the look directly. The message, as I understood it, was that I was an annoyance barely worth notice. And that I would have no impact at all on his actions.

14

I followed the casket down a paved path to the chapel. Jenny was waiting well to the right of the entrance, looking a little forlorn. "Where's Fay?" I asked.

Jenny hugged herself. "She kind of left me behind. I didn't want to go in there with all those people thinking I was . . . Bill, it's so weird. I'm starting to feel like I *am* guilty."

I squeezed her hand. "Don't let them do that to you."

As we went in, arm in arm, I noticed a stairway leading to the choir. "Let's go up," I said. "We'll look down on them for a change."

From our perch, we watched the mingled elements of the crowd separate out like colors in a printing process. The family sat in the front. It was not a large group. Mrs. Harros was in her wheelchair on the aisle, shoulders slumped. Mr. Harros sat bolt upright next to her, then Abe, then the aunt and uncle. A set of younger people, cousins probably, were with them. Behind them were Fay and Marion, then Frederick McKinnon, Doug Englehart, and the bunch we'd met on the steps.

On the other side of the aisle was a group I'd seen only from the corner of my eye. Most of them appeared to be in their late twenties. A man with white hair sat at the end of their bench.

Neil Dugan was behind them, and in the same row, separated by plenty of space, was Jill Nikano, Sheila's allergist.

Farther back was a scattering of people, alone and in pairs. I wondered if the mysterious Karen was among them. As the chapel slowly quieted, I heard a faint sound coming from a man in the rear, just below us. He looked to be in his mid-fifties and wore a pilled brown jacket. He was sobbing softly. I'd want to speak to him.

The service was short and simple. The family didn't strike me as being especially religious. The minister mentioned the fact that Sheila was in some sense returning to home ground, the place where her mother had been born and her grandmother was buried.

Abe got up to speak about his sister. He was three years older than her. He described the science experiments they'd conducted when they were young, and the fact that when they played "doctor" it was to simulate and diagnose actual medical conditions; the other kids in the neighborhood gave up on playing with them. This got a chuckle from the audience. Abe and Sheila read biology books and delighted in regaling each other with bizarre tales from the microbial world. He spoke with the affection of an older brother, but his face remained rigid. His voice carried the same force and righteousness I'd heard in his words to me.

Then the white-haired man on the other side of the aisle got up. He turned out to be Harry Salzmann, Sheila's mentor in graduate school. He used the same phrase McKinnon had to describe her: a natural scientist. He talked about her devotion to discovery and her attitude of cooperation with other students. It was tragic for her to be taken now, when she'd found such a happy research home with his former colleague, Dr. McKinnon. By the end of his remarks, tears were streaming down Salzmann's face. Sobs could be heard elsewhere in the chapel, too—though, I noticed, no longer from the man below us.

As the service came to an end, I stood. Jenny stayed where she was. "I just want to sit here for a few minutes," she said.

"Okay. There's someone I want to talk to. I'll see you up at the main building."

I caught the man in the pilled brown jacket as I came to the bottom of the stairs. He was trying to make a quick exit. I paced along with him out of the chapel and up the path. He reluctantly exchanged greetings with me. I extracted a name: Carl Steiner. I asked how he knew Sheila.

"We worked together." He'd put on a straw sun hat, which he had to hold down against an afternoon breeze. Skin sagged at the corners of his mouth.

"You were in her group?"

"No." His eyes were fixed on loaves of fog thickening in the sky to the west. "I was in another division. She liked to come to the garden I tended, out in back. Watch its progress . . ." His voice trailed off.

"Very sad about her."

He stopped, fastened his nimbus-gray eyes on me, and said with conviction, "She was a wonderful girl. Those people have no idea. They act like they care—but they'll just go on with their lives."

"And you?"

He shook his head and jammed the hat down tighter. "I can't live with it."

He ducked away from me and strode off. I began to follow. He raised a hand to ward me off and disappeared over the hill. I turned to see the casket being borne from the chapel, then returned to join the gathering. As the casket moved off in the direction of the green lawns, I saw McKinnon split off. He marched back up the path. Dugan followed about fifteen feet behind. I took off after Dugan.

The door to the main building was propped open. As I came up the steps, I glimpsed McKinnon at a table with a large urn of coffee. His expression when he looked up to see Dugan was not what I expected. It was cold and distrustful. They might have been executives in the same company, but they were not allies.

McKinnon turned away when he noticed me. I needed to be a fly on the wall. Having the two men alone in a room was one of those experiments that would be ruined by an observer. I acted as if I'd forgotten something, spun on my heel, and sidled back along the wall outside. After a few seconds, I edged closer to the door again.

Silence, then voices. I couldn't make out what they were saying. I'd been lugging my briefcase around like a nerd. It was time to use it. Quietly I opened the latches. Setup took only a minute. I slid a wind baffle over the mike and screwed it into its battery base. The rig was unobtrusive, about the size of a slim baton. After plugging the cord into my portable DAT recorder, I inched close enough to set the mike just inside the door frame. A shotgun mike, it ought to pick up enough of the conversation for me to hear it later.

I hit RECORD. The dB indicator spiked in synch with the murmurs. I pushed the levels, covered everything but the mike with my jacket, then sat back against the wall, trying to look casual. Now and then a mortuary employee bustled by. They were preparing for the return of the mourners, or perhaps getting ready for the next funeral. I smiled stupidly at them, and did things like dig my finger in my ear or inspect my arm. Anything to look busy. I was glad they were trained not to bother the bereaved.

A few minutes later, the voices stopped. McKinnon emerged with his jacket slung over his shoulder. He stared out over the hills, dotted with markers, and his muscles went slack. His long frame lurched to one side, like a willow in the wind. He sighed, turned, and gave a start when he noticed me. It was only a glance; I registered as neither friend nor foe. He straightened, checked his watch, then strode off to the parking area.

I used the cord to reel in the mike. People were starting to file back up from the burial ground. I unscrewed the mike, put the whole rig into the briefcase, closed it, and shrugged on my jacket.

Abe was the first to return. He gave me a long, hard look. Jenny straggled along at the end, ahead only of Mrs. Harros, who was being pushed in her wheelchair by a man with a carnation. Jenny's face was puffy. When I asked if she wanted to leave, she gave me a toss of the head and pushed past me. She'd expected me to be down at the burial with her.

I followed her into the reception room. She made a beeline for the corner. There, beside a vase of pussy willows, stood Mr. Harros. Next to him was Neil Dugan. Jenny marched right at them. I wanted to stop her, to tell her it wasn't time for Harros yet. Professor Salzmann was across the room, getting coffee. He was the one we wanted first. Or Karen, if she was there.

But Jenny was resolved, and I couldn't stop her without causing a scene. I hung a few feet back, listening. "We'll have it all ready for you tomorrow," Dugan was saying to Harros. "Come by whenever you like."

Dugan had the courtesy to step away as Jenny approached. He perched on the arm of a nearby sofa. Swaddled in the cushions, whispering together, were Marion and Fay.

Jenny planted herself. "Mr. Harros, I want to say how very, very sorry I am, and how badly I feel—"

"Who are you?"

She swallowed before answering. "Jenny Ingersoll."

His blunt features stiffened. His brows gathered like thunderclouds. "You dare to come here?"

"Well, yes, I feel involved. We were the ones who went to the hospital—"

"You're involved, young woman. Up to your ears."

Jenny flushed. "What, you think I poisoned your daughter?"

His hands quivered. He looked ready to throw her out. "We'll settle that soon. You'll own up to your responsibility!"

I moved in. "It's true the dinner party was at her house. But Jenny and Fay were very careful about the menu."

Harros's eyes flashed on me. Their fleshiness turned imperious when he opened them wide. "What does this have to do with Fay?"

"She hosted the party with Jenny. Didn't she tell you?"

Fay sprung up from the sofa. "Jenny, what are you saying?"

Jenny set her jaw. "Don't listen to her," she said to Harros. "She's misled you."

"Fay's helping us."

"That's exactly wrong!" Jenny cried. "Fay was the one who stole your daughter's diary!"

Fay's mouth hung open. She had talent, all right. "Is this how you thank me, Jenny?!" She gave a glance of appeal back to Marion. Marion wagged her head sadly, as if dismayed at the depths to which Jenny had sunk. "Is this really about Sheila's death, or is it about you and your guilty feelings?"

Fay had struck a nerve. Jenny's eyes were liquefying. I took her arm just as Harros was about to loose his thunder on her.

"You want to help, young woman?" he said. "Then we'll sit down together and you'll tell me everything. What you did all that day, and the day before, in your kitchen. Who brought what to your party. You'll tell me the truth, and you won't wait for me to get an order to scour your apartment. You'll let us come and do it now."

"This *minute?*" I demanded.

"Whenever I'm ready!" he exploded.

I steered Jenny away from him. "Come over anytime," I said over my shoulder. "We'll tell you what we know. But you're going to have to do some listening, too, Mr. Harros."

His shoulder muscles relaxed a notch. But if Harros was appeased for the moment, his son was not. Abe had circled and was zeroing in on my briefcase again.

"While you're coming clean," Abe said, "how about letting us see what you've got in there? It's been glued to your hand like a nuclear trigger."

"It's nothing that concerns you."

"No, I saw you. When I was coming back up the hill, I saw you closing it. Come on, open it!"

Under other circumstances, I might have let him look, just to show him up. I could invent a good reason for the camera. But the audiotape was too valuable. With one hand keeping a grip on the briefcase, and the other crooked into Jenny's elbow, I had to use my shoulder to push past him.

"Show some respect to your guests," I said.

Abe jabbed his finger at me. "You're up to something, Damen. I'm going to find out what it is and I'm going to nail you."

We marched from the room. Jenny turned to shoot Fay a look. Dugan's eyes bored into the briefcase. Salzmann looked baffled, the LifeSciencers skeptical. The aunt had a worried expression that fell short of sympathy. Whether it was for us or Harros, I couldn't say.

Once we were in the parking lot, Jenny jerked her arm away from me. We'd come in her car. She thrust the keys into my hand without a word. I put the briefcase in back and turned the ignition. Jenny jammed herself into the passenger seat as if trying to crush it.

As I spun by on my way out of the lot, I saw Mrs. Harros sitting in front of the building in her wheelchair. For some reason she'd been left outside. Her head bobbed slowly in our direction, though she didn't really see us. Her neck was tilted at an awkward angle. The wind flailed her hair, and a gnarled hand reached for some object that did not exist.

15

"What do you mean inviting him to *my* house? Since when do you have the authority?"

Jenny had been silent the whole way back to her apartment. I'd been preoccupied with the events of the funeral. I knew she was angry, but I figured it was at Harros.

She threw the keys on the dining room table. They slid across it and fell off. She stomped into the kitchen, filled the teapot with water, and slammed it down on the burner.

I unpacked my briefcase in the living room. Jenny came and stood in front of me, waiting for an answer.

"What can they find? We'll have the Harroses on our ground," I said. "Let them poke around all they want. They'll have to listen to us while they do."

"There it is again. *Our* ground. You don't live here, Bill."

"You want to deal with the guy yourself? Be my guest."

Jenny stamped her foot. "See? I knew you'd leave me to handle this alone. You're not serious about us."

I didn't recall saying either of those things. I tried to get to the real point. "Jenny, I'm sorry I didn't come down to the burial with you. I had other things to do."

"What if it was me in that box? Would you even care?"

"Don't say that. Of course I'd care."

The teapot whistled. Jenny didn't move. She just sat there staring icicles at me.

"What is it, Jenny?"

"Well? Are you going to move in or not? You talk about it, but you don't do anything."

The teapot was screaming. I got up to turn it off. "What do you want?" I called to the living room.

"You know what I want!"

Either chamomile or a marriage proposal, I figured. I tossed the tea bags into the cups, took them to the coffee table, and sat down. "If we do live together, I don't think it would be here."

"Of course not. We'd get a bigger place. I hate these curtains."

"No, I mean here on the Peninsula."

"You're not thinking we'd live in your flat."

"What's wrong with my flat?"

"It's old and mildewy. Besides, the work is down here. The parties, the Frisbee games, people you see in cafes. All your connections."

"No, no. My work is not down here. I do industrials when I have to, but they're not my work."

"You don't even have a cell phone. It's still broken from two weeks ago."

"Yes, and I don't miss it a bit."

She folded her arms. "When are you going to get a real job? Or start a real business?"

"I don't need a real fucking job! I'm doing fine as a camera operator. It's enough for now. I'm thinking about what I'm going to do next, and no one's going to rush me."

Her anger hardened into sarcasm. "Yeah, you're real good at that. *Thinking.*"

I opened my mouth to say she could be better at it. To say that while I very much wanted to resolve the question of what happened to Sheila, the question of whether or not Jenny and I were right for each other in the long run was one I was not ready to take on yet.

In the end, I closed my mouth. She scowled at the steam curling from the teacups, stood up, marched into the bedroom, and closed the door.

"This tops off a really pleasant day," I said to no one.

My machines sat mute on the couch. The white curtains stared at me. Jenny was right. They were repellent. I packed up the equipment and went out to the Scout.

I wasn't ready to drive away just yet. I opened the briefcase again, plugged headphones into the DAT recorder, and listened to what I'd gotten at the funeral home.

After some bumping and rattling, the voices started to come through. They were distant and echoey, but by cranking the volume I could make them out. The first one was McKinnon's.

"... put into the ground. Too painful. I have to get back to the lab in any case."

"It's a tough break." This was Dugan. "Extraordinarily bad luck. This kind of thing doesn't happen very often, does it doctor?"

"It's rare. It takes the right—or wrong—mix of circumstances."

"Yes. She had an adrenaline injection with her, but apparently it spoiled. What would cause that?"

"Heat. Time."

"We don't know how long she would have lasted anyway," Dugan said.

There was a pause. "Meaning—?"

"I don't suppose it matters now. Well, I should get back, too."

"Busy time for us."

"More than I'd like. Why did you tell the board we're ready to start Phase I on MC124?"

"Simple. We are. The IND determination is due back from the FDA on Friday. That'll clear the way to start testing it on human subjects."

"Yes. But wait for it. The chief hasn't signed off yet."

"The results are solid. I'm the scientist, Neil."

"But it's my job to verify. There's some loose data floating around. I think you know that."

"It's nothing to worry about. An anomaly. There's one—many—in every program."

"I hope you're right. I hope it has magically disappeared, because I can't undo your announcement." Dugan cleared his throat. "Tell me, what's your theory on what happened to this girl?"

"It looks pretty straightforward." McKinnon paused. "Unless you know something you're not telling me."

More silence. "There's plenty I don't tell you, Frederick. You do not have the same privilege. I'm the COO. You answer to me. If there are *any* red flags on MC124, you must write them up. Human trials will not commence until we're sure. We *will* put a hold on the program if necessary. No matter what it costs the company in the short run."

"The big pharma money is ready to come in, Neil. They've been knocking down the door."

"Oh, I know. I keep an eye on you. But I'm warning you—don't make any premature moves. We have to do this right."

"You don't actually want to see this fly, do you? You'd be happy if I just went away. Oh, but don't forget to leave behind the science that started this company. Look, if you don't step lightly, I *will* leave. And I'll take the program with me."

Dugan chuckled. "We want your program to succeed. Very much. There's no rivalry here, Frederick. We all know what it would do for the company. Pave the way for the IPO. The biggest monoclonal breakthrough in years."

"And I think you have a problem with that. With the credit I'll get."

Another laugh. "No, I've only got a problem with the huge crater you'll leave if you're wrong."

"On the contrary, I think you might enjoy it. As long as it's my crater, not yours."

"It's the *company's* crater, doctor. That's my sole concern. This is not a lab experiment you can throw out if it goes wrong. We have obligations. You take the risks in science. We take the risks in business. That's what we were brought in for."

McKinnon's voice, under control to this point, turned angry. "You want to know how safe MC124 is? I'll demonstrate. I'll inject it myself. Would that satisfy you?"

Dugan laughed. "Don't be ridiculous."

"You just proved to me how little you know about the field, Neil. It's an old tradition. My team will administer it to ourselves. It won't give us results on the target, of course, but it *will* address toxicology. That all right with you, Mr. Dugan?"

"Be my guest."

"*Thank* you for your permission. I guarantee the effects will be negligible. *Guarantee* it."

"Nothing would make me happier. But one more thing. Don't broadcast it up and down the industry. Your announcement of MC124 at the medical conference in San Diego was unacceptable."

"It's my work. My call when to publish."

"I understand you're giving Doug top billing on the paper."

"Christ, Neil, does your snooping never stop? This program has turned LifeScience into a money magnet. We could become the next Genentech. What exactly is your complaint?"

"True, the product will be huge—if it works. True, it has attracted investors, short term. Our pipeline is filling up. But if MC124 fails, if there's a problem, the damage to the company in the long run will be equally huge. With so much at stake, we don't need the backdoor tactics you pulled with the board. Never do that again, Dr. McKinnon."

The clump of footsteps followed. This must have been when McKinnon came out on the porch. The rest of the tape was room noise, then the skittering of the mike being reeled in.

I clicked off the recorder. Somehow I felt better. Other people's problems can do that for you. I was less inclined now to drive off, at least not without speaking to Jenny. More inclined than ever to find out what was really going on at LifeScience.

That meant I'd have to play my Gregory Alton card. I thought back to my day of shooting with Rita at Kumar Biotechnics yesterday. Gregory had been lurking in the parking lot late in the afternoon. We watched him from Kumar's window. By the time we packed up, though, Gregory was gone.

I finished stowing the DAT recorder in the briefcase and went back inside. Jenny's door was closed. Taking a nap, maybe. She'd slept poorly the past two nights. We'd gotten up while it was still dark on Monday morning to go to her office and scan Sheila's journal. I didn't know how big a force Dugan had following us, but no one appeared to be on duty at that hour. Once we had the diary digitized, we could produce copies at will. I instructed Jenny to package up the two photocopies we had and mail them to the police, just so Dugan couldn't get us on that one.

I went to the dining room and called Rita to make sure work had gone all right today, since I'd been replaced by the new DP. She described it as splendid. "Best DP I ever had," she said.

"Ha ha. Well, I'll be in to check on you tomorrow. Will you put those items I left with you in the camera case?"

"No problem," Rita said. She still had the zip disks and the tape of Sheila in the parking lot. The security of my flat and of my jeep were questionable, and I trusted her as much as anyone to keep them safe. "I need the HD cassette, though, so I'll transfer it to video for you."

"Thanks a lot."

I called Wes next. He wasn't happy about what I wanted him to arrange for tomorrow night, but he couldn't turn me down.

Then I dug Gregory Alton's card out of my billfold. I hated doing this. I tried to block out the image of his smug blond mug on the other end of the line.

"Hello, Gregory. It's Bill."

"Bill! Where were you today, buddy?" Apparently he didn't mind admitting he was stalking me.

"I had to go to a funeral."

"Oh, gee. I hope it wasn't anyone—"

"How much do you actually know about LifeScience, Gregory? Did you know a researcher named Sheila Harros?"

"Not specifically. But I can bring you up to speed on the company. I've had a few meetings. Scoped them out, got some juicy confidentials. If, that is, you can—"

"Yeah, yeah. I know what you want. Okay, you got a deal. I want to see you tomorrow. You'll tell me about LifeScience."

"And you'll bring some goodies for me."

"Hold on. I missed today's shoot, you know. I don't have the footage. Give me another day or two on the job."

"Whoa, whoa, Bill. This isn't what I call even-Steven."

"You're going to go first, Gregory. That's the way it is."

I heard just enough of a pause. "Why should that be?"

"You need what I've got more than the other way around. That's the fact. I hate to be like this, but I'm going to be like this."

He gave in with a knowing chuckle. "Film people are all about deals, aren't they? Okay. I'll give you the data dump on LifeScience. And by Friday you'll give me what I need on Kumar."

We agreed to meet for lunch. I hung up the phone and bounced onto the couch, feeling magically lighter. Pushing Gregory around had improved my mood even more than listening to Dugan and McKinnon duke it out.

Still, I was buying his information on credit. I didn't know if I'd actually follow through on my end of the bargain. Kumar had been incredibly decent to us so far. I didn't want to betray him. But I needed Gregory's "juicy confidentials" right now, and I'd worry about paying the bill later.

16

I met Gregory Alton at Perry's in downtown
Palo Alto on Thursday. What a difference a year had made. I had
stopped even trying to come down here at the height of the boom.
University Avenue traffic had stood still then, like a pipe clogged
between Stanford at one end and Highway 101 at the other. Now
I actually found a parking spot on my first pass. The sycamore
trees along the avenue were curled a dusty yellow. I strolled the
sidewalk without being knocked over by lines of marching MBAs.
Attendants at the salons and spas loitered by their doors, wondering where they'd have to move for their next job.

I got a table right away. Once upon a time I would have
waited outside, along with the mostly male clientele in their
polos and striped shirts. Cell phones, PDAs, and laptops would
have been arrayed on the blue-checked tablecloths like pieces on
a chessboard, the buzz of electrons and venture capital in the air.

Gregory swaggered in and took a look around. "It's a good
thing biotech is happening, huh?" he said as he joined me.
"Otherwise I'd probably be doing egregiously trivial sys admin
for some corporate suit." He said *suit* in a manner meant to
imply he and I were brothers-in-arms. "And you'd be—what,
shooting weddings?"

I ignored this. "You new to biotech?"

He shot me a sneaky grin. "I majored in computer science in college because I loved video games. Got an MBA so I could speak the tongue of the suits. I was in the first wave in South Park." South Park was the epicenter of the Web boom in San Francisco. "Dude, in those days it was like a gumball machine. Put in a penny idea, turn the knob, and get a wad of cash. You jump on that?"

I gave a sort-of nod. I did get mesmerized by those candy colors, until I had to factor in consorting with the Gregorys of the world in order to turn the knob.

When the waiter came around, I ordered the Chinese chicken salad. Gregory didn't look at the menu. "I'll have the grilled ahi sandwich," he said. "The tuna should be crisp, very crisp, on the outside, like bacon. Soft on the inside, like jelly, but not raw. And keep the capers off it, okay?"

His attention came back to me. "So you know the L curve. Big drop and now we're bumping along the bottom. I give myself credit, though. Never promised eyeballs. Never made a B-to-C play." He meant business-to-consumer. "I always got the quick flip, then slid over before any of my ventures turned up on fuckedcompany.com. I wasn't going to be no dead man driving."

"Dead man driving?"

"You know the guys. Instead of doing something smart with their severance, they buy a Jag. So they can look good driving to their nonexistent job interviews."

"Keep looking like a big man, and maybe the world will treat you like one."

"So anyway, this guy, my partner Ron, he clued me in on biotech as the next exponential industry. Guess who are some of the major individual investors? Bill, Paul, and Larry."

He listed them on a first-name basis, as if the trio was as familiar as Moe, Curly, and Larry. Gates, Allen, and Ellison. "Curing disease must be hot," I said.

"End users can ignore a banner ad. They can't ignore cancer."

"How did you get up to speed on molecular genetics?"

"Well, Ron's got the bio side. I've got the information architecture. That's our play, bioinformatics. We got cooking last year. Once the human genome was sequenced, boom! It's a race to monetize the genome, just like the Internet."

"Explain bioinformatics to me."

"There are mega databases of genetic information out there. Somewhere in that galactic cloud is precisely the data a lab or pharma needs to define their disease target and test their drug candidate. We penetrate the cloud for them."

"With some kind of specialized search engine?"

"It's way more gnarly than that, Bill. We've got some proprietary code in the works. Let's say you're looking at a particular stretch of DNA. You've got an idea that it's involved in, I don't know, cancer of the cuticle. Now, this gene is maybe four thousand base pairs long. Base pairs are the rungs on the twisted ladder of DNA. They're like a very long address. Now, people out there have researched what goes on at this address. They might be able to give you codons, receptors, promoters, protein sequence assembly—the kind of stuff you can use to design your drug. But that data is dispersed. All *you've* got is the address. It's like having a house number, but you don't know the street, you don't even know the city. That's where we come in. We use our tools to put you in touch with what everyone else can tell you about this address."

The food came. Gregory lifted the top of his sandwich, inspected the ahi like an Olympic judge, then tore into it. I said, "And this is what your company wants to do for LifeScience."

He showed me a chewing version of that smug smile of his. "Oh yeah, your buddies at LifeScience. What's so fascinating about them anyway?"

"It's a personal thing, Gregory. A friend of mine worked there."

He took a gulp of soda and eventually got around to swallowing. "We're playing for an alliance with LifeScience. They've got a new molecule that's supposed to be monstrously effective against cancer. It'll be in trials soon. It's already bringing in big bucks for new programs. Their pipeline's going to be stuffed. Meaning new targets, new drug candidates. We'll help them find both. Later, if we grow like I think we can, we'll test the candidates *in silico*. Find out what the compound does in various tissues, cell processes, metabolic pathways. All of these human functions are being modelled. The computer is the lab."

"LifeScience is on the verge of going big time."

"Yup. They've been up and down. The new cash machine is a monoclonal antibody. Their science guy, McKinnon, was big into them back when. Didn't pan out. They were gasping for air, got some new management, a new target, and now they've got this hot candidate, MC124. McKinnon dropped the bomb at a med conference. Cheesed the crap out of his bosses. By the way, you heard none of this from me."

"Don't worry. Who do you deal with there—McKinnon? Dugan?"

"I've heard of Dugan. He's COO. I met McKinnon. He's got an underling named Doug Englehart who's set to get his own program there soon. Plus, LifeScience has acquired a new agri division. What exactly do you want to know?"

"Hear about any problems with MC124? Troublesome lab results? A researcher named Sheila Harros?"

Gregory shook his head. His eyes narrowed. "You got some money riding on this?"

"None whatsoever. But you did see Sheila, that first time you and I met in the parking lot. Why do you think she looked so startled?"

Gregory tongued some food from his back teeth. "Not because of me, pal. Probably your camera scared her."

"How does this monoclonal antibody, MC124, work?"

He waved a hand. "I don't keep up with the trivia. All I know is that monoclonal candidates can be produced faster and cheaper than your average drug. Large pharma is hot for LifeScience. The money pump is running. Meanwhile, I've got Bigfuckers breathing down my neck this minute. We gotta have the LifeScience deal. That's why Kumar is pissing me off so bad. If he steals my technology *and* this gig—"

"It's hell being stuck at Littlefucker level, isn't it?"

A look of suspended disbelief crossed Gregory's face. He might have gotten up and left right there. I wouldn't have minded. Instead he decided to break out laughing. "You've got some sense of humor, Bill."

I smiled. "Pretty much my only good point, isn't it?"

"Buddy, you got to come through. Here I've been spitting data all through lunch. What have you got for *me?*"

I crunched on some crispy noodles. "Is there a woman named Karen working at your company?" It had occurred to me that that would explain Sheila in the parking lot—she was meeting Karen. Karen might work at either BioVerge or Kumar.

"Maybe. It's a common name. Now come on. Give me something. *Anything.*"

He pushed his plate away, locked his hands behind his head, and heaved his feet up onto the chair next to me. I stared at the soles of his expensive boots and weighed my options. "You're right to be worried about Kumar. The software's deep in beta.

Our film's wrapping next month. That means they'll be making an announcement."

Gregory sucked air between his teeth. "I know all that. It's the fine grain I need. Screen shots. Documentation."

"I told you I missed the shoot yesterday. I'll be back on it again tomorrow," I lied. "I'll try to copy some footage."

"Why aren't you there today?"

"It's just second unit stuff." As if Rita *had* a second unit.

"I want to see the goods tomorrow night. No later."

The waiter dropped off the tab. I snatched it. "This one's on me, Gregory."

He made a smirk of agreement, then stood to leave. "Ciao. I'll see you tomorrow, when you'll have you-know-what in your hand."

"You'll get it, all right."

I was glad to pick up the tab. What he'd told me was worth the price of lunch. But no more.

As I waited for my change, a pattern kept dancing in my head. The big diagonals on the soles of his boots. Bits of mud stuffed in the crannies. I'd seen the pattern before. Now I remembered where: in the moist soil of my backyard.

>> >> >> >> >>

I stayed at Perry's a little longer. I wanted to make sure Gregory was clear of the area. Then I headed for the business park shared by Kumar and BioVerge. I didn't use their parking lot. Instead, I put the Scout in another manicured lot on the far side of a four-lane divided boulevard.

The reception desk at Kumar Biotechnics paged Rita for me. Five minutes later I was upstairs with her. She was shooting in a third-floor conference room. The chief technology officer was getting ready to go on camera. Monitors, flasks, pipettes, and circuit boards were set up behind him. My replacement DP and the gaffer were fussing with the lights. Rita came with me into the corridor, through which the crew's gear was scattered.

"What's all that stuff doing in a conference room?"

Rita chuckled. "They actually use some of it for presentations. But we brought in some extra for background. We need something more than computer screens."

"Silicon Valley action picture. Guys working a mouse with their tongues sticking out."

"We did get some cool probe lens shots yesterday. These chips are incredible—one day they'll carry your entire personal genome."

"Sorry I missed it. Is the new DP doing all right? He looks like a tweaker."

"Yeah, I love it. He's cute, too."

She was still trying to make me jealous. I gave the proper frown, then said, "I left a couple of things I need in the camera cases. I'm going to poke around for a minute."

"No problem. Just don't step in front of any cameras."

The DP called Rita into the conference room. I made sure he was watching as I blew her a little good-bye kiss. Then I picked through the maze of padded bags until I found the one in which she'd put my things: the tape of Sheila, along with the computer disks from Sheila's apartment. I deposited them into a wrinkled plastic grocery bag I'd brought.

Inside the conference room, Rita gave directions to lock down the set. I took the opportunity to pick through some of the other bags. I'd unzipped a million of these things, and could do so with hardly a sound. I looked until I found two DAT cassettes with yesterday's date scrawled on them. They went into my grocery bag. No HD videotapes, though—Mr. Perfect must have hidden them away good.

Rita's fanny pack was by the door. I found her cell phone in it and scurried down the corridor. I called information, covered the mouthpiece, and mumbled that I wanted the number for BioVerge. The operator didn't hear me. As I mumbled it louder, Arun Kumar came around the corner. I froze. He smiled at me and put out his hand. I got the number and clicked off the phone.

"Are you back on the job?" Kumar asked. He had a fleshy chin and round, inquisitive eyes. His thick black hair fell across his forehead in a double wave.

"I'm afraid not. Just came by to see how it was going." His gaze fell to the crumpled plastic bag in my left hand. "And pick up a few items of mine," I added, mentally kicking myself up and down the hallway. If Rita noticed the missing DAT cassettes, and she and Kumar put two and two together . . .

"We're very pleased with Rita. Very pleased."

"It's good to know she can get along without me." I smiled and resisted the urge to hide the plastic bag behind my back. "I've been meaning to ask—do you have a woman named Karen working here?"

"I believe we have a Karen in accounting."

"Hmm, probably not her. Maybe she works across the way." If he'd heard my phone request, I might as well cover myself. Kumar showed no reaction at the mention of his competitor, so I pushed a little more. "What do you hear about BioVerge?"

His laugh was gentle. "I don't lose any sleep over them."

"Does Gregory Alton have any idea what he's doing?"

Kumar shook his head. His tone was almost regretful. "Very little. It makes my job easier in one way, but in another it reflects poorly on the sector as a whole."

"Thanks a lot. Good to see you."

"Drop by anytime."

I hoped he'd still feel that way in a few days. Flipping open the phone again, I called BioVerge and asked for Karen. The receptionist gave me a choice of two. "The bioscientist," I said.

That would be Karen Harper, the receptionist said, and connected me.

I started right in. "Karen, this is Bill Damen. I'm a—"

Click. That was as far as I got. But it confirmed I'd found the right Karen. I redialed and asked for her. The receptionist told me she wasn't in. What did Karen Harper have against me?

I returned Rita's phone. She was still shooting in the conference room, so I left without saying good-bye. I was outside waiting to cross the boulevard when I heard footsteps pounding in my direction. They belonged to Gregory Alton. His sunglasses were pushed up on top of his brushed-up blond hair.

"Bill!" he said, breathless. "Aren't you coming to see us?"

"Not until tomorrow, Gregory." How did he know I was here?

He eyed the crumpled plastic bag. "Second unit, huh? It looks like you've got some goodies right now."

"I told you. Friday. And when I do come, I want to see Karen Harper."

As a grin spread over his face, I realized how he'd caught me. I'd used Rita's phone to call Karen. Caller ID showed Rita's number. Karen told him I'd made the call, and he knew Rita was at Kumar.

"Karen might have accidentally heard the wrong things about you," he said. "I'll have to set her straight. After you've made your delivery."

I hated to do it, but I needed Karen. I reached into the bag, drew out the two marked DAT cassettes, and held them up for him to see. He made a grab. I dropped the tapes into the bag and brought my right elbow up hard into his solar plexus. He staggered backward with a grunt, his shades flying off. I took a stance. He thought about it for a minute, then stooped to pick up his glasses.

"Easy, buddy," he said. "I just wanted to look."

"I have to copy them first. Don't push me, Gregory. They'll be ready tomorrow. At noon. I want to see Karen at the same time."

He jabbed a forefinger at me. "You're not getting near Karen until those tapes are in my hands." He shoved the glasses onto his face, spun, and walked away.

I noticed his feet again. "Hey Gregory," I called. "Where'd you get those boots?"

He turned. "They're German. Hard to find. Got them on the Net."

Clearly he was proud of them.

17

I hurried back to Jenny's apartment, not knowing whether I was on my way to a peace parley or war council. At four o'clock, George and Abe Harros were scheduled to arrive. I prayed they were late.

George Harros had called Jenny's last night to arrange the meeting. Jenny wasn't thrilled about it, but I wanted to find out what they knew. I'd taken her to dinner later and we'd reached a truce of our own.

It was four on the dot when I parked the Scout. I bounded up Jenny's stairs, and after a quick knock, let myself in.

I did not like what I saw. The two Harros men occupied one of the living room sofas. Fay, in a short skirt, legs crossed, sat on the other. There was some activity in the kitchen. Jenny was at the dining room table, twirling a strand of hair into a knot. Her eyes filled with reproach when she saw me.

"They just get here?" I asked softly.

"They've been here for *half an hour.*" She didn't bother to lower her voice. "Look at what they're doing to my kitchen."

Although their backs were turned to me, the shapes of the two men in the kitchen shot a little dagger of panic through my gut. They were the ones who'd been after us in the copy shop. Harros must have hired them, not Dugan.

One of the men was up to his elbows in the refrigerator, filling up a trash bag of evidence. The other was scraping something out of the microwave. The latter looked over his shoulder and gave me a little smirk.

I said, "What are you guys, private investigators? You find the smoking gun yet—or did you bring it with you?"

The smirk needed only a couple of millimeters to turn into a scowl. His complexion was light and sand-freckled, his eyebrows nearly invisible, but the scowl had unexpected menace. He stabbed his chisel-like instrument into the side of the microwave.

"Whoops," he said.

"Don't worry. Mr. Harros will pay for it."

I was torn between staying in the kitchen—to make sure they didn't do more damage, plant evidence, or install some kind of listening device—and dealing with Harros in the living room. I went for Harros. The kitchen guys had probably already done their deeds, and I couldn't leave Jenny alone any longer.

I motioned for her to come with me into the living room. She answered by making a face, but moved to the steps between the two rooms. My cordial greeting to Mr. Harros brought a cool nod. He wore a tie and vest. His steel-streaked hair was slicked back. His prominent features jutted into the room. Abe sported some nice Italian shoes.

"I need the names of the two men in the kitchen," I said.

"No, you don't," Abe answered.

"I need their names or they are leaving *now*."

George Harros gave a disgusted sigh, took a card from his wallet, and thrust it at me. William Pratt Agency, the card said.

"Looks like you've got two Bills in your life," I remarked. "The good one and the bad one."

Fay giggled, but the observation did not have the relaxing effect I'd aimed for on the others. "His name's William," Abe said coldly.

I gazed at him long enough to make him look away. Then I grabbed a side chair, plunked it at a right angle by Mr. Harros, and launched into my version of events. I started with the dinner party and ran through our visit to the hospital, adding that we went to Sheila's apartment with Fay only to get contact information for Abe.

"I don't see what we've done to deserve hostility," I concluded. "We've been here to help from the beginning."

Harros cleared his throat. His voice had an even keel now. "That's all very well. But perhaps your efforts derive from a sense of guilt."

"A point," I allowed, "but off the mark. We do feel terrible about what happened to Sheila. We feel grief and regret. But not guilt. Jenny was impeccably careful about what she served."

"I'm a doctor," Abe said. "I've got the autopsy report. The swollen tissues, angio-edema, hyperinflated lungs, they all add up to the fact that Sheila ate something in this apartment that killed her."

"Sheila may have ingested or somehow got the stuff that produced anaphylactic shock that night. That doesn't mean she got it here. I'll tell you what. Let's review her last night step by step. Does anyone know what else Sheila did that day?"

"She left work early," Abe said. "Doug Englehart and others confirm she departed around 4:30."

"She arrived here at about seven. I also happen to know she was in a parking lot at Kumar Biotechnics around six."

Both Abe and George Harros looked at me in surprise. "Why didn't you tell us?" Abe burst.

I let a long stare sink in. "At what point did you give me the opportunity?"

"The more I hear you talk, the less I like," Harros rumbled. "But go on, take some more rope."

"Sheila was nervous about something in that parking lot. It's shared by two companies that are bidding for a contract with LifeScience. She must have been there for work."

Abe shook his head. "No. Dugan and Englehart said nothing was on her agenda."

I remembered Sheila's startled look when I turned the camera on her. I wondered if, when I looked at the tape, I'd find Neil Dugan lurking in the background. "Anyway, the next time I saw Sheila was when I let her in here around seven."

"So you were the last person to see her in the lot and the first when she got here?" Abe made it sound incriminating.

"I'm sure *someone* saw her *somewhere* in between. I myself was talking to Gregory Alton, the CEO of BioVerge. You can check on it."

"We will," Harros assured me. "Now, the dinner party. Fay has told us what was on the menu. But we'd like to hear your version, Jenny. Tell us precisely who provided what item."

Jenny was on the step between the dining room and living room, her chin cupped in her hand. She looked like a captured villager brought before an inquiring colonel.

She listed, in a careful voice, what went into the dinner. She had bought the salmon at the Fish Market on El Camino. Potatoes, dill, and green beans had come from the Gilman Street farmers' market. Fay had gotten the cheeses. Marion brought mozzarella and basil for the salad, and Sheila herself brought tomatoes. Another couple provided ice cream and berries for dessert. Various guests brought wine.

"So you were allegedly throwing this party with Fay, yet you bought most of the ingredients yourself?" Harros asked.

"Fay was supposed to share the cost with me. She did help cook."

Fay recrossed her legs. "During the party, Bill's friend Wes tried to pick up Sheila. I guess she told him to get lost. Bill ended up talking to Sheila during the entire dinner. I don't think Jenny liked that."

"Excuse me?" Jenny objected.

Harros held up his hand. "Marion has confirmed this. Now let's move on. What did Sheila eat and drink?"

I repeated the list that Jenny had just recited. "She ate and drank the same things the rest of us did."

"But you noticed Sheila was unwell," Harros said.

"Her eyes became red and swollen. She said it was just hay fever. She excused herself and went into the bathroom. I went to help Jenny in the kitchen. When I came out, Sheila had left."

"So again, you were the last to talk to her."

"No. Fay and Sheila had an argument while Sheila was getting her coat. Marion saw it."

"Fay has assured us it was insignificant. Marion concurs."

Fay knitted her brows innocently at me.

I said to Harros, "Are you aware that Fay and Sheila were both pursuing a guy named Simon? And that Simon was doing his best to win Sheila back?"

Harros got a hard little twinkle in his eye. "And how is it that you know this?"

He had me there. There was no point in denying the diary. We were the ones who'd given it to him, after all. "I've been trying to figure out what happened to Sheila, just like you."

Harros's twinkle turned into a small, satisfied smile. "Let me get this straight. You had talked with my daughter all night about something you've yet to disclose. You saw she was feeling unwell, yet did nothing. Then, once you saw for yourself that she was dead in the morgue, you broke into her apartment and stole her diary. But first you cleaned your kitchen in order to remove incriminating foodstuffs."

"That was Fay's idea!" Jenny objected. "If anyone had a reason to hurt Sheila, it was Fay!"

Harros shook his head. "No, it's your role in this, Mr. Damen, as well as Miss Ingersoll's, that needs to be explained."

I began to see how it was with him. He was like a film director who already saw the whole picture in his head. It would not change, even if none of the actors fit their roles. "Fay and Jenny mutually decided to clean the kitchen," I said. "It was a natural, and innocent, reaction. Fay was the one who knew where Sheila's apartment keys were hidden. Fay was the one who stole the diary from Sheila's bedside. We took it out of her bag."

Fay's hands were folded like a perfect lady. "I wanted to make sure you got it, Mr. Harros. Bill said Sheila's computer had been broken into. I was worried the diary might be taken, too."

"Someone had been in the apartment before us," I said. "I'm certain the manager will identify the man as Neil Dugan of LifeScience. He took Sheila's hard drive."

"Again. You *said* someone took the hard drive. Yet you did not allow Fay to see to confirm. That someone could have been you."

"Dugan as much as admitted it was him," I said.

"He did no such thing. Even so, he has a legitimate claim to her work. The company is at a crucial juncture."

"I'll say it is." I took a small leap of speculation. "Sheila had uncovered serious problems. Neil Dugan was trying to make sure she didn't reveal them. If someone did—I mean, if Sheila's death wasn't accidental, Dugan is the man to look at."

Harros consulted his watch. "He'll be here in ten minutes. You may elaborate at that time."

My brain did a little somersault. Dugan had gotten the inside track with the Harroses already. Dugan, Fay, and Marion had all thrown in with them. I could see why the first two did, but not Marion.

"Until now, we had assumed Sheila's death was an accident, albeit not without culpability," Harros went on. "We assumed you and Jennifer were guilty of criminal negligence in the first place, and covering up in the second. But your own words lead me to suspect otherwise. Perhaps you didn't mean to let slip that she did not die by chance. But here you clean up evidence. You violate her privacy. Then you point the finger at others. Fay. Miss Roos. Mr. Dugan."

A voice was reading me my rights in my head. Anything I said was being used against me. But so would silence. "I understand your grief, Mr. Harros. I understand the urge to blame someone. But you're reaching far beyond reason. What possible motive could we have?"

"We don't know what you were doing in that parking lot before the dinner party," he shot back. "We don't know what you talked to my daughter about all night. We have only your word that you did not know her before. Perhaps you are involved in ways we have not discovered yet. Or perhaps the motive is not yours. Perhaps it is Jennifer's, and the motive is jealousy."

"Read the diary," I blurted. "You won't see my name."

"Not on the pages that still exist. But you ripped out some pages, didn't you?"

I shook my head. It all felt like a dream. "No. This is ridiculous." It was amazing how weak the truth sounded.

The doorbell rang. Everyone looked at one another. I forgot, for a moment, whose house we were in. Then I went to get the door.

Neil Dugan stood there, teeth exposed in a wolflike smile. My eyes did not leave his as I stood aside to let him in. He went directly to the kitchen.

The two men were tying up their garbage bags. Dugan's tone with them was cheerful and familiar. My stomach sank a little further. What if Dugan and Harros had hired the PIs together?

"We're done here," said the sand-freckled one. I assumed he was Pratt. "We'll get you a report by the weekend, Mr. Dugan."

"Tomorrow, please," Dugan said. He gave Pratt a little pat on the back as he and the second man went to the door. I locked it behind them, and we proceeded to the living room. Abe and George Harros had warm handshakes for Dugan. He gave Fay a little bow and a wink and took a seat next to her.

"We were just discussing the diary," Harros said. I was standing next to Jenny, who'd squished herself to the edge of the step. Harros fixed his stony eyes on me and commanded, "Give Mr. Dugan the missing diary pages."

"You're letting *him* read your daughter's diary?"

"He has intellectual property concerns." Harros's voice was firm, as repeating a reprimand to a child. "He will have access to Sheila's notebooks and any other potential LifeScience IP."

I couldn't keep the desperation out of my voice. "That's exactly the wrong thing to do. Anyway, I don't have any diary pages, missing or otherwise."

Dugan tsked. "You expect us to believe that?"

I nearly made a jump for him, and everyone could see it. My pulse raced. I unclenched my fists and forced myself to take a deep breath. Fighting to control my voice, I said, "You transferred her out of the MC124 program, Mr. Dugan. It's not her work you want. It's what she knew and you didn't want her to know. What she was about to expose."

Dugan drew himself up. "You have no idea what you're talking about."

"Sheila was not the only one. There's at least one other person who knows about it, isn't there?" Saying so was a real risk. But I needed to know if such a person existed, and if Dugan knew she existed. If she did, I thought it had to be Karen Harper, the woman Sheila had an appointment with before the dinner party. Her name had also appeared in the diary.

Dugan's expression did not shift at all. But I could see his mind working. He didn't know who I meant, but he'd be hunting right away. I wished even harder that Harros would not let him read the diary.

Harros directed a little harrumph at me. His trust of Dugan appeared to know no bounds. But Abe had been tapping his finger against his nose as I'd spoken. "What about that, Mr. Dugan? There are some things in the diary—"

"Employees can make mistakes with company IP. Inadvertently, I assure you, Abe. No serious wrongdoing on Sheila's part. Nevertheless, in addition to finding any unreported research on the program, I also need to make certain security was not compromised."

Mr. Harros straightened. "Neil, I give you my assurance Sheila would have done nothing to harm your company deliberately. But she was not the most, let us say, practical woman in the world. It was ideas, knowledge that excited her. She loved to share it, but she never would have done so in an improper way— not on purpose."

"My thoughts exactly." Dugan's voice was practically a coo.

Harros clapped his hands to his knees. "Let's bring this to a close. We've learned a great deal here today. Now, Bill, there's one more question I'd like to ask."

I leaned against the archway and folded my arms.

"What else haven't you told us? What else did you steal from my daughter's apartment?"

"Nothing." My answer was quick and dismissive.

"Then we're done." Mr. Harros exhaled loudly and pushed himself to his feet. Abe followed, then Dugan and Fay, like a row of ducklings. Jenny and I went to the entryway to show them out.

"Wait a minute," I said as they filed toward the door.

They turned with a certain eagerness, as if to receive some kind of confession. "We never finished the timeline. What happened after Sheila got in her car? There's a big hole there."

"That's what we'd like to know, Bill," Abe responded. "Of course, once Fay left, we don't know what you and Jenny did. Sheila was found in her car on Page Mill Road."

The insinuation didn't deserve a response. "Page Mill is between her apartment and the hospital."

"Yes. The pathologist put time of death after midnight. That leaves about enough time for her to have gone home, searched for epinephrine, and then driven part of the way to the hospital. That makes it a near certainty she received the toxin here. If something did happen after the party, we'll soon have witnesses. The police are investigating. We ourselves have put up posters in the area asking people to come forward."

"The police were here, Bill," Jenny said in a quiet voice. "They asked me questions for about twenty minutes." She shot a look at Harros. "They were very nice to me."

"They're not taking it seriously enough," Harros declared. "But they will. Once they see the evidence we've collected today."

"Whatever you found in the kitchen will be useless," I said. "The analysis will be biased. You should have let the police do it."

"Pratt's reputation will be sufficient," Harros sniffed.

Dugan had already opened the door for Fay. Abe was about to follow them out. I wanted to take one last stab. The younger Harros had shown a small gleam of independence. "Abe, take a minute to think clearly about the facts. Don't you see what's happening? Dugan is using you."

Abe's eyes flashed mock gratitude. "Do you really think a man in his position would harm Sheila, with all he has to lose? Just come clean with us, Bill. It'll be better in the long run."

I stared a hole through the middle of his forehead. "I thought doctors waited until all the tests were in to make a diagnosis."

"By the way," Abe added, as if playing a trump card, "the autopsy report showed needle puncture marks in Sheila's arm. Injections." His gaze shifted to Jenny. "You might want to think about that."

George Harros bent slightly at the waist and extended a hand to Jenny. "I thank you for your hospitality." He turned to me. "And I suggest you follow some advice. Don't take any trips."

I held the door open for him, but didn't bother to respond. His words had no meaning to me anymore. Abe's mention of the injections in Sheila's arm were far more important. I wanted to know who'd administered them and what was in them.

Jenny wouldn't take Mr. Harros's hand either. Instead, she stood with her arms folded across her chest, looked him in the eye, and said, "You have one very *fucking* weird way of mourning your daughter."

The venom in her voice took us all by surprise. But I felt some pleasure in watching the rage tremble and spread over Harros's face. I slammed the door behind him.

18

I gave myself a minute at the door to cool off, then took a tour of the area around Jenny's apartment to make sure all of our guests really had left. When I came back inside, Jenny was sitting on the couch, legs crossed, staring daggers of spite at her cream curtains.

"Why are they like that?" she demanded.

"I guess the landlord felt safe with a neutral color."

"No, those people! Why are they against us? What did we ever do to them?"

I sat next to her. "Nothing, Jen. They've decided to see the situation in a certain way. They're fixated on their own goals, and they see others as either helping them or getting in their way. If you don't help them, you're their enemy."

"That's so unfair."

"Well, I intend to get in their way a little more." I looked at my watch. "I've got a meeting with Marion at the Brentwood."

Jenny's foot wiggled madly. "Great. Leave me here alone. Why didn't you toss their self-righteous asses on the street?"

"If we were guilty, that would have been a logical thing to do. But we need to stay in the game. Stay on some kind of speaking terms with Harros. Otherwise Dugan's got free rein."

"It's not a game. It's my life. My reputation."

"You're right. It's not a game."

"So what am I supposed to do, sit around and wait for those two belly-floppers who ransacked my kitchen to come back?"

"You could come with me to see Marion. Or maybe you need a break from this business. You could go up to your mother's house in Sacramento. You'd be safe up there."

Jenny lifted her chin. "I might do that."

It didn't sound like a bad idea to me, either. The whole business was wearing on her. I got the feeling she'd prefer that I just drop it, which was not going to happen.

She picked up the remote and switched on the TV, making a point of ignoring me. I said good-bye and took a slow walk to the Scout, wondering if her real peeve didn't still come down to my continuing failure to move in with her.

» » » » »

The Brentwood Lodge, halfway between Palo Alto and the city, was a monument to the grand era of ersatz elegant American dining. The entryway and great hearth were built of flagstones laid atop one another. A dark oak counter made a big undulating sweep in front of the bar. A fire roared in the hearth. The bar had a small stage in one corner and plenty of room for dancing to the old tunes, now belted out on Saturday nights by a guy in a velvet jacket with a portable synthesizer. The restaurant served old favorites like beef burgundy and crab à la king. The bow-tied waiters and their shoe-polish hair were monuments in themselves.

I put on a little double take when I came upon Wes and Marion at a table in the bar. Wes was rotating his beer glass in nervous circles. He pressed forward in his seat as if trying to get some difficult words out. Marion sipped a drink with an umbrella. Her head was erect, her neck and shoulders draped artfully with a checked scarf.

Wes leaned back and stretched his arms with relief. "Bill! What are you doing here?"

"Meeting Jenny. Wow, what a surprise!"

I pulled an imitation leather chair right up to their table. Marion turned a briny eye on me. I sat down anyway. I signalled to the cocktail waitress, ordered a Manhattan, and beamed at Wes and Marion with a whaddya-know smile.

Marion turned away from me and tightened the scarf on her shoulders. "Finish what you were telling me, Wes."

"Oh . . . well, never mind," he stammered. "But I think it can be easily—uh, easily treated."

He looked at his watch and I looked at mine. Seven-fifteen. Wes's cell phone chirped. His secretary was punctual. After a few uh-huhs into the phone, he gulped down his beer. "Something's come up. Sorry, I've got to go. Good seeing you, Marion."

Marion stood to protest. I stood with her. "What is this?" she demanded. "You set me up!"

I blocked her way out. "Stay just a minute, Marion. Let's talk about Sheila."

Marion sank slowly into the chair. Her eyes burned holes into Wes's receding back, then turned on me. "You're a couple of creeps."

My face remained innocent and blank. The waitress set a perfect brimming amber cone of Manhattan before me. I lifted it in Marion's direction and savored a spine-shivering sip. She looked into her own drink, then picked the umbrella out and twirled it. "You still have a copy of the diary, don't you?"

I was impressed with her ability to shift gears. "I know what's in it," I allowed, "and I'm willing to share. But first, I want to know why you ganged up with Fay against Jenny and me."

Marion gave a naughty-girl tilt of the head. A strand of hair fell across her face. "Don't take it personally. It was just something I needed to do. George Harros was in a position to shed light."

I held her eyes. They'd gone opaque again, reflecting neither hostility nor sympathy. She was all about her own agenda. "I'm glad to hear you use the past tense. As you know, there's a lot more to it than Harros thinks. You know that Dugan is in deep, and he's got Harros snookered."

"I had to keep Dugan off my own ass, Bill."

"Maybe so, but you've used us as decoys long enough. Jenny's about to have a nervous breakdown." This did bring a flicker of concern. "Let's just talk. We're both trying to figure out what killed Sheila, right?"

Marion tilted her head in a qualified yes.

"I count five ways Sheila could have died," I went on.

"Only five?"

"Feel free to add to the list. One, Jenny had the shellfish antigen in her kitchen. Unless she's totally mistaken, this isn't it. Two, Sheila ingested the antigen on her own before or after Jenny's. This is highly unlikely. She was very careful. Three, someone brought the antigen to the meal in a deliberate attempt to poison her. Four, someone injected the antigen or forced it on her outside of Jenny's apartment, before or after dinner. She had puncture marks in her arm. And five, the cause of death is something other than the antigen. Factor X. Probably from the lab at LifeScience."

Amusement played on Marion's lips. "You're so charmingly naive about causation. You think we can pin it on one little smoking-gun protein."

"So you're saying it's number five. Factor X."

"No. Bill, I don't know what killed her. Honestly, I don't. I'm trying to make you see that there could be a multiplicity of factors. Cellular interactions so complex we'll never disentangle them."

"Don't pull the scientist stuff on me, Marion. If I need to learn something new, I will."

"I didn't mean it that way. I'm saying we really may never unravel it. It's the nature of the new world we're creating. We're rearranging the alphabet of life."

"Well, isn't biotech just a more precise way to do what farmers have been doing for millennia? Animal breeding, grain hybrids. They're pretty much the cornerstone of civilization, right?"

"Sure. But we're transferring genes between kingdoms now, not just species. For each little step we take, there's a logical purpose. Put them together, though, and they add up to something bigger than any of us can grasp. People only latch on to the immediate dangers. The Institute of Science and Technology is funding research into mass-produced, high-throughput, high-value cloned chickens for the poultry industry. Animal welfare people worry that the chickens will suffer. Sure, that's an issue, but it's miles from the real point. The leap we're taking is epochal. It's metaphysical."

"Metaphysical?"

"On the scale of Prometheus stealing fire from Olympus. In the old days, doctors were like mechanics repairing a vehicle. Now we're becoming more like co-creators of the vehicle. Look at the other realms we've conquered. Once upon a time, the heavens belonged only to birds and gods. Now we zoom through them drinking cocktails. Then, when we divided the atom, which was thought to be the irreducible unit of the universe, we gave ourselves the button to apocalypse. Over and over, we usurp the powers of nature, or the gods, or whatever name you want to use. The question, of course, is whether we have the *wisdom* of the gods."

"From what I remember of Greek mythology, the gods had more power than wisdom."

"You two have *got* to need another drink," the waitress said from over my right shoulder. The lines around her eyes said she knew more about the whims of the gods than the two of us put together.

"Rum and bitters," Marion said. "Over, with a twist."

I tapped my glass for another Manhattan. "How'd you get into biotech anyway, Marion?"

"I started in botany, way back when. Silly thing, I loved flowers, their role in evolution. 'The weight of a petal has changed the face of the world.' But I slowly found out that if you really wanted to know *why* a plant survived a drought or resisted a pest, you had to go into the lab."

"So you switched to molecular biology."

"I'd thought mo bio was all about yeast colonies and fruit flies. When I saw what it could tell me about petals, I was hooked. Fifty years ago, most people thought proteins were what we now call genes. Now we can manipulate them to assemble our own bestiary."

"Didn't someone plug a firefly gene into a rabbit, so that the rabbit glowed in the dark?"

"Mere epiphenomena. We can go much deeper now. We can engineer male fruit flies to spend their whole day doing mating dances with each other in a big conga line. If you alter a gene called *disheveled,* a normally neat mouse turns into a slob. Humans share 80 percent of our genome with fruit flies, 90 percent with mice, and 98 percent with chimps. That means we'll be able to engineer human behavior, too. Stephen Hawking and others say we have no choice, or we'll be left behind by our machines."

The cocktails arrived. We touched glasses. I took a long sip and said, "We've got the power to engineer ourselves into obsolescence."

Marion swallowed some rum. "Accelerated evolution into cyborgs or transgenic superhumans," she said. "The ones left behind will be curiosities. Like Ishi, the last Yahi Indian."

"But people later realized he had a lot of knowledge we've lost. I wonder if the preterite humans will be valued and consulted for their appreciation of, say, a Tarkovsky film."

"If they're lucky. They may have no survival value. The direction we're going, survival will be measured by efficiency and shareholder value. We'll still have entertainment, but it will come in the form of adrenaline jolts. Religion will be packaged as pharmacologically managed inner peace."

"They're both guaranteed box office. But I'm not so sure it's going to happen, Marion. I mean, look around." A silver-haired man in a crimson cravat was playing liar's dice with the bartender. Two women with their white hair done up in cochlear curls were chatting over martinis. "The dot-commers used to flock to this place. Now it's retro'd back to the days before retro. You never know when the future's going to go bust."

"Markets may rise and fall, but the underlying technology takes root. The Internet certainly has. The groundwork is being laid in bioengineering right now. Real estate in the genome is being staked out the same way it was on the Web."

I let some more of the Manhattan warm my throat. "Okay, so biotech is where it's happening, and you want to influence its direction. What exactly do you do at LifeScience?"

"I'm in the agri department. Bioremediation. Engineering crops that help the environment instead of depleting it. For example, a guy in Davis has a tomato that can grow in salty soils and alleviate soil salinity at the same time. That's potentially revolutionary."

"What about MC124?"

"Another department altogether. I don't know a whole lot about it, to tell you the truth."

"How about helping me find out, then? Let's say some mysterious combination of microbes from the lab killed Sheila. Okay, maybe we can't get all the details, but at least we can find out where it came from."

Marion tapped the side of her glass. Her nails were short and unlacquered. The right thumb had been chewed. "Sheila's death is kind of beside the point. I'm sorry for it, but she is, after all, dead. The question is, can we make it count for something?"

I regarded Marion's pale Nordic face. She was Dutch, Wes had said. At this particular moment she seemed bloodless as a stone. Maybe she was already part of the future. "Don't you think her family deserves to know what killed her? Don't you think Sheila herself deserves it? She was on to something at LifeScience."

"She was *into* something, Bill. She may have stolen some company secrets, or sold inside information, I'm not sure. I'd let it go, if I were you. Whatever you find will only muddy her name. Is that what you want?"

"What is it that *you* want, Marion?"

She shook the ice in her glass. "Something bigger, Bill. Something necessary. It's not personal to Sheila or you or Jenny."

"And you expect me to let you see the diary based on this?"

"What were you talking about so intensely with Sheila that night at Jenny's?"

"Nothing sinister, Marion. Just life. Allergies. Genetics. Not her work, but general stuff. That's all."

Marion folded her arms and regarded me. "Well, I could be wrong. Maybe I should trust you. I just don't know."

I folded my arms back at her. "Why am I even talking to you?"

"You tell me. You're not the only one with the diary."

"Yeah. There's Dugan." This got a good wince from her. She leaned forward. I went ahead and told her about the interrogation this afternoon. Actually, I wasn't certain that Dugan had read the journal, but I was willing to bet Harros would let him. "It's them or us," I said. "Who are you going to let take control?"

She frowned. "I'm sorry, Bill. It's just too risky for me to tell you more."

"I know that Frederick McKinnon is feuding with Dugan. I know that he's planning to start human trials soon. I know that MC124 will be very big for LifeScience if it pans out." The idea was to make her feel that she'd be adding only a small scrap of information to a large pile.

"Good for you." Marion loosened the scarf and re-draped it on her shoulders. I could see the down on her arms. She looked more human now. Her voice was softer. "You'll understand one day."

I ate my second cherry, red dye and all, and signalled the waitress for the check. Marion opened her wallet, but I stopped her. "So where's Jenny?" she asked.

I wasn't quite fast enough. "Um—"

"She was never coming to begin with. You really are a creep, aren't you?"

Marion stood and put her arm into a long cable-knit sweater. I couldn't resist a little smile. "We've got to stop meeting this way."

The corners of her mouth folded down, which I took to be an effort not to smile back. She took a couple of steps, then turned. "Does Wes really have some kind of—should I see a doctor?"

I wondered if she had strong feelings for him. I hoped not. I wasn't sure he could handle her.

"Nah," I said. "He just wanted to see you."

19

"So what did she say about me?"

Wes handed me a beer. We were at a party in a loft in the South of Market area of San Francisco. Much of the neighborhood was landfill, an area of mixed industry that slowly became more of a skid row after the 1906 quake. In the eighties artists started moving in and it became known as SOMA, then in the nineties, with the rise of digital media, Multimedia Gulch. Magazines like *Wired* and *The Industry Standard* had started here. Many had ended here, too.

People in flared hip huggers and platform shoes clustered near outposts of bean bags and neobrutalist sofas. This was more the city Web crowd, what remained of it, than the Silicon Valley chip crowd. The latter tended to be true geeks, or else suburbanites in polo shirts who felt cool because they worked in high tech. The dot-commers were the ones with the sideburns and soul patches, nose posts and Buddy Holly glasses, the weekends on E and techno.

This party hosted the hip middle between the original idealists—the ones who were deep online before the run-up and had remained so after it evaporated—and the legions of well-scrubbed graduates who'd roved the city in packs in the late nineties, sucking up real estate and bar stools.

Wes reclined in a hammock hung between two pillars of iron. A sculpted car crash, painted remains of mangled metal, was affixed to the concrete wall above. I kept out from under it.

"Marion didn't really mention you," I replied. "Except she did want to make sure you didn't have any diseases."

Wes shook his head slowly. "The bonds of friendship run deep here, Damen. You owe me."

"And here I am, drinking beer with you, as promised." I gave him a toast. "Thanks again. I'll definitely cast you in the next script."

"Just as long as you rewrite my scene with Marion."

"Is it over between you two?"

Wes had himself a long gulp of beer, then scanned the room. "I don't know. Her arms were too long. I felt like I was being grabbed by a tree." He was a connoisseur of faults, particularly if he sensed a woman was losing interest. "You find out what you needed?"

"I'm starting to think that whatever killed Sheila came out of LifeScience Molecules."

"Like maybe Sheila brewed up something that came back to bite her?"

"I don't know. Whatever it is, Marion says it will make Sheila look very bad."

"Maybe you should just drop this thing, Bill."

"You and Marion agree on that. But I can't, not as long as Dugan and the Harroses are still all over Jenny. And me." I put my beer down. "I need to call her. Can I use your phone?"

Wes handed me his cell. I got only Jenny's machine. Either she'd gone out or she was refusing to pick up.

I sipped my beer, and suddenly realized it was the last thing I wanted right now. "Wes," I said, "I'm sorry, but I got to go."

"No way. A belly dancer is coming out."

"Sorry, no bangles for me tonight. I got tapes I gotta view." I clapped Wes on the shoulder. "Thanks again. You're an excellent guy."

Wes shook his head. "I can't believe it. Leaving just when the fun is about to start. You're obsessed, Billy."

I stumbled into the dark warehouse streets. As I had been doing since Sunday, I approached the Scout warily. The only activity came from a couple of street people down the block, having a smoke beside a shopping cart. Maybe Dugan thought he was in control enough now not to bother with me. Either that or the PIs were still following me and I was too tired to realize it.

» » » » »

At home, I went straight to the answering machine. Gregory had called, of course, to remind me about our meeting tomorrow. Rita had checked in to ask how I was doing. A couple of other people I was supposed to see this week had called to ask where the hell I was. But no message from Jenny.

I found a couple pieces of stale pizza from last weekend in my refrigerator, popped them in the microwave, and took the soggy results down the hall to my video player. I put in the tape I had retrieved today, rewound it, and settled back.

There was Gregory in the parking lot, mugging for the camera and talking about buying an island in the Caribbean. What made him say something like that when his company was so desperate? The same bravado, I suppose, that got BioVerge funded in the first place. The bravado that had fueled the Internet binge, driven by youngsters like Gregory who hadn't been around long enough to know their conjurings were only vapor, and by investors who'd been around long enough to know better than to be bewitched by the vapor. The two got together to produce dreams of a new alchemy, one that transmuted money into silicon and back into exponentially multiplied money via arcane coding rites known only to the young magicians of bits.

I hit myself on the side of the head, trying to knock my own personal bitters and about five ounces of Manhattan out of my ear. As the camera shifted away from the grid of Gregory's teeth, I tracked the image in slow motion. The block geometry of the BioVerge building loomed in the distance. The foreground was a blur of parked cars—black tires, reflective windshields, chunks of color. Then sudden, reflexive focus on a small figure emerging from behind a black Range Rover. Sheila was eerily resurrected.

The pause button gave me a still of the dark ringletted hair, the startled brown eyes, mouth caught in an O of worry. She was up to something. You could see the tension in her body, the tightening of muscles, one hand rising to ward off the camera's intruding eye. Her right shoulder was weighed down by the large brown leather bag, something like what a mail carrier might use.

I tracked ahead in slow motion. As her left hand rose, the other arm pulled the bag protectively close. The eyes narrowed. She was trying to gauge us. Her gaze shifted right of the camera to where Gregory and Ron stood. I hit PAUSE, then scrolled ahead frame by frame. She must have seen Gregory's grin and realized he didn't recognize her. Her mouth relaxed into a frown, one of displeasure more than fear. Her eyes stayed on him for a moment, as if to be sure, and then scanned back to the left. Then came a moment when they changed again. I hadn't noticed it in real time. Sheila's gaze caught on something. Her lips drew back in alarm. She turned and disappeared quickly behind the Range Rover.

On the soundtrack, Gregory chortled and made his comment about her. Then the tape went blue.

I rewound past Sheila to Gregory's teeth, stopped, and scrolled forward again. Nothing in the background—the BioVerge building—was noteworthy. Nor did I see anything special in the parking lot middle ground—until after Sheila had moved away and I'd swung the camera to my right.

I peered closely at the blur of metal, rubber, and glass. There it was. That maroon. The same color I'd seen at the office shop where Jenny I had copied the diary. The car was not in a parking space, but moving down a row. That's what had startled Sheila, not Gregory. Dugan had hired Pratt after all, and had hired him before anything happened to Sheila.

I rewound and squinted. I couldn't make out who was inside, nor any other details. Just the blur of maroon.

Then Sheila, and the leather bag. I thought hard about it, replaying the moment when Sheila had arrived at Jenny's. Her smooth and certain denial of having been in the parking lot. The way she'd unwrapped the scarf with both hands. The small bag on her shoulder. The linen jacket I'd hung in the closet. The tomatoes. But no large brown leather pouch. I was sure of that. Sheila showed no signs of having endured a struggle, so she must have succeeded in delivering it wherever she'd been going.

A string of possibilities filed through my mind. Maybe Sheila had stolen LifeScience intellectual property, as Dugan claimed, and I'd caught her in the process. If that was the case, the PIs were tracking her for legitimate reasons.

Or Sheila had taken something from the lab, and her success in delivering it had enraged Dugan and Pratt. Possibly so much so that they came after her following the dinner party. Or before, but whatever toxin they'd given her hadn't yet taken effect by the time she arrived. Maybe they'd even gotten their hands on the bag, and Sheila was seeking refuge at the party. But she'd looked calm enough when she arrived that I had to dismiss the latter two possibilities.

It was equally possible that the bag was Sheila's own property. That would mean there was still a tangle to unwind, a knot of people and factors I hadn't yet found.

Such as Karen. She was the missing piece. More and more counted on meeting her tomorrow. If only I felt better about what I had to do to get that meeting.

I got to work transferring the DAT tapes I'd pilfered from Rita earlier in the day. I had to run several samples before I got the levels right.

While the tapes were transferring, I tried Jenny once more, and once more got her machine. A sudden pit of panic gaped in my stomach. She should have been back by now.

I dialed her cell number. As it rang and rang, the pit deepened. Then suddenly there was Jenny's voice. I asked if she was all right. Yes, she was out with some friends. Restaurant din clattered in the background.

"I got worried about you."

"That's sweet." Her voice was back to its perky self. "But I'm fine. I'll talk to you later."

"I have to stay here and—" I started to say. But the connection was lost. "Transfer some tapes."

I put down the phone and stared at the floor. A congealed piece of pizza sat on my plate. It tasted a lot like I felt.

20

It was ten minutes after twelve on Friday when I careened into the BioVerge parking lot. Knowing Gregory, he'd chewed his cell phone to bits trying to find me: our meeting was set for noon. He'd have to chew a little longer. I dashed into the Kumar building to return, surreptitiously, the DAT originals to Rita's sound bag, praying no one had noticed their absence. Fortunately Rita was busy and only had time to give me a quick nod.

I ran across the lot to BioVerge. Sure enough, there was Gregory, pacing in the lobby. I caught a flash of relief on his face before he set it sternly.

"Dude, I thought you were going to leave me hanging."

"Would I do that to you, Gregory?" His eyes fixed on the same plastic bag I'd been carrying yesterday. I kept a tight grip and scanned the lobby. "Where's Karen?"

He held out his hand. "At her station. Rikki will take you." The receptionist, a girl with three pigtails, looked up.

"I think you should introduce me to Karen," I insisted.

Gregory pointed toward a conference room. "I've got two execs and a lawyer waiting for me. The lawyer is on the clock."

This was plausible. I handed over the bag. Inside were two DAT cassettes and a videotape. Gregory bared those big dental rows again and clenched a fist. "Justice will prevail, buddy."

He was gone before I could answer. Rikki regarded me, removed her headset, and motioned for me to follow. She wore a pleated skirt, tights, and boots. She took the stairs two at a time, turned left on the second floor, and entered a large space divided into a maze of cubicles. Rounding the corner, she stopped abruptly at one.

"Oh! Karen's not here?"

I went in and scanned the papers on the desk. An interoffice envelope had Karen's name on the bottom. This seemed to be her station. Rikki peeked in the next cubicle over. "Lian's gone, too?" In fact, the whole space was strangely quiet.

"I'll wait here for Karen," I said. When Rikki hesitated, I added, "Gregory will be upset if no one's at the front desk."

"I'll go and, like, page Karen?"

I plopped down in Karen's chair. Maybe she'd just gone to the bathroom or something. But I got a sick feeling in my stomach when I saw that her computer was off. I conducted a quick search of her stuff. A hairbrush in her drawer yielded dark strands about eight inches long. Judging from the height of her desk chair, she was half a foot shorter than me. A picture of two parent-age figures tacked to a small bulletin board showed a woman with sharp brown eyes and a thin, intelligent mouth. A completed crossword puzzle had been tossed on top of a row of binders.

The phone buzzed. I stared at the blinking light, then picked up the receiver and waited. "Hello?" an uncertain voice asked.

"It's Bill, Rikki. Go ahead."

"Oh! Well, someone said Karen was in a conference?"

Before I could ask where, a harsh voice near Rikki demanded who she was talking to. "Uh, you better come down?" she said. The voice sounded like Gregory's. I slammed down the phone. He'd double-crossed me. I went into the main corridor. Two employees gave me a curious look. Gregory was not going to leave me to my own devices up here, I was sure of that. I turned right, away from the central stairway, and went in search of an exit. As I reached the end of the corridor, a voice yelled at me, "Hey! Stop!"

I tried an unmarked door. To my relief, it gave onto a concrete stairway. I plunged down the stairs. They ended in a stale vestibule on the first floor. To my right was a door that would take me back inside. In front of me was a door labelled, EMER-GENCY EXIT. ALARM WILL SOUND.

This counted as an emergency. As I reached for the door, I had the bizarre precognition of hearing the fire alarm go off before I touched it. But the head-splitting bell was real enough. It propelled me out the door.

In front of me was a small walk, landscaped with grass and low bushes, and beyond them a strip of parking spaces. The main lot was around the corner of the building. I sprinted down the walk.

As I turned the corner, the first thing that caught my eye was a woman running for her car. At the same instant, I saw Gregory near the building entrance, speaking frantically into his cell phone. The woman was about five foot six, with straight brown hair that fell to her neck. She had to be Karen.

I followed Gregory's line of sight and my blood ran cold. A maroon sedan was speeding into the lot. Karen reached a white

Honda and dug for her keys in her bag. The sedan screeched around the corner. I raced across the asphalt, entirely underestimating the car's speed. The next thing I heard was the shriek of tires. The sedan was in a skid and coming right at me. At least Pratt, or his partner, had been nice enough to hit the brakes.

I dove out of the way and rolled into a gap between two cars, still one space over from Karen. Propelling myself under the car, I scraped along the pavement. Tires squealed behind me. I popped out on the other side and knocked on Karen's passenger window. She gaped at me, terrified, from behind the wheel.

"I'm a friend of Sheila's!" I shouted over the scream of the fire alarm. The maroon car had blocked Karen's exit. I motioned for her to get out. "Come with me!"

Either I had an honest face or she made a quick calculation between the lesser of two evils. Karen sprang from her car. We dashed in parallel rows away from the sedan. "Sheila was a friend of mine," I repeated, yelling across the space between us. "I've got a Scout over here."

We slowed in the lane between parked cars. The fire bell ceased abruptly, leaving us in a gaping silence. Karen kept her distance, eyeing the line of trees at the end of the lot and the boulevard beyond it.

A car door slammed. The head of Pratt's partner bobbed among the glittering cartops.

"They'll catch you if you run," I warned. "They were hired by Dugan at LifeScience."

That did the trick. Without saying a word, she joined me, angling across the lot. The maroon car peeled out, coming our way. The Scout was a few spaces over, in the last row of the lot. Karen and I met at the passenger door. I jerked the keys from my pocket, sorted frantically, and fumbled the right one into the lock.

Karen climbed in. Pratt's partner was hurrying across the last bit of pavement as fast as his stomach could shake. There was no time for me to get to the driver's side. I pivoted and stood inside of the passenger door, pulling it most of the way closed. My posture relaxed, as if I was going to surrender to the fact the man had caught me. I gauged his approach: six feet, four, two . . .

I swung the door out as hard as I could. Twenty pounds of steel hit him square in the stomach and sent him sprawling to the ground. He gasped for breath. I caught the door on its way back and dove into the jeep over Karen's lap, into the driver's seat. She slammed the door shut and hit the lock. Again I fumbled with the keys, trying to will the tiny tip into its slot in the ignition.

By now the maroon car had arrived. It blocked my rear exit. I heard the partner gasp something to Pratt. The next moment Pratt was at my window, pounding on the glass.

"Open up!" he commanded. "Open up!"

I turned the key. The engine cranked, and cranked, and cranked. Please don't be ornery, I pleaded.

"I've got mace," Karen said.

It was the first time I'd heard her speak. Her voice was clear, pragmatic, and perfectly calm. I stared at her. She gave a little nod. Her hand was in her bag and had already closed around the canister.

"I'm going to roll down the window and duck," I said.

She nodded again. I held my arms up in surrender to Pratt. He'd just cocked his elbow to smash in the window. "I'm opening!" I shouted.

I rolled the window down fast, inhaled, and ducked away. Karen leaned across me and gave Pratt a quick shot. He screamed and staggered against the car next to me. I rolled the window back up.

I pressed the gas pedal to the floor and cranked the ignition again. At last the engine roared to life. Over my shoulder, I saw that the partner had regained his breath and was getting into the maroon car behind us. I didn't intend to wait to find out if he was going for a weapon.

Only one direction was open. In front of me was a high curb and a tree, about ten feet tall, newly planted on the grass embankment between the parking lot and the boulevard below. I gunned the engine and pushed the tires, in first gear, up to the curb. More gas, and they jumped it. Sad to say, the little tree wasn't much of a match for the Scout. It cracked and went down. When my rear tires hit the curb, the jolt shot both Karen and me up out of our seats.

The Scout skidded down the grass slope. I held on to the wheel, pumped the brakes, and wrestled the jeep to the right to avoid the cars parked along the street below. Now I found myself driving down a narrow sidewalk, one wheel still angled up on the grass bank. Luckily, this was not the kind of place where people actually walked.

As soon as I found a break in the row of parked cars, I bounced down between them. When traffic was clear, I swerved onto the boulevard. I knew the maroon car would be coming out of the lot to head us off. I crossed two lanes and hit the median at an angle, jerking the left wheel up to help it over the curb. Again we were thrown into the air and pitched from side to side as the other three tires dealt with the median. Something scraped horribly on the curb as I came down into the opposite lane.

"Ouch," I said, but still managed a smile to myself.

The Scout had come through. I accelerated and we headed away from BioVerge.

"Who are you?" Karen asked in that same steady, purposeful voice.

I looked over at her. My smile disappeared. She still had the mace in her hand, and it was pointed at me.

21

"Sheila tore the pages out of her diary because she was afraid. At least, that's my theory."

Karen Harper paused to lift a cup of coffee to her lips. She sat across from me at a small tottery table in a cafe in downtown Santa Clara. Her blue-jeaned legs were crossed. Her finger curled around the handle. The cup was perfectly steady.

I sat facing the door of the cafe, just to be on guard. Chances were, though, that Pratt had not been able to track us through ten miles of surface streets.

"Afraid of Neil Dugan?" I asked.

"Yes. Afraid of what would happen if *anyone* found out what she was up to."

"So, Karen, what *was* she up to?"

Karen took another sip. She had those sharp brown eyes I'd seen in the photograph at her desk. Her lips compressed in a thoughtful line. I'd told her enough about Sheila, and what had happened since her death, to convince her to keep sitting with me. I'd also hinted she might get a look at the journal.

"Sheila and I went to graduate school together. We understood each other's style. Some of the people in mo bio are really wound up, very secretive about their work. They view every gain you make as a loss for them. I think it's a carryover from physics. You know, in the early part of the twentieth century, a lot of physicists got into the field. Erwin Schrödinger wrote a book called *What Is Life?* They'd gotten matter down to its basic building blocks; now they set out to do the same for life. The stakes were high. Lots of Nobel prizes. Sheila and I preferred the old, more cooperative approach. When she found some peculiar results in her program, she came to me."

"The MC124 program. The monoclonal antibody that Frederick McKinnon designed to fight cancer."

"Designed in a manner of speaking." Karen's lips curled for a moment, and then her face returned to its default expression. There was something appraising and yet plain about it, unsettling yet reassuring. Most people revealed more in their faces—softness or hardness, wariness or openness. Karen simply seemed aware. *Ready.*

"McKinnon does deserve credit," she went on. "He conceived the program, he directed the research. Sheila was loyal to him. She thought he was brilliant, and I'd guess the feeling was mutual. He was the one who'd spotted her at Stanford. But according to Sheila, it was really Doug Englehart who made the big steps in identifying the monoclonal."

"And he's not getting credit?"

"Not what he deserves. That's the way it works in this business. The senior scientist takes primary authorship. Our advisor, Harry Salzmann, was different. He put us in alphabetical order. The work inspired him more than the glory. Don't get me wrong, the work inspires the others, too. But they live for the glory."

"And McKinnon's got plenty of that coming. Not to mention good old cash."

"If MC124 works. It did well in vitro and in animal tests, but you never know what will ultimately show up in the clinical trials."

"And that's what got Sheila worried?"

Karen nodded slowly. "I'd say so. But for the time being she was worried about a mouse. One little knockout mouse. Dead."

"Knockout mouse?"

"A mouse with certain genes knocked out. It's often done to determine the gene's function. Recently it was found that a mouse lacking a gene for brain development will also keep hair longer. Whole lines of knockout mice have been created for testing purposes. RAG1 mice are immunodeficient in a way that allows tumors to grow quickly. In nude mice, the tumors can be seen growing under the skin. You can knock in genes, too. Human immune genes might be knocked into a mouse to get it to produce a more humanized antibody."

"So a knockout mouse got knocked out in Sheila's lab . . ."

"This mouse was in the trial population for MC124. Anything could have killed it. It happens all the time, you know. Organisms die. You look for the pattern. McKinnon and Englehart assumed this mouse was merely an anomaly. But Sheila thought there was something special about it. Its eyes were a little farther apart than the others. She was sure it came from a different, more humanized population than the other trial mice. If that was true, it didn't belong in the test group. It may have been mixed in by accident. On the other hand, the humanized mice have a certain marking on their feet, which this one lacked."

"If MC124 is fatal to human immune systems, that sounds like a problem. Did they test it on more humanized mice?"

"I assume they will. But McKinnon and Englehart are just as

sure as they can be that it's safe. Sheila still wanted to look very closely at this particular mouse."

"And then she got transferred out of the group."

"Yeah. McKinnon told her she was wasting her time. Actually, it was Sheila who asked to be transferred. She never did tell me why."

"That's weird. Wasn't she excited about the program?"

"Very. It was good work. I was envious."

"What does MC124 do, exactly? What's a monoclonal antibody?"

"MAbs, we call them. You know what an antibody is, right? It's a type of protein that responds to an antigen—an invader—in your body by going around and tagging it for destruction. Most antibodies have a single antigen they bind to. Their molecular receptors fit each other like a lock and key. One antigen, one antibody. So you can design a MAb to hunt out and bind with certain parts of cancer cells instead of with the usual pathogens like bacteria or a virus."

"What makes it 'monoclonal'?"

"Mouse and rabbit populations are induced to produce the particular antibody you want. The antibody is fused with a myeloma cell. This allows you to reproduce it in what are called immortal cell lines. The antibodies are all clones. From these you derive therapeutics, such as MC124, to inject in patients. The antibody does its tagging work and recruits the immune system to attack the cancer cells. This kind of monoclonal is called a naked MAb. Others are conjugated with toxins or radioisotopes to kill the pathogens. MAbs to treat breast cancer, non-Hodgkin's lymphoma, and transplant rejection, among other things, are already on the market."

"It sounds like they do the same kind of thing to cancer cells that an allergic immune system does to a pollen or shellfish protein."

"In certain ways. I always felt Sheila had her own personal reasons for getting into this field. You saw her mother at the funeral? She has lupus, which is a different kind of immune disease—autoimmune. Her system mistakes her body's own cells for antigens. MAbs are being developed for autoimmune diseases, too."

"I think Sheila was afraid she'd inherit it from her mother."

"It's certainly possible. Sheila didn't like to talk about it, though. Maybe she opened up about it more to her diary."

I affirmed with a nod. Karen stared into her empty coffee cup. "She had these depths of—I don't know, pain. I tried to reach her, to be a friend. She was one of the best, the most inquiring, the most genuine people I've met. But she kept so much bottled inside." Karen touched a finger to the wet corner of her eye and averted her gaze.

"I only knew her a little," I said. "But I saw that, too."

We sat in silence for a few moments. "Anyway," Karen said, "monoclonals have been around for a while. They were big in the eighties: someone called them 'magic bullets.' Two scientists in Cambridge won a Nobel. But the drugs didn't work the way they were supposed to in humans. Frederick McKinnon was a young dynamo at the time, poised to make a name with a small company. He had to go back to the bench before new techniques made the treatment feasible again. This is an incredible comeback for him."

"And he wouldn't want anyone getting in the way of it."

"Yes, but—well, if there's a snag, it's going to come out sooner or later. Better sooner. The earlier problem they had with MAbs was that they were essentially mouse antibodies. Humans in turn developed their own antibodies against the murine ones. The therapy could only be used once before the patient became 'immune' to it. These new monoclonals are better targeted and more highly humanized—a few of them are fully human."

"So humanized just means the antibody is made partly of human genes."

"Yes. You take whatever antigen you want to attack and inject it into a transgenic mouse whose immune genes are either partially or wholly human. The mouse produces the antibody, which you isolate from its spleen cells. You then fuse the antibody with human bone cancer cells, which tend to proliferate like mad. This allows the hybridoma, as it's called, to divide and multiply. You select the most effective hybridoma culture, propagate it in the lab or in mice, and then purify your MAb from them to use as a drug."

"So where in that process did Sheila think MC124 went wrong?"

"That's the big question. McKinnon is truly convinced it works and is safe. But Sheila had such a thorough mind, she insisted on getting to the bottom of whether it killed this mouse. I still don't know why she left the group. I don't think McKinnon forced her."

I remembered my tape. "So what exactly did Sheila bring to you? Was she carrying a big leather bag?"

Karen blinked a few times, taking herself back to that day. "I guess she was. All her data on the mouse. Samples, ELISAs, amino acid sequences, immunoassays, notebooks, printouts. Maybe—well, probably she didn't have permission to take them from the lab."

"I have a feeling that's why those two guys were trying to trap you and me like rabbits. Neil Dugan wants that stuff."

"Yeah, it could be someone reported her. It's all at my house right now. You don't think they'd go after it, do you?"

"Yes, I do."

Karen jumped up and went to a phone in the back of the cafe. She returned with a relieved look. "You were right. They came. Tried to push their way in. My roommate called the police, and they backed off."

"It's good to know they'll stop at something."

"Well, they'll have to stop some more. I'm going to get a restraining order slapped on those guys. You've got their names?"

I nodded. "What about Gregory? And your job?"

A sudden laugh erupted from Karen. "At that company? The axe is about to fall anyway. BioVerge is going nowhere."

I gave her Pratt's card. "How did you get hooked up with Gregory in the first place? You seem like—"

"I should have known better?" She let out a mock wail. "Don't remind me! At the time, bioinformatics was the hottest pot boiling on the stove. I came in with Ron, Gregory's partner. Ron's a top-notch guy, but he didn't know the IT side. Gregory acted like he had it licked. He totally evangelized us. We signed on the dotted line."

I gave a wry smile. "I know the feeling. I got drawn into all this doing film work for Kumar Biotechnics. Gregory tried to make me believe they were stealing some software of yours, and I should hand over Kumar's footage."

"What a joke. Kumar's got BioVerge licked from here to Toledo. I'm sure they'll get the LifeScience contract. Then Gregory's little shell game will be kaput."

"Certain things are starting to fall into place."

"That little rat. I *knew* something was up. He told me to come down for some mysterious meeting today. Then he stuck me in a side room and disappeared into the conference. When I heard him railing at Rikki, I got worried. He was out of control. I went for the exit."

"We can go rescue your car later tonight."

"Don't worry. I'll get a few friends together to do it."

I sat back. Karen had that ready look on her face again. She had trusted me. It was time to trust her. "I have a copy of Sheila's diary. I also found some disks in her apartment. If we put them together with what you know about her research, we might come up with some answers to how she was killed. What do you say?"

We were alone in the cafe now. The handful of people who'd been lingering from lunch had left. Karen's mouth curved into a small Mona Lisa smile. I took it for agreement, and smiled back. Then her eyes wandered over to the glass case by the cash register. "God, wouldn't you just love a piece of chocolate cake right now?"

22

There was only one way Gregory could have gotten Jenny's address: Neil Dugan. The same connection, I figured, that had resulted in Pratt busting into the parking lot to get me and Karen. Gregory had set me up completely. Yet I'd played a part, too: I was the one who'd told Dugan and Harros to call Gregory to validate my reason for being in that parking lot on the night Sheila was killed.

And I knew it had to be Gregory. I knew it before I saw the boot print. After leaving Karen, I'd come to Jenny's. I rang the bell and pounded on the door. No answer. I used my key to get in. There was a strong alcohol smell. I went straight to the kitchen. The back door had been kicked in. Crockery and glass were in shards all over the floor.

I called for Jenny, knowing I wouldn't get a response. The dining room was untouched, but the white curtains in the living room were torn down. The rods were in pieces in front of the window. Lamps were broken and lolling on the floor. For a moment I wondered if Jenny had had a massive tantrum.

Then the huge stain jumped out from the cream white carpet and sofa. Blood, I thought. I knelt to touch it. No, it was too purple, too aromatic. I noticed the jagged shards of a wine bottle. It had been smashed against the coffee table. The liquid was splattered everywhere. The diagonals of a boot print confirmed my intuition of who'd done it.

I checked in the bedroom and bathroom. They'd been similarly wrecked. The shower curtain was ripped from its rings. Toiletries littered the tile. But there was no sign of Jenny.

I rushed to the Scout. It never occurred to me to call the police. My only thought was to find him. He wouldn't have taken her to the office, I was sure of that. But I'd force Rikki to give me his home address. And then I'd find Gregory and wring his neck like a dishcloth.

Rikki just about jumped out of her chair when I barged into the BioVerge lobby. She opened her mouth without speaking. "Where is he?" I yelled. I slapped my hands on the counter and leaned toward her without lowering my voice. "Give me his address!"

"He's—he's—in his office?"

The direction of her glance told me which way to go. I marched down the corridor. If any of the employees I passed had any sense, they'd have tried to stop me.

The door to Gregory's office was closed. I paused just a moment, then burst in. I had no intention of stopping at the threshold to talk. I plunged straight for his desk. But his chair was empty.

The telephone was buzzing. That would be Rikki, announcing my arrival. The sound of running water came from behind a closed door across the room. I rushed through the door and into a large bathroom. The carpeting was plush, even more cushy than in the office. I never did like people who carpeted their bathrooms. Gregory stood in front of a sink, reaching for a towel.

He caught sight of me charging him in a mirror framed like a big painting that hung above the sink. He turned, holding up the towel in defense or surrender—I didn't care which. I took his left wrist in both hands and wrenched it up behind his back. He bellowed. I used my body to shove his hips hard against the sink. Now I had a good enough hold on his arm with my left hand to use my right to grab his hair. But it was too short to grip, so I twisted his right ear. In the mirror I could see his forehead, corrugated in pain.

"Where is she, Gregory? Where's Jenny?"

"Fuuuuck!" he screamed.

"Speak softly, please." I wrenched his arm harder behind his back. He screamed again. I looked around. The glass-enclosed shower was empty. The treadmill was quiet. She wasn't here.

I jerked his ear up so I could see his face full in the mirror. Relaxing my hold on his left arm a tad, I said in a calmer voice, "Just tell me where Jenny is, and I'll leave you alone."

His eyes widened. Not with fear, nor anger, but with puzzlement. This had been Gregory's shortcoming all along: he was too easy to read. It was written like a headline across his face. He didn't have Jenny. She hadn't been there when he trashed her apartment, either.

My eyes fell to a familiar shape on the counter. I had a weird flash of Jenny's bathroom, and didn't understand why—until I focused on the small bottle of expensive hand lotion next to the soap. It was Jenny's.

"You idiot," I said.

I was saved from having to decide what to do with him by three guys who burst through the door. Gregory screamed for help. They were on me fast. They weren't exactly athletic, but there were three of them. I had to let Gregory go to fend them off. The room was all elbows and knees for about thirty seconds. Then they got control of my limbs. Gregory slapped me in the head, someone else kicked me in the shins, and a knee to the groin left me gasping. They pinned me hard against the wall next to the towel rack. I couldn't even bend over. All I could do was suck in big howling gulps of air. The knee had not been a direct hit, but close enough.

Gregory quivered before me, bent at the waist. His fists closed into tight knots. When my vision cleared enough to make out his face, I saw that it was red, all the way down to the roots of his bleached hair.

"You shithead, you double-crossed me!" His eyes bulged at me until he was sure my attention was back with him. "The tapes you gave me are worthless."

"It's not like you came through on your end of the bargain." My words were punctuated by small gasps. "Anyway, I can't help it if you don't know how to interpret the data."

"The audio level is too low to hear anything, and the video is nothing but a bunch of test shots at Kumar's."

"Plus you in the parking lot. Telling me how great your penny-ante company is. That's a bonus."

My breath was returning to normal—as normal as it could be with three guys bolting me to wall. Gregory's face was fading from red back to bright pink, but his eyes still burned. He shook his right fist.

"Hold him good." He zeroed in on me. "I just want one shot. This is going to feel so good, buddy."

He cocked the fist. He didn't really know what he was doing. The idiot went for my face. I watched his eyes carefully and jerked my head away at the last moment. His fist smashed into drywall.

Gregory howled in pain again and hopped to the other side of the bathroom, hand clutched in his armpit. The guys pinning me were startled enough to loosen their grip. I broke free, though not before one of them stomped on my foot. I got to the door, threw it open, and found a crowd waiting in Gregory's office. They retreated a few feet as I stumbled out.

Rikki stared at me with an incredulous face. "Like—?"

Two of the guys spilled out after me. They slowed at the sight of the crowd and their wide eyes. I hobbled to the edge of Gregory's desk. He appeared a moment later, leaning on the third guy. Gregory's face was wet. His right fingers hung in front of him like gnarled clothespins. "Jesus, I think they're broken."

"Likely," I agreed.

He snarled in my direction. "Has someone called the cops?"

"Um, I can?" Rikki said in a small voice.

"You're finished, Bill. You're *finished!*"

I was too busy deciding which part of my body hurt the most to reply. My ear, my foot, my shin, and my ribs all throbbed. My white shirt was streaked with dirt and wine, and I could feel something wet on my face. I must have looked like I'd just come in from an especially exciting hunting trip.

Rikki had gone behind the desk. "Put down the phone, Rikki," I said over my shoulder. "Unless your boss is ready to be arrested for breaking and entering. Twice. You left prints all over my flat, Gregory. The police have them, plus you're stupid enough to keep Jenny's lotion in your bathroom. There's plenty of evidence you broke into her apartment today."

I watched him closely. If we'd been alone, he might have given in. But not in front of all these people. "You're full of it," he said. "Make the call, Rikki."

"Let's see the bottom of your boot, Gregory. Let's see the red wine on it. If it's not there, you've got a whole room of people to back you up."

"You're finished," Gregory repeated. But his voice lacked conviction. His face had turned a sort of moldy yellow, and he was forcing down swallows. He'd be rushing to the toilet any minute.

I pushed up from the desk, wobbled, and got my feet under me. "I'm sorry about your hand," I said. I moved slowly toward the door. Gregory retreated to the bathroom. "You'll have to learn how to sign checks with the other one. The bill for Jenny's apartment will come next week."

No one moved to stop me as I reached the open door. The receiver in Rikki's hand started to honk its off-hook signal. I caught sight of Ron—Karen's friend who was also Gregory's partner. His expression was suspended somewhere between disbelief and understanding. "Give Karen Harper a call at home," I suggested. "She'll tell you what this is all about."

23

In Silicon Valley, when the nucleus of a new company was being formed, when it was abuzz with the infinite potential of dense code, sticky interface, and parturient markets, only a glimmer of which could be allowed to escape into the light of day, the company was said to be in stealth mode. That meant the startup was assembling resources, gathering capital, developing technology. No one outside the nucleus knew yet what it *did:* concepts were too easily lifted. Outsiders saw a spiffy logo, a history-making yet vague promise, and a lot of feverish activity, cloaked in darkness. The unveiling would occur the day the site went online, at which point the idea was to break on the world like a new virus, the kind that sucked money out of bank accounts.

It was time for me to come out of stealth mode and go public. I was tired of doing all the work on my own. Some other people needed to contribute now.

I returned to Jenny's place and cleaned up the best I could, pouring a whole box of salt over the wine stains in the living room. The look on Gregory's face before I left had told me I didn't need to get the police involved. He wasn't going to bother me anymore. I didn't need the headache of filing charges, and besides, there were too many things for which I could still get nailed. I didn't want to call the police just yet.

When I called to check my answering machine in San Francisco, I found out that I could have saved myself a few bruises. Jenny had left a message around noon saying she was going to her mother's in Sacramento and taking the cat with her. I didn't mind, though. My accounts with Gregory would have needed to be settled sooner or later.

My next steps were to tell Kumar about Gregory's scheme and to control the damage at LifeScience. Gregory no doubt had defamed my character to Dugan, but zero from zero left zero. It was the others at LifeScience who counted. The people handling the bioinformatics bid, for instance, ought to hear about Gregory. But that was a small point. I wanted to get to Marion Roos, Frederick McKinnon, Doug Englehart, and Carl Steiner, the peculiar man at the funeral. I wanted answers from them about MC124 and the knockout mouse. I also wanted them to know that Dugan and his hired hands were stalking me, threatening me, and generally lurking with intent to loom. So far they hadn't actually laid a hand on me—either to keep their record clean or because I hadn't given them a clear shot—but if the worst happened, I wanted people to know who to blame.

And then there was the Harros family. Every innocent move Jenny and I had made had been turned against us. I'd dug a hole for myself with them and there was nothing to do but keep digging. They'd want to hear about the knockout mouse, too. Perhaps it would force them to ask Dugan some questions.

I sat down in Jenny's dining room with the phone and a folded piece of paper on which I'd been keeping numbers. My first call was to Jenny in Sacramento. Already she sounded happier. She was pleased to hear I was at her apartment, until I told her there'd been a little break-in. I described my set-to with Gregory, and she made a lot of nice coos of concern. She wanted me to join her in Sacramento. I said I would try to make it tomorrow or Sunday.

Next up was Rita. "Are you all right?" she asked with some urgency. "We heard the fire alarm across the way. Suddenly there you were being chased by those two guys."

I gave her the playback on Karen and our escapade with Pratt. Rita was enjoying it until I got to the part about needing her help again. "I already owe you a dinner, Rita. Boulevard, Chez Panisse—it's your choice. I need you to hook me up with Kumar. I'm going to tell him what Gregory was up to, but I also want him to get me inside LifeScience."

"Is Fleur de Lys on the restaurant list?"

"They're *all* on the list."

"Right answer. Okay, I'll give you his private cell number. But give me a chance to talk to him first."

Five minutes later, I got the all clear from Rita. Kumar answered in a friendly tone. He said he was happy to name his contacts at LifeScience for me, one of whom turned out to be Doug Englehart. Not only did Kumar give me Englehart's direct number, he promised to call him on my behalf. Kumar also thanked me for warning him about Gregory's scheme. He'd keep an eye out for any spies Gregory might have inside the company.

I braced myself for the next call. Abe Harros's voice had been on my home machine. He reported, snidely, that my story about being with Gregory in the parking lot last Wednesday had not checked out. Abe wasn't in his hotel room, so I left him a voicemail inviting him over to view my tape of Gregory. As soon as I hung up, I regretted the message. My words had been just as snide as his.

My last call was to Dr. Nikano, Sheila's allergist. I wanted to catch her before she left for the day. She'd reviewed the pathologist's report and had managed to get a sample of Sheila's blood.

"I did some further analysis," she said, "and saw elevated levels of mast cell tryptase. That points to an allergic reaction, so anaphylactic shock seems certain as the cause of death. Knowing her history, we have to assume some kind of shellfish is the culprit."

"It may be *a* culprit, but it's not *the* culprit. The culprit is whoever gave her those proteins. Abe Harros said there were needle punctures in her arm."

"That's correct. I'd like to know where the punctures came from. She wasn't receiving allergy shots. If she'd been vaccinated recently, it would explain a lot of things—but she wasn't. I checked her records."

"I'll look into it. Meanwhile, if I can get you more information on what compounds Sheila was working with in the lab, can you test whether they connect to her death?"

"Absolutely. Something very peculiar happened here."

"You're right, Jill." I told her a little bit about Dugan, LifeScience, and Karen. I also warned her about what the Harros family was likely to say about me. Jill said not to worry. She'd gotten a dose of George's temper herself. "You'll be the first to hear when I find out more, Bill," she promised.

I thanked her, glad to have one more person trust me.

I rose from the dining table and realized how stiff my body was. My adrenaline had drained away and my muscles had contracted into soreness. A bruise the size of a softball had bloomed on my left thigh. My ribs screamed when I raised my arms. The toes on my right foot throbbed. My lower lip was swollen. I needed to soak in some hot water.

I drove north to the city in the gathering dusk. Darkness was coming earlier every day. Fall was here. I felt myself floating in the river of taillights.

Back at my flat, a message from Doug Englehart was waiting. He wanted to see me in his office. He'd call back in the morning to tell me what time. I gazed at the blinking light on the machine for a moment, thinking about what that meant. The game was on. I'd be inside LifeScience tomorrow, a Saturday, and with any luck I would be able to do some poking around in a mostly empty building.

I limped into the shower and let the hot water pound me until the tank ran out. By the end of it I was lying under the barrage in the tub. I used my foot to turn the water off and lay until it drained out. The tub still was warm, but cool night air eddied over me. The flat was silent. My skin tightened into a shiver.

What was I going to find inside LifeScience tomorrow? With my body still aching and my energy ebbing, I felt a twinge of fear. I was gambling everything on this move. I'd be on Dugan's turf, and I didn't yet know how far he and his security staff were willing to go. The working-over I got at BioVerge might be a mere appetizer. Or the ranks within LifeScience could close against me, cutting off any chance of finding answers.

As a boy, hunting with my father, I'd had the fear I'd be mistaken for quarry. When my parents split up, the fear was I'd be left without shelter or food. The fear I felt now was more nebulous, more diffuse. The danger might take any form and come from any direction. Dugan or Harros could well find a way to turn the people I now trusted against me. Everyone seemed to have a hidden ambition, an ulterior motive. Everyone but Sheila.

Sheila and Karen. In many respects, Karen was my best hope. I suddenly felt very afraid for her. I rose from the tub, threw on a robe, and dialed her cell number. Relief flooded my veins when I heard her voice. She was fine, taking refuge at a friend's for the night. She'd started to look over the materials Sheila had given her. They looked promising. I told her I hoped to get into LifeScience to speak to Doug Englehart tomorrow. She asked me to come over to her hideout afterward.

I agreed, then hung up and called Wes. I wanted at least one other person to know where to come looking for my body.

"You know that this is kind of crazy, don't you?" Wes said. "I've been in some tight places, dealing with VCs to fund my company, but I never went prowling into enemy territory. This guy Dugan sounds like the type who'd slip you something invisible that rearranges your DNA. You wouldn't figure out what hit you until months later."

"That's exactly what I think he did to Sheila. I'm not saying I'm looking forward to this, Wes, but you know better than to try to talk me out of it."

"Yeah, you've got your teeth sunk into this one, Billy. Okay, just act like you belong in the building. Fake it till you make it. If you don't call me by three tomorrow afternoon, I'm coming to find you myself."

"Thanks, Wes. Don't be afraid to call the police, if you think you have to."

"Same goes for you, Bill."

"Right."

But as I clicked off the phone, I knew it wasn't an option. Dugan and Harros had all the pieces on the board arranged against me. If the police showed up, it would mean I'd already failed.

24

Doug Englehart woke me up. He was ready to see me. Could I come right down?

I looked at my clock. Seven-thirty on Saturday morning and this guy was already at work. I mumbled something that even I couldn't understand and said I'd be there by nine. That gave me forty-five minutes to get my wits about me and forty-five minutes to drive to Palo Alto.

As I rolled over to get to my feet, a stabbing pain in my ribs reminded me of the fun I'd had yesterday. At least I could take satisfaction in visualizing Gregory's pain reliever intake this morning.

Two cups of coffee and three ibuprofen later, I was on the road to LifeScience. The water of the bay winked and glittered beside the parking lot. The sun was not yet high enough to be blocked by the band of cirrus clouds skating in from the northwest.

I chose a space behind the annex as the least likely to be spotted. My orange Scout would stick out like a common poppy among roses in the main lot.

I walked around to the front entrance. Doug had told me to dial his extension from an intercom outside the door. There was no receptionist today and, I hoped, a minimum of security.

I reached Doug's voicemail and told him I was at the door. It was not quite nine. A quick look through the glass showed the lobby was empty. But the red light on the camera above the reception desk was on. I looked up over my shoulder. Another camera affixed to a column was aimed at the door. I pressed myself against a wall, out of reach of the lens.

The nerves in my stomach were starting to jumble when a kiwi green Volkswagen zipped into a space in front of the building. A woman popped out of the door. The sleek black hair, the bolero jacket, the brisk walk—I recognized Fay immediately. She jumped with a bark of fright, nearly dropping the portfolio under her arm, when she saw me in the shadow of the portico.

"Bill! God, you scared me. What are you doing here?"

"Visiting a friend. And you?"

"I'm just—just showing my work."

"Are you all right?" In spite of the outfit, in spite of the makeup, her shoulders sagged and her eyes were puffy and red. Her voice didn't have the usual swagger.

"I'm not doing too great, I have to admit. Simon—" She stopped, a catch in her voice. "Simon called. You were right about him and Sheila. I feel so badly. She helped me get this contract."

The door opened. The woman holding it said hello to Fay and asked if she had brought the sketches. Fay greeted her, then turned to give me an imploring look. "Please don't mention this to Jenny. I wanted to do a job on my own."

I followed her in. Doug Englehart was just entering the forelobby. He gave Fay an inquiring glance before fixing on me. "You're Bill, right?"

Fay was still waiting for an answer. I just smiled at her, then turned to shake Doug's hand. "Yes. Thanks for inviting me over."

"Come on up." I followed him to an elevator on the left side of the atrium. We rode to the third floor. Doug tapped the side of his leg the whole time, as if preoccupied with some calculation. He wore a short sleeve yellow-checked shirt. His balding head stood out on his thin neck like a light bulb. Two shoots of a mustache crawled across his upper lip. His long arms drooped from his shoulders, and his large feet were encased in running shoes.

"Lots of people working today," I commented as the doors opened.

"Lots happening." He kept a step ahead of me as we walked. He didn't seem to want to talk in the open. We passed labs on either side, sets of long work benches in long rooms cluttered with tanks, jars, flasks, beakers, tubes, titers, centrifuges. A cart in the corridor contained more glass stacked like dirty dishes. We took a corner and passed a glassed room containing a small black box.

"That's our PCR machine," Doug said offhandedly.

In another lab, machines resembling grocery scales undulated in perfectly symmetrical hulas. Doug said they were vortexers.

We got to the end of the linoleum corridor and took a right to a space cloverleafed with work stations. On one wall was a big metal door with a window that looked into his lab. I saw a couple of scientists at the benches, and recognized their faces from the funeral.

Doug's office was a drywalled box next to the lab. He gestured for me to shut the door behind me. "You can put your coat anywhere."

"Thanks." I kept it on. It was a heavy canvas jacket. Tucked into one inside pocket was a mini-DV camera. In the other was the DAT recorder, cued up.

Doug went behind his desk. I looked for a place to sit. A cheap loveseat was pushed back against the wall by the door. Books, binders, and manuals lined the walls. There was one window in the room, partially blocked by a bookcase, to the left of Doug's desk.

I moved a stack of reprints off a hard chair. While I was turned away, I slipped my hand in my inner coat pocket and clicked off the DAT's pause button. Then I pulled the chair close to the desk.

Taped to the edge of a metal shelf to Doug's right, above his computer workstation, was a multihued image, a muscular humanoid sort of figure that might have come out of a cartoon. It had two bulging bow legs and two massively biceped arms with what looked like giant double-claws for hands. There was no head. A line connected the legs to a legend in the margin that read Fc. The arms were labelled FAb. The claws, a mix of green and red, were labelled M; the legs, in blue and silver, H.

I stared at the image. "Is that MC124?"

Doug glanced at it. His eyes dilated, and he flicked at his mustache with his thumb. "You said you had something to tell me about Gregory Alton?" His voice was sharp, all treble.

I laid out what I knew about Gregory and his attempt to steal software from Kumar. Doug nodded along with me. He seemed in a hurry, so I wrapped it up quickly. When I was done, he sat with his eyes slanted toward the window. I waited for a response, then asked, "This information isn't helpful?"

His head turned back, but his eyes focused somewhere behind me. "Somewhat. BioVerge keeps claiming they're about to unveil some new technology."

"Now you know where it would come from," I said. He shrugged. "Of course you can't take only my word for it," I added. "I have someone who just quit the company who will confirm it."

"All right." He put his elbows on the desk. His eyes slid back toward the window.

"I appreciate your talking to me," I said. "I have some questions about Sheila, if you don't mind."

He gave a perfunctory nod.

"Did you know her well?" I asked.

"Yes, of course." He spoke into his hands. His head didn't move. "She was one of my best people."

"What do you know about the problems she found with MC124?"

His gaze quickly locked on me. He lost his distracted tone. "There are no problems. She got stuck on an anomalous result. One of the trial mice died. It happens all the time—both things. Random mortality, and a researcher mistaking it for important data."

"Do you think *her* death was a random mortality?"

His eyes grew wide. He slowly pressed his palms to his desk. "What are you saying?"

"Sheila's allergist has been running some tests on her blood serum. People will want to know how her findings match up with MC124."

"An allergist doesn't have the training," he scoffed.

"She's doing research at UCSF."

"I don't care where she's from. It's perfectly obvious what caused Sheila's death. You'll find no connection to MC124."

"Sheila herself did. It's in her notes and some other materials. There are people following up on her research."

"That's just wrong!" He slammed a fist on the desk. The window rattled with the force of his voice.

If I'd exaggerated what Karen and I knew, his reaction told me we weren't far off. "I understand you're the principal designer of the antibody," I continued. "You probably know better than anyone what it can do and what it can't. Don't you want to find out if someone in this company misused it to hurt Sheila?"

Doug put his forehead in a bunch. His hands locked in front of his mouth again and he blew a little air between his thumbs. He was not one to hide his thought processes. "Like who?"

"Neil Dugan has been doing everything he can—legally and illegally—to get his hands on Sheila's notebooks and diaries."

I hoped for, and got, a ping of recognition. "Dugan, huh?"

Doug was showing what might be the start of a smile. I didn't know why that thought would amuse him, but it did. Then I remembered Dugan's battle with McKinnon. "Do you think he might be trying to use Sheila's death somehow to derail MC124?"

Doug frowned. "Neil is an ignoramus, scientifically speaking. Company politics, the dirty kind, are his specialty. When the new regime came in, he read a couple of articles and decided monoclonals were dead. He had no idea about the work being done on the Fc region. Now that MAbs are making a comeback, Dugan looks bad. I never thought he'd go to such lengths, though."

I leaned forward and waited for Doug to look me in the face. "Let's stop him. Help me out. Tell me what happened to that knockout mouse. Tell me how MC124 could be misused."

Doug bit his fingernail. The wheels were turning in his head. I looked at him more closely and saw the signs of wear and tear from the rush to complete this program: the newly etched lines around his eyes and mouth, the fuzz of gray above his ears. He was on the verge of speaking when a sharp rap came at the door. It opened before he could ask who it was.

Frederick McKinnon's tall, angular frame loomed in the doorway. "Oh, sorry Doug." He peered at me. "I know you. Where have we met?"

I stood and shook McKinnon's hand. "Here and at Sheila's funeral. I'm Bill Damen."

"He had some information on the biocomputing deal," Doug said. "It cinches our decision. I'll fill you in."

"That's fine, Doug. Just pass it on to the department. You know we need to have the results locked down for the meeting on Monday."

Doug's mouth twisted in a brief grimace of resentment. McKinnon was busy scanning some papers on the desk. "What are you looking for, Frederick?" Doug asked with some irritation.

McKinnon glanced up. "Nothing, Doug. Just trying to help."

"I'll give you my usual update at lunch."

McKinnon chuckled gently. "Of course. Sorry to intrude. You won't have to put up with me much longer, eh?"

Doug started to act busy. He opened a folder on his desk and began poring over its contents. "Let's get the work done. The sooner we can celebrate, the better."

McKinnon smiled in commiseration. Doug wouldn't look up. McKinnon shifted his glance to me. "Stressful time for all of us."

I responded with my own smile. I wanted to hear what Doug was about to say before McKinnon came in, but I had a feeling he was not going to unglue his eyes from that folder anytime soon. Not while McKinnon was here. I took my next best opportunity. "Dr. McKinnon, do you have a minute? I'd like to talk to you about Sheila Harros."

"Ah, now I remember. You visited us last week." He shook his head. "I am so sorry about Sheila. What a loss. I'm—"

The old beg-off was coming, I could tell. I didn't give him the chance. "Her death was not an accident. People here at LifeScience were involved."

McKinnon straightened. His hands moved up, started to slide into his pockets, then stopped. "That's a serious statement."

"It is. I'd like to speak to you."

He nodded toward the door. "We'll go to my office."

We both turned at the sudden clatter of a chair. Doug was on his feet, coming around his desk. McKinnon gave me a small push out of the room, then positioned himself in the doorway. "Don't stop your work, Doug. I can handle this."

25

Frederick McKinnon's office was a different story than Doug Englehart's. It was in a tower attached to the annex, at the fulcrum of the company's three departments. Windows looked east over the bay, now green under the shadows of clouds, and west over the mottled landscape of Palo Alto. The bookcases were built into the walls, their contents stacked neatly. A pair of couches faced each other over a glass coffee table, which was arrayed with scientific journals. The rear of the office was dominated by McKinnon's walnut desk, nearly empty of clutter. A single folder was open next to a slim black laptop in front of his Herman Miller desk chair.

I took a seat in one of the cushioned chairs facing the desk. McKinnon closed the folder and punched up a double-helix screensaver on the computer display. On our walk over, he'd asked for the background on my connection to Sheila. He asked intelligent questions and drew out various details about my film work. His voice was genial and refined, his gait loping, quite a contrast to Doug. Doug was a driven lab rat who didn't have much of a life away from the bench. McKinnon, on the other hand, had the air of a man of the world. The wave in his hair, angled rakishly across his forehead, reminded me of a hero from a British movie, an RAF pilot perhaps. While Doug was perpetually distracted, McKinnon listened with what seemed his full attention. He gave the impression of being utterly concerned about you and your words—a technique, I knew, that certain executives cultivated. It worked nonetheless.

Once we were seated, though, the casual chat was over. His sky-blue eyes lasered in on me. "Now tell me. What do you have to link LifeScience to Sheila's death?"

"She found a problem with MC124. The dead knockout mouse. Someone here was very upset about that. They wanted to make sure it didn't get out."

McKinnon sat back and gazed out the window, wondering perhaps how I knew about the mouse. Whatever he decided, he didn't let me in on it.

"Yes, the mouse," he said smoothly. "It concerned Sheila. I took it quite seriously myself. She had an intuitive feel for the work. I had such hopes—" He caught himself, then turned back to me. "We did a careful investigation. MC124 has no significant problems."

"I have some notes from her that say otherwise." This was a stretch, but I wanted to gauge how close my theory was to being right. "These reactions are so complex—isn't it possible something unexpected happened?"

McKinnon leaned forward and folded his hands on the desk. "The unexpected is more than possible, it's inevitable. This is what makes the field so challenging. I feel a personal responsibility to detect potential danger. We have only the beginning of a grasp on these processes. When you alter one pathway, you can alter many others down the line. We don't always know what produces a reaction. You have to study the effects minutely, in vitro, in silico, in vivo."

He tapped his manicured fingers on the desk. "I've been working with monoclonal antibodies for fifteen years. The first time around, the subjects' immune systems attacked the chimeric hybridomas as invaders. Monoclonals went out of favor, but I knew that with ingenuity they could succeed. Now, at last, we understand the role of the constant region more clearly, and we can be far more exact with the antigen-binding regions. MC124 is 90 percent humanized. It took some hard work to develop the framework and many versions of the antibody—124 to be exact—to get it right."

"And you're sure that it *is* right?"

McKinnon's eyes blazed into me. "No one has more depth in this field than myself. Myself and Doug. We've reviewed every result. Who could have more incentive to insure its safety than me? I've staked my career on it."

"You really can't afford to have a mistake uncovered, then."

"True." He indulged a smile. "Does that turn me into the prime suspect?"

He was so smooth. He'd managed to disarm my thrust with a combination of honesty and style, even make it look a bit silly. My eyes strayed to the art on his walls. None of the usual suspects, meant to assure the executive of his taste, but mixed media tableaux that turned the letters and icons of genetics into children's building blocks. His willingness to install such an ironic twist on biomedical symbols showed McKinnon had confidence in his choices. And in his style. Silicon Valley's climate was Mediterranean, and his dress was calibrated to it—rather than to the power suit mode of the East Coast or the slick casualness of Hollywood. Accessible, jaunty, but still elegant and in charge.

I dodged his question and said, "I appreciate your answering so fully."

He waved it off. "I'm not giving away any company secrets. We're about to publish our paper on it."

"You sound very confident."

He inhaled deeply, arching his brows. "Frankly, yes. I have been injecting myself with the drug to test for safety." He smiled and exhaled. "So you see, I have reason for confidence."

"And you're going to have the rest of your team try it next? Doesn't that violate some code of ethics?"

I finally broke the surface of his cool. He blinked a couple of times. "Only if they withhold assent. But they haven't. Now," he added with a trace of impatience, "you mentioned notes of Sheila's. You'll need to give them to me immediately. We can make revisions to the paper if necessary."

"Neil Dugan must have given you the hard drive from her home computer already."

Now he was flustered. "*Neil*—? I don't know a thing about this."

"He took the hard drive just after Sheila was found. He's been trying his damnedest to get more documents from me. His private detectives have assaulted me twice."

"*Dugan*, dammit. He's out of control. He—" McKinnon stopped and glared at me. "I can't vouch for anything Neil Dugan does. Sometimes I wonder if we even work for the same company. If you think Dugan is somehow involved with Sheila's death, come out with it. I want to know. I'll examine those documents, and we'll take any evidence you have to the police."

"Thank you for cooperating. I'll be in touch with you."

The blue eyes hardened again. "Now look, you can't come in here and lay down these accusations and then just walk away. I need to see those materials. We need to take action."

"I agree," I said in my most polite voice. I wanted to remain on good terms with him, but I didn't want him to take over.

"I don't have the materials here. Others have some of them. I'll pull them all together."

McKinnon relinquished as gracefully as he could. "*Quickly,* please, unless you'd like a visit from the police. Time is of the essence."

"One other thing—why did you transfer Sheila out of the group?"

McKinnon collapsed back into his chair. "She requested it herself. Terribly disappointing to me. I never fully understood her reasons. Something personal, perhaps. She was a bit troubled, I think—not by our work, but in her emotions."

"Did she test out MC124 on herself?"

McKinnon stared out the window for a long moment. "I suppose she could have."

"Thanks for talking to me." As I stood, the DAT recorder clicked off. I covered it with a cough. McKinnon gave me a long, hard look. I switched to a new subject. "Oh, I also meant to ask you about Carl Steiner."

McKinnon stood with me. "Steiner? The gardener?"

"Yes. He was at the funeral. Had an attachment to Sheila."

"Ah . . . he tends to do that. I didn't realize Sheila was his latest object. Well, he works in the agri department, you know. That part of the company was acquired by the new management. I can't tell you much about it."

"All right. Thanks again. I can find my own way out."

"I'm sorry, I'll need to accompany you." He touched my arm and moved me toward the door.

"Oh, you know what—I left my bag back in Doug's office. He can show me out."

McKinnon simply smiled and waited for me to walk with him down a floor to Doug's office and the lab. Just outside the office,

Doug and two white-coated researchers were engaged in a heated conversation over a series of printouts. McKinnon got drawn into the discussion. I sauntered over to Doug's office, paused by the door, and waited for Doug to glance my way. When he did, I very deliberately closed the door.

It burst open a few moments later. "What the—?" Doug demanded.

"Close the door," I said in a low voice. "Don't you want to hear what Dr. McKinnon said to me?"

His shoulders relaxed. It was clear he did. My hypothesis was correct. Some kind of fissure had opened up between mentor and protégé, and I intended to exploit it. If Doug believed I was on his side, he might cough up some new information.

"Just a minute," Doug said. He went back to the group, leaving the door ajar. I sat on the couch, out of sight of the scientists. I couldn't follow their discussion, so I poked into a stack of papers next to me on the couch. On top was a book about golf, but underneath were reprints of technical papers. The words that appeared most often in the titles were *phage display* and *Escherichia coli*.

The sound of my name brought my attention back. It was McKinnon, asking Doug where I was and telling him I needed to be escorted from the building.

"I'll do it, Frederick," Doug said. "I want to speak to him again. The biocomputation matter."

"That's not our priority, Doug. The Curaris Pharmaceutical people arrive at ten on Monday morning. This is it for us. Once they sign the licensing deal, Dugan has no choice. But everything must—"

"I'm *on* it, Frederick." Doug's voice was curt. "Please, just leave me to do my work."

Even from my position on the couch, I could feel the tension. All conversation had ceased. I pictured the two men glaring at each other, McKinnon towering erect and imperious, Doug bristling below.

Doug came into the office a moment later. He closed the door, then paced the small area in front of his desk.

"You need a bigger office," I said.

He froze and stared me. "I'm getting one."

"Once MC124 is a success?"

"Very soon."

"I imagine that will put you on more equal footing with Dr. McKinnon. You two have been very close, haven't you?"

He turned away and began to straighten papers. "I was his grad student. It's long past time for me to have a program of my own."

"Will you still be working with monoclonal antibodies?"

He spun on me. "What do you care? Just tell me what Frederick said to you!"

"He said he's tested MC124 on himself to prove its safety. I thought that was noble of him."

Doug stretched his neck and scratched. He had some kind of rash under his jowl. "I've tested it, too, but I don't go around bragging about it."

"Did Sheila?"

"Maybe Frederick tricked her into it," he said after a pause.

"Did Neil Dugan know about this?"

Doug shook his head slowly. "No one did. You shouldn't either. What do you want, anyway?"

"I just want to know what killed Sheila."

His forehead bunched again. "All right. I'll see what I can find out. I'll check up on Dugan. But not until after Monday."

"Anything helps. I have some notes from Sheila—"

His eyes widened and the phone buzzed at the same instant. Doug picked it up. "Yeah, I talked to him. No, he's not here. Yeah, I know what he looks like."

He put down the phone. "Dugan. He's looking for you."

I stood up. Doug appraised me for a minute, then said, "Go back down the corridor to the center of the building. Past the elevators, into the wing opposite this one. Turn right. Look for a stairway. It'll take you down to the atrium. Turn left and go out the door in the back. A guard will be watching for you at the front."

"Thanks. Do you have a cell phone?"

He scribbled the number on the back of his card. I took it and took off. The stairway was where he said it would be. I went down the stairs and opened the door into the atrium very slowly. The guard, near the reception desk, was looking the other way. I slid out and walked quickly toward the back exit. The guard called to me as I got to the door. I picked up my pace.

The door led onto a patio bordered by a line of raised flower beds. I stepped around them and broke into a run. I had to turn right to get around the annex, the agri division, which stood between me and my car. As I came around the blind corner, I nearly ran straight into a high wire fence around a garden tall with corn. I cut left into the parking lot and got in the Scout. As I was backing up, I saw the guard huffing his way around the building. By the time he yelled at me to stop, I was already pulling away.

26

Karen answered the door in shorts and a red T-shirt. She was hiding out at her friend's condo in Redwood City, about five miles north of Palo Alto. Yesterday, she and a posse of friends had managed to rescue her car from Gregory's lot and to retrieve Sheila's leather bag from Karen's apartment. I thought it was a good idea for her to stay put for a while. I was more concerned than ever that Dugan and Pratt were hunting for her, and I'd watched to make sure no one was following me as I drove over. Scrutinizing my rearview mirror had become second nature lately.

The condo's owner had gone out for the day. On a table in a nook of the kitchen, Karen had spread what Sheila had given her: notebooks, disks, and printouts. I'd brought the diary and the zip disks from their hiding place in the Scout. We sat next to the humming refrigerator. Karen plunked some leftover Chinese food and a Coke in front of me and said, "So what did you get?"

I told her about my visit to LifeScience. "McKinnon had a strong case for MC124 being safe. Both he and Doug Englehart tested it on themselves. The autopsy said Sheila had needle puncture marks in her arm. Doug as much as admitted she'd been dosed too."

Karen shook her head in disapproval. "She should've told me about it. Then again, she knew what I'd say. I would have chewed her out. She might have felt like she had no choice but to test it."

"To keep her job?"

"To keep McKinnon's respect. To show her loyalty to the team. There's an intense togetherness on a project like that. Sheila cared so much about being part of it. She cared what McKinnon thought of her."

"Well, her injecting it cuts both ways," I said. "On the one hand, I want to look even harder at MC124. On the other, the fact that her two superiors have tried it and are fine so far means it's a less likely cause of her death."

Karen stopped with a string of noodles in front of her mouth. "Wait a minute. What does this remind you of?"

"Someone about to make a big slurping sound?"

Karen went ahead and slurped. "It reminds you of the knockout mouse. One died. The others that we know of are fine."

"Right. The question is, what is it that got that one?"

We sat for a minute, pondering the mouse. The only insight that came to me was that it was time for lunch. I shoveled some food onto a plate, then managed to spray soy from a little packet onto a printout.

"Try to control yourself," Karen said in a dry voice.

"It's a boy thing," I said. Then a small pang hit me as I recalled my dinner conversation with Sheila.

"Are you all right?"

I shook it off. "Tell me what you've learned about this mouse."

"I've combed through Sheila's research. MC124 was being tested on three populations. One was mice with tumors. Another was mice without tumors, a control group. A third was a population with and without tumors that was receiving high doses of MC124. The focus in that group was toxicity. Our knockout mouse was in the third group. Sheila named her Smidge because she had just a smidgen of white on her back foot. The necropsy showed the mouse was strangled by her own immune system. Doug declared that she'd simply been overdosed or had a reaction to some other antigen. It didn't matter which, because it was an anomaly: no other mice died. Sheila wondered if the problem had more to do with the bit of white on the foot."

"What does the foot have to do with it?"

"Very little, of course, except that the white was a marker. It designated a mouse population that was humanized. Smidge had a number of mouse immune genes knocked out and human ones knocked in. Sheila conjectured that a technician put Smidge in the wrong cage because the white mark on her foot was so small. You could easily miss it."

"How sure are you that Smidge didn't belong in the test population? If the marking was so clear on the others but not on her, maybe she was in the right place after all."

"You're right. That's the biggest flaw in Sheila's hypothesis, and the biggest question we have to answer. Anyway, McKinnon backed Doug's interpretation. He said fine, at worst it means we need to be careful about the dose regimen. The lower dose seemed to do the job on tumors, so there was nothing to worry about. Sheila thought that conclusion was a little too convenient."

"A problem with MC124 would be phenomenally inconvenient for LifeScience right now. McKinnon's got everything riding on it. I heard him say they're set to sign a licensing deal with Curaris on Monday. It's already been drawing new capital to develop more programs."

"I hope they know what they're doing," Karen said. "The problem is, I'm kind of stuck. I can't say I know for sure MC124 is dangerous until we know the origin of Smidge, the knockout mouse."

"That's what I'm here for." I drew the diary and the zip disks from a folded paper grocery bag. "The file names on these disks look promising. I also remember seeing the name Smidge in the diary. I didn't know what it meant at the time, but I'll go back to it."

Karen took the disks as if accepting a fragile specimen. "There's a computer in the living room."

We moved to the next room. Karen leafed through the photocopy of Sheila's journal while the computer booted, then put in the first of the disks. I took the diary and sat on the couch.

"Uh huh . . . uh huh . . ." Karen repeated as she inspected the files. "Most of this data confirms what we've already got. It's good, though; it gives us greater granularity on the mechanism of MC124."

I was working backward in the diary. "Here's another reference to the mouse. *I've got to make the move, or Smidge's fate may be my own.*"

Karen's face clouded. "She was right about that one."

"The first time I read it, I thought Smidge might be some kind of nickname for her mother, which seemed very odd. Now I think the move she was talking about was transferring out of the MC124 group."

Karen nodded and punched some keys. "We're getting warm. I'm doing a global search on Smidge's line." The computer hemmed and hawed. "Here we go. Yes. Databases on all the mouse lines. I wonder if Sheila had a chance to review these."

I kept looking through the journal. Carl Steiner's name popped out at me. I asked Karen if she knew who he was.

Her face was glued to the screen. "Some guy who had a crush on Sheila or something."

The diary entry agreed:

Simon thinks I'm lying to him. I don't want to stand there making excuses, like I'm guilty—yet I am guilty, he can see it. How can I possibly explain? No one wants to hear excuses, they're boring. I'm sick of my own excuses. I should just resign myself to the nunnery of the lab. If only there was someone who understood this life, someone I could get interested in there. Aside from Carl, I mean. It's flattering, but I have a feeling he gets a wicked crush on every new female scientist that walks in. I don't know if I should keep accepting his little gifts. They're almost too delicious to refuse.

"Here we go," Karen said. She turned in her chair. Her face had lit up in an unexpected smile. "Smidge was one of thirty-five pups in her line. The traits of the humanized population were less visible in her, but she had them: wide-set eyes, bit of white on the foot, the rest. We found it!"

"You're going to have to explain," I said. "What did we just find?"

"You need to know how Smidge was humanized," Karen said. She stood and did a kind of two-step in front of the couch as she spoke. "Smidge was engineered to help test another antibody, one that targeted inflammation. See, there are two parts to an antibody. If you visualize an antibody as a Y-shape, one part

consists of the arms. These are denoted FAb, the variable binding regions. They're what recognize and bind to only one specific
antigen. The stem of the Y is called Fc, the constant region. It
calls in the body's immune effector cells to destroy the target.
It's also the part that can be most completely humanized, as
Smidge's was. The reason you want it to be more human is so
that human immune systems don't treat the antibody itself as
an invader. While the other MC124 test mice had weakened
immune systems, Smidge's was transgenically strengthened."

"So she should have been even better at killing tumor cells
with the help of MC124."

Karen put her hands on her hips. "Well, her cancer wasn't
very far advanced to begin with. But this is the strange thing
about MC124. Sheila confessed to me that even McKinnon
wasn't actually sure why it was so effective. Somehow the Fc
region of the antibody managed to signal receptors that exist in
a number of kinds of tumor cells to initiate programmed cell
death, also known as apoptosis."

"Cell suicide."

"Exactly. That's why the drug will be so huge. They weren't
sure how the apoptosis and effector cells were linked, though.
They just knew the binding regions sought out the tumor receptors, and the constant region initiated apoptosis. There are ten
billion cells in the immune system and complex signalling pathways we don't begin to understand. A small inhibiting or stimu-
lating signal can be amplified throughout the system. As long
as it has no serious side effects, you've got a killer drug. Don't
question your good fortune, just run with it."

I grimaced at Karen's double meaning. Her expression
showed she was aware of it. "So MC124 is killer in more ways

than one," I said. "In most mice, it just works on tumors. But in a humanized mouse like Smidge, it makes the immune system go crazy. Which means it could do the same to human beings."

"Especially human beings like Sheila, whose system was already hypersensitive."

I shook my head. "So the cure might be worse than the disease. I can't understand why Smidge's death didn't inspire LifeScience to extend the tests to humanized mice."

"I imagine they're doing that next, before Phase I begins, now that they've established the effectiveness of MC124. I'd hope so. Even if McKinnon thinks Smidge was an anomaly, he's got to cover himself. And if she wasn't, I'm sure he's counting on the dose regimen to prevent disaster. But the fact is, there's no perfect model for treating human cancers until you get to actual clinical trials."

"We both suspect McKinnon is wrong," I said. Karen nodded, and I went on, "But we need to know how and why. We need the mechanism if we're going to take this to the authorities."

Karen plunked back into the computer chair. "Very good. You're starting to think like a scientist."

"I'll take that as a compliment."

"It is. We do need to explain how MC124 caused the reaction. Here's what I think, based on what I've read in Sheila's notebooks. The immune system has two main branches. Let's call them Th-1 and Th-2 for short. Th-1 is involved with fighting things like viruses and cancers. Th-2 is active in allergy. Sheila speculated that something changed between mice and humans in how MC124 stimulated the immune system. Her big fear was that the Fc region changed the way signals and mediators were propagated and amplified through the network of immune cells. It turned the Th-2 branch hyper-hyperreactive."

"So MC124 pushed Smidge's immune system to the edge. But what killed her?"

"Smidge was getting a high enough dose that it could have gone off by itself. But Sheila wouldn't have injected a proportionally heavy amount. Something still had to set it off in Sheila."

"Like the shellfish protein," I said.

Karen drummed her fingers on the table. "I'd like to know more about what the assays showed about Sheila's blood, she said"

"I've got just the woman for you. Jill Nikano, Sheila's allergist. She's been running more tests."

Karen thrust a cordless phone at me. "Call her."

I dug Jill's home phone number out of my billfold. That gave me only a machine, so I tried her office number. She was there. As I began telling her what we'd discovered, Karen made grasping motions at the receiver. "Gimme."

"Isn't there another phone?"

She dashed into the kitchen. Once we got the introductions done, Karen launched into her reconstruction of Sheila's theory. I could hear the excitement rising in Jill's voice. "What you're telling me makes sense with everything I've seen so far."

"She must have injected MC124," Karen said.

"Yes, with those puncture marks in her arm."

"Any way the drug could have killed her by itself?" I asked.

There was a silence on the other end of the line. "Noooo, I don't think so. I've done immunoelectrophoresis on Sheila's serum. I got stains for proteins whose molecular size matches shellfish allergens. There's no doubt in my mind the anaphylactic event was induced by these proteins. MC124 may have primed her immune system, but it didn't trigger the blow."

"Could it have induced a new sensitivity?" I said. "Maybe she hadn't been allergic to salmon before, but was now?"

"I doubt it. There's virtually always a mild initial reaction to a new allergy before the big blow."

"Right," I said. "Thanks very much, Jill. We'll let you know as soon as we have something new."

"Glad to help. Say, Karen, can you email me what you've got?" Karen hesitated.

"Not all of it is in digital form," I said, "but we'll send what we have."

As we hung up, I glanced down at my watch. It was four o'clock already, an hour past the time Wes was expecting my all-safe call. I dialed his number. Karen came in breathless from the kitchen, but when she saw I was on the phone again, she made a U-turn.

Wes picked up. "It's me," I said. "Sorry I forgot to check in. I'm safe and sound."

I grunted apologetically as Wes listed the symptoms of anxiety he'd endured for the past hour. He'd been on the verge of phoning the police.

"I really am sorry," I repeated. "I meant to call you."

"How's it going with Marion?" he asked out of nowhere.

"About the same. She's not a whole lot of help. Why?"

"I don't know. She called me. Got me thinking about her legs again. I guess I'm forgiven for the Brentwood stunt."

"It's your love life, Wes. Just let me be the one to talk to her about what I'm up to. You know nothing."

"I certainly do, Damen. You've told me nothing except that your life is in danger. Then you forget to call. What are you chasing after, anyway?"

"We're getting close. I'll let you know when we're there."

"You mean Jenny's actually following you on this goose chase?"

"Are you kidding? No, I've got some expert help."

"I assume she's smart, yet naive enough to join up with you."

"Your confidence means a lot to me, Wes. Talk to you later."

I joined Karen in the kitchen. She clattered the plates into the sink and angrily wrenched the tap open to rinse them. I asked what was bothering her.

"If we don't know how Sheila got the allergen that induced her reaction, we're right back at the beginning!"

"That's not exactly true," I said. I stacked the food cartons inside one another and tossed them into the garbage. "We know that MC124 primed Sheila's immune system. Let's assume for a minute that whoever gave her the antigen knew that, too. If this person was familiar with the antibody, all they had to do was give Sheila the right protein. It could have come in any form."

Karen put both elbows on the counter. She wedged her chin between her palms. "But what if they didn't? What if the whole thing was just blind accident, coincidence?"

I contemplated that void for a moment. "It was orchestrated. It had to be."

Karen wagged a finger at me. "Don't make assumptions. That's how bad science happens. Look at McKinnon. He had something to prove about MC124. It turned out he was right, but the drug might also have fatal side effects. We have to get him to open his eyes to these results. He wouldn't before, even when Sheila pointed right at them. That's what happens. People see what they want to see. Especially when their career is at stake."

"Okay, then. What I personally want to see is how Neil Dugan got that protein into Sheila's system. It only had to be a small amount. Could there have been something in the lab—?"

"Like a lobster tank?" Karen said sarcastically.

"Wait a minute. They don't have a fish farm, but LifeScience does have a farm. A big garden out back. They acquired some agri company doing transgenic plants. The corn in that garden was growing mighty high."

"It's a possibility. A remote one, but still . . . The timing of the attack means it has to be something Sheila ate at the dinner party."

"What about this: What if someone at the party is working with Dugan? Fay or Marion gets the food into Sheila's mouth that night. Dugan supplies it—the agri company was acquired under his regime, so Dugan knows its products. Fay has a motive to get back at Sheila. And Marion, I don't know her motive, but she's up to something."

Karen lifted her chin at me, a kind of challenge. "Can you get either one to talk?"

"They're pretty tough. I might have a spy in Marion's house, except I'm not sure whose side he's on."

Karen squinted at my remark, but let it pass. "We need people at LifeScience, people who know more."

"Like Carl Steiner, the gardener."

Karen punched my arm. "Right! Sheila's not-so-secret admirer. She said he was a sweet guy, but—"

I finished the sentence for her. "They're the ones you have to watch out for."

27

I had to twist Marion's arm to get her to tell us that Carl Steiner lived in Menlo Park, which was between Redwood City and Palo Alto. She twisted back, making me promise I'd let her in on new information. I agreed to do that this evening, hoping that by then I'd be in a position to force her hand and get her to tell me what she was up to.

Two C. Steiners were listed in the phone book. The first one, Karen and I discovered, was a young woman named Cindy who lived in an apartment complex. No relation. The other lived in a neighborhood of narrow leafy streets. The 1950s-vintage one-story house looked tired, its plaster chipping. We tried the doorbell with no result. I opened a dented aluminum screen door and pounded on the front door. Still no answer.

We went down a walkway to the back. A tall redwood fence blocked our view of the yard. But as soon as I chinned up the fence, I knew we had the right place. "There's a small farm back there."

Karen cocked her ear. "I hear digging."

We knocked on the fence and called Carl's name. After about the tenth try we finally heard the click of a latch. The gate opened. Carl Steiner stood before us in a gardening cap with a giant sun bill. Fringes of brown and gray hair curled out from under the cap. He wore an ancient khaki shirt and even older pants. His shoes were covered with dirt.

Recognition flickered in his eyes. After introducing Karen and myself, I reminded him that he and I had met at Sheila's funeral. Steiner pulled off his gloves and put out a hesitant hand. Karen took it and turned on a charm I hadn't seen before. Beaming at him, she said, "Sheila told me about you. She said that you were so very nice to her."

He turned his head and looked down at the ground. When he looked back up at Karen, he said, "She was a really special girl. It's terrible what happened."

"That's just what we wanted to ask you about," I said. "May we come in?"

"I suppose. Not many do. Sheila never did." He held the gate open for us. We filed into what seemed a jungle of corn stalks, tomato plants, bean vines, and growth I didn't recognize. It was a neat jungle, though. Narrow but well-defined paths marked the lines between each crop.

He picked up his hoe and used it as a kind of staff as we walked. Corn stalks, now dry and stripped of their ears, rattled in the breeze. Steiner described the plants to us, their germ lines and characteristics, how they'd produced this summer, how the weather influenced the flavor. "Change coming," he added, raising the handle of the hoe toward the cirrus clouds. "Our first rain, tomorrow maybe. Hope so. It'll wash off the dust."

"I see you've made use of every square inch of your backyard, Mr. Steiner," Karen remarked.

"Just call me Carl. You'd be amazed by my harvests. I could open a grocery store. I prefer to give it away, though." He smiled ruefully. "Can't eat it all myself. You like zucchini?"

"An old favorite," I said. "I'm surprised you grow so much here at home. Isn't this what you do all day at work—gardening?"

"I've got my degree in biology!" he objected.

"You're a scientist-technician," Karen said diplomatically.

"Exactly. I work at the bench. I work in the garden, too. Got a feel for everything we're growing. I know more about it than any of those PhDs. You can't replace hands-on knowledge. How a leaf smells first thing in the morning, its temper in the afternoon. These plants are my life. Why would I leave them behind when I come home?"

"So you grow some of the company's plants here?"

"Just the ones we're not actively working with."

We'd come to the tomatoes. I bent down to look at them. There looked to be four different varieties, each in its own plot where the south sun hit the back fence. I reached for one.

"Don't—don't touch!" Carl barked.

"Is it valuable?"

"No, it's just—off limits." We looked at him, waiting for more. A ripple of anxiety slowly curdled across his face. "I didn't develop it. The line's from Tomagen—the company LifeScience acquired for our agri division. Best tomato you ever tasted in your life. It can grow anywhere, survive the frosts." An unexpected bitterness came into his voice. "They call it the *heart* tomato."

He shook his hoe at the plant, as if it offended him. Some of the fruits were still mottled green and red and some were ripe enough to drop. I recognized the lovely little heart shape, about the size of a tennis ball. The film word "continuity" popped into my mind: the tomato had appeared earlier. I was trying to remember when and where. It was Jenny's dinner party. This tomato was a perfect stand-in for the ones that Sheila had laid on the counter.

I asked Carl delicately, "Did you know that Sheila brought some tomatoes to dinner the night she—"

Carl exploded. "Of course I knew! Where do you think they came from!"

Veins pulsed on his nose. The knuckles gripping the hoe were white. Karen and I took a step back. Carl stood there shaking. After a moment I realized it was as much from grief and guilt as from anger.

Karen's voice was even and kind. "You gave them to her?"

"Yes. I mean, no, not directly, I left her a message telling her she could have some and asking when I should drop them off. They're no big secret. I just don't usually give them out. Well, anyway, she never called back." His throat tightened. "If only she did. I could have warned her . . ."

"About what?"

"It was an experimental line engineered by Tomagen, before we bought them. They set themselves the task of making the best tomato ever—the tastiest, the hardiest, the juiciest. If they hit all the marks, they'd have an incredible product. It was like entering the lottery. Well, they won—except they couldn't collect. Turned out they'd used a gene from some fish to help the tomato resist cold. See, the same protein that helps a crustacean survive frigid water is the one that causes allergy in humans. Anyway, the protein was still being expressed in the heart tomato. They couldn't take it to market."

I opened my mouth, but Carl jumped quickly to the question. He ticked off his points on soil-crusted fingers. "So why did I keep growing it? I told you about the taste. Why did I give it to people? I didn't give it to many. A few in my department. The chief wanted to try it, too. Didn't hurt anyone, not so much as a cough. So then Sheila. Why should I keep it from her, if she wanted to try it? I didn't know she had an allergy. I would have told her, though, I would have warned her, even though the protein showed up weak in the bioassays."

"But the company had to pull the tomato, in spite of that?"

"Oh yeah. They didn't even bother asking the FDA. You can't go around selling food that looks like an apple but really it's an oyster. You can't sell soy that's really Brazil nut proteins. Company that did that in 1996 had to pull it for the same reason: allergies. There were no solid documented cases of adverse reaction, but you've got to be double careful. Triple."

We stared, stunned, at Carl. "Why would a company use a shellfish protein like that?" I managed to ask.

"Lots of people have used fish genes to help crops stand the cold," he said. His shoulders were slumped, but with a kind of relief. He'd been carrying this knowledge around all on his own. He was dying to share it.

"Carl," I said gently, "you said you didn't give Sheila the tomatoes in person. You also said you didn't talk to her about them. So how did you know Sheila wanted to try them?"

Carl screwed up his face and clutched at his hat. "Jesus, I don't know!" His fingers slowly released the hat. "It was Dr. McKinnon. He thought she'd enjoy them."

Karen and I stared at each other. McKinnon.

Carl knew what the look meant. He shook his head vehemently. "No, Dr. McKinnon's a good man. He wouldn't knowingly give Sheila something dangerous. The chief neither. But that Dugan—he's another basket of onions. Listen up, I'm going to tell you right now he will try to pin this on me. Because they got to find someone to blame. The family's gonna sue, I heard that. And what I think is maybe *Dugan's* the one who told the doctor about the tomatoes. Tricked him or something."

"Dugan likes to spread blame around," I agreed. "As long as it lands on anyone but himself."

"In any case, it's likely the shellfish protein didn't do the job alone," Karen said. "We think there was another factor."

Carl's brows rose in a hopeful wrinkle.

"How much do you know about MC124?" I asked.

He shrugged. "I know it's Dr. McKinnon's big program. But that's not my field."

I curled my fingers round one of the tomatoes. "We'd like to take this and analyze it. Is that all right?"

"Take the whole damn plant," Carl said. "Burn it."

Karen smiled sympathetically. "I understand how you feel. We'll let you know what we find out."

The three of us shuffled slowly back to the gate, each lost in our thoughts. If Carl had been annoyed at our entrance, his face grew sad at our departure. He looked hollow and exhausted, as if an enormous weight had been briefly lifted from his chest—but now he was about to be left alone with it again.

"I could offer you some lemonade," he said. "I grow Meyers."

Karen put a hand on his arm. "Another time."

I shook his hand and promised to be in touch. Karen leaned forward to give him a kiss on the cheek. "Thank you for speaking to us."

We turned to leave. I took a couple of steps, then stopped. "The heart tomatoes—do you still eat them, Carl?"

A cold, distant look came into his eyes. "Not anymore."

28

"It wasn't Fay who brought the toxic food to the dinner party," I said. "It wasn't Marion. It was Sheila herself."

"And someone used Carl Steiner to get her to do it."

I was still stunned by the idea. Saying it made it a little more real. We were back at the kitchen table in Karen's home away from home in Redwood City. Karen had brewed coffee. She set a mug in front of me. "Drink up. Did you know coffee increases your IQ?"

"That's the best news I've heard all week. But it can't be true, or I'd be a genius."

"Do we assume that Carl's aboveboard? That he was just a pawn?" Karen asked.

I stared into the black cup. "His emotions were real. I suppose he could be pulling some kind of ruse, figuring the truth about the tomatoes would come out eventually. It's possible he wanted to get back at Sheila for not returning his attention—but it's not like she broke up with him. They were never even together."

"What if he's one of those stalker types who thought he owned her just because he was infatuated with her?"

I shook my head. "Do you really think he was capable of murder?"

"No. Not Carl." Karen paused, then added, "You know who that puts in the hot seat, don't you? Frederick McKinnon."

I nodded. "Have you met him?"

"At the last LifeScience Christmas party. Very charismatic, I have to admit. I see why Sheila was inspired by him. He's smooth, smart, cultured, completely dedicated—everything we always thought a scientist should be. His team is incredibly loyal."

I looked up at her through the coffee steam. "Maybe most are. Not Doug Englehart. He's ready to be king of his own realm."

Karen sipped her drink. "I've wondered about that. I've met him only once, and it was hard for me to get a reading. He's been with Frederick for so many years. I thought maybe Doug just didn't have the ambition to strike out on his own."

"Oh, he's got the ambition. It's more narrow than McKinnon's, but just as strong. Sheila wrote about it in her diary. Doug was a fountain of ideas, always pushing the frontiers. She said McKinnon acknowledged that in the team meetings. He raved about how brilliant Doug was. She liked that about McKinnon."

"Now that I think about it, Sheila told me that when McKinnon announced MC124 at the conference, he gave the whole presentation himself. Sheila said Doug looked stricken. He thought he'd at least get to explain the antibody to the session."

"McKinnon's generosity could also have been a way to keep Doug right where he was," I said. "Use his brains, stroke his ego, but take the credit. Maybe the conference was the last straw. Gregory Alton told me Doug's about to get his own program now. McKinnon dropped hints about it, too."

"Did he say what it is?"

"No. But I noticed some articles in Doug's office on topics I haven't seen before. Phage display, I think, and a lot of stuff about *E. coli*."

Karen barked with laughter. "Aha! A completely different approach to monoclonals. See, MC124 had to be produced by a mouse population. It's tough to do, and tough on the mice. With this other approach, you engineer the antibody into *E. coli* bacteria. The bacteria act as a carrier to reproduce the antibody-carrying phage inside the subject. If that's what Doug plans to do, it'll make McKinnon's fur stand up."

"I wonder how far Doug's resentment goes. If McKinnon really is our man, maybe Doug will help us nail him."

Karen shook her head. "Hard to imagine. It's one thing to spread your wings and fly. It's another to stab the man who helped get you there in the back."

"It's still hard for me to believe McKinnon is our man. He might be more capable of murder than Carl Steiner, but he's not the one who sent private detectives after us. I have to think Carl is right: Dugan's behind it all."

Karen swirled the grounds in the bottom of her cup. "You don't harass people like Dugan did unless you've got something big to hide."

I finished the last of my coffee. "Karen, I've been meaning to say—I'm really sorry about getting you in trouble at BioVerge."

She waved it off. "You did me a favor. My work was going nowhere. I spent most of my time trolling the Web for journal articles and important facts—like the one about coffee. This is much more exciting." Her smile gradually fell. Her brown eyes turned muddy. "When I heard about Sheila, I couldn't fathom it. Nothing made sense anymore. Science seemed useless. If we can uncover how Sheila was killed—I don't know, at least I'll have accomplished something."

A pair of tears tracked down her cheeks, in no hurry to get to the bottom. It was the first time she'd shown her real feelings in front of me. My instinct was to put my arms around her, but I held back. I wasn't sure how she'd take it.

"I'm afraid I've put you in some danger," I said. I wanted to make sure she knew I was concerned about her. "Dugan knows you're a biologist, a friend of Sheila's who can put all the science together. If you want to get out of town for a little while, to be safe, I'd understand." It was the same advice I'd given Jenny, though I was hoping for a different answer from Karen.

Her moist eyes slowly narrowed to sharp black points. "I'm not going anywhere. I want to know who did this to Sheila. I want to look them in the face and ask why."

I nodded. A look of understanding flashed between us. Karen took the cups to the sink and washed them as if she was trying to punch through their bases. "What's next?" she asked.

"Let's talk to Marion. She's in the agri department and knows more than she's been telling me. I might be able to talk her into a data swap now. She definitely is not on Dugan's side."

Karen handed me the phone. I pulled out my billfold for the piece of paper on which I had all my numbers written. "You know what?" I said. "I need to call Jenny first."

"No problem. Is it all right if I look at the diary?"

I nodded, then dialed Jenny's mother in Sacramento. Jenny answered the phone herself. She started talking about how she'd been outside gardening and how good it was for her soul. I hated having to tell her the story of the killer tomato.

She reacted with a stunned silence. "That is so freaky," Jenny finally said. "Someone deliberately gave her the tomatoes."

"Yeah. But the good news is that you're in the clear."

"I don't think you should stay there, Bill. It's too dangerous. Take this to the police."

"Don't worry. We're in a safe place. I'll go to the police as soon as I figure out—"

"Who's this we?"

"Karen, that scientist friend of Sheila's. We're about to visit Marion. I think she can fill in some more pieces for us."

"You said you were coming up here."

"Well, that was before I knew how Sheila was murdered. I'm not going to walk away from this."

"Who said this is for you to solve, Bill? I don't understand why you're so fixated on it. Is it about some kind of ego battle with Dugan? Maybe you think you can get a film out of this."

It was my turn to be stunned. I didn't think she really meant what she said. She just felt left out—left out of a party she didn't really want to attend. I knew there was hurt underneath her anger, but I'd have to try to take care of it later.

"I'm sorry, Jen. I'll see you as soon as I can," I said.

I put down the phone to find Karen at the kitchen door. "Sorry," she said, "I thought—"

"Don't worry about it."

"I've never met Jenny. Sheila was kind of in awe of her. She thought Jenny had so much life, sparkle—a winning way, I guess."

"She does like winning."

A bit of mock pity played on Karen's lips. It cheered me up. "I just had a conversation of my own," she said. "Harry Salzmann, on my cell phone. I saw his name in the diary and should have thought of calling him sooner. He told me something really bizarre. Smidge was an offshoot of a line in Harry's lab. Sheila herself developed the line. It was what got McKinnon interested in her in the first place. So, guess whose human DNA was knocked into Smidge's chromosomes?"

"Sheila's," I said immediately. "Is that ethical?"

"It's perfectly common. Researchers have to get human DNA from somewhere, right? I've known people who hang around maternity wards asking for spare placentas. All Sheila had to do was scrape a few of her own cells. Sheila must have realized the mouse's origin when she wrote about Smidge's fate being her own. If MC124 killed Smidge, she had good reason to worry about what it would do to her."

I nodded. "It's coming together, Karen. We're getting close."

She nodded back. I checked my watch. It was getting late. "Look, we better get going. Marion wanted to see us today. I'll call to tell her we're on the way."

"Good. I'll find a place to hide the research," Karen said.

"Right. There's no way we're taking it to Marion's."

After I'd talked to Marion, my last call was to Abe Harros at the hotel. I came back into the living room when it was done, and Karen and I headed out to the Scout.

We crawled across the bay on the San Mateo Bridge. I got off 580 at State 13, a cute little grass-lined highway that snaked along the base of the Oakland hills, almost exactly on top of the Hayward fault. A winding hairpin lane took us from 13 into the steep, redwood-shaded hills. Marion's place was about halfway up. I pulled into the carport, a wood platform built into the hillside, and parked next to a Volvo.

Marion lived in a classic wood-shingled Berkeley bungalow. The trees whispered in the breeze as we followed a stone walk down to the front door. Marion treated us like old friends. She kissed me on both cheeks. We went into a long, narrow living room. Marion had her own little indoor forest, consisting primarily of ferns. The walls were decorated with magical-looking tribal objects.

"You're a world traveller," I commented.

"What can I say, I'm Dutch. Sit down. I'll bring you something—tea, wine?"

Karen and I both declined. We sat on a wool couch that faced a picture window. The bay, visible through the branches outside, was gunmetal gray and sullenly still under the clouds. Marion plunked down in a rocking chair. She was wearing tights and a long, loose shirt.

"Nice place," I said. "Long drive to work, though."

"You'd have to clamp me in chains to get me to live in the valley. What I paid for this place would buy me a studio in Palo Alto." She crossed her legs, shook a slippered foot at us, and grinned. "So, here we are. Come on, out with it. Don't be shy."

"Here's what we'll do, Marion. We'll take turns. I'll go first and tell you that Sheila gave Karen her notes on MC124. We know what's wrong with it, and we know how the knockout mouse died."

"And that is?"

As Karen explained, Marion's mouth puckered into a kind of grudging acknowledgment. "You may be right. Of course, it's not my field, and I don't have all the data."

"Tell us about the agri department," I said. "Tell us about Carl Steiner."

Marion started to ask another question, but I wagged my finger.

"Carl's probably the best man at the whole company." She paused to enjoy our dubious looks before adding, "As long as he's not in love with you. He's harmless, really, but I meant it about his talent. He knows plants like no one else. He was just as upset as I was when management decided—but I'm getting ahead of myself. Why don't you tell me something."

"All right. MC124 wasn't enough to kill Sheila by itself. Something had to trigger it. Maybe something from your department."

Marion clucked her tongue. "Could be. It's scientifically feasible. And those people are capable of it. The division has taken a wrong turn. It's getting into dangerous territory. Dugan's regime—they're not scientists. They're not even responsible executives. Short term profit, that's all they're about."

"What do you know about the heart tomato?"

"It was Tomagen's, before the acquisition. So packed full of exogenous DNA I half expected it to sit up and start barking."

"Are there any tomato plants left in the company garden?"

"No. Everything we're growing now is for drug production. That's the new direction. They're aiming to steal some of Frederick's thunder. It's expensive to produce monoclonals in quantity using mice. But if you engineer a plant, or even a goat, to produce it, you've got a cheap source. The drug is produced in fruit or in milk."

Marion's rocking chair was rolling now. She motioned to hear more. It was my turn.

"Carl's still growing a few of the tomatoes in his home garden. He likes to share his crops," I said.

"Yeah, some of his zucchini is sitting in my fridge. But what about these tomatoes?" Marion said.

"They had certain shellfish proteins engineered into them, to help them survive cold," I said. "The same protein humans are allergic to. Sheila brought some to the dinner party, remember? I recognized it right away in Carl's garden. He said he didn't know about Sheila's allergy. But what are the chances that he—"

"Nope," Marion cut me off. "Not Carl. Not to Sheila."

"He says someone asked him to bring them in for her." I didn't want to tell her who just yet.

Marion's brow furrowed. "Now you're starting to make sense. Someone who knew about the allergy."

"Someone who also knew the truth about MC124," Karen added. "Someone who knew how it would react with the tomato. Neither would do the job on its own."

Marion stood up. "I have to say, you're turning up some good soil. This calls for some wine, don't you think? It's getting to be dinnertime."

Karen got up to help. I slumped into the couch and let the wool scratch against my neck. Marion seemed to have chosen the precise moment when I'd revealed the most and she'd revealed the least to break off the conversation. I still hoped to bring her over to our side, but it looked like her allegiance remained only to herself.

The tree branches had turned to dark fingers. A few lights twinkled out in the bay. I let them drift out of focus, then noticed a stack of magazines under the wicker coffee table. I picked up a few. They were standard fare: *Science, Nature, Annals of Botany.* A couple, though, reflected a more definite point of view: *Living Planet, Earth Island, The Greenpeace International Newsletter.*

The doorbell rang, followed immediately by a sharp knock. I jumped up to get it.

Marion met me at the entry. "It better not be Wes," she warned.

I shook my head. I knew it wasn't. She swung open the door to find a sullen face staring back at her. It was Abe Harros. And standing right behind him was Neil Dugan.

29

I slid past Marion to shake Abe's hand. "I see you've brought a friend."

His expression remained flat. "Why not? Sounded like a party."

I looked at Dugan and said, "I was hoping you were a waiter on wheels."

Dugan, in his own special way, smiled. He hadn't shaved, and yesterday's five o'clock shadow smothered his jaw. "The party will have to wait."

Marion's mouth hung open. It seemed for a moment that she had lost her touch. But then she turned and disappeared into the kitchen, leaving the three of us in a standoff. It only ended when she returned and stuck a glass of wine into each of our hands. They were flat glasses, European style.

"Go sit down," she ordered.

I led the way into the living room. Dugan and Abe took the couch, Dugan on the far side. I planted myself in the rocking chair across from them. Marion and Karen reappeared with glasses of their own. Marion put a plate of Gouda on the coffee table and sat cross-legged on the floor. Karen gave Abe a friendly greeting and pulled up a chair between me and him. I had a bite of cheese and smiled, hoping to force Abe or Dugan into the first move.

Abe didn't touch his glass. His eyes had not left me since we sat down. "You asked me to come here," he said. "Now tell me why."

I ignored a seething glance from Marion. "There are some facts you should know about your sister's death. It would be better if we could talk without Mr. Dugan, but what the hell."

Abe's face was set like stone. Karen seemed about to burst. "Listen to him, Abe!" she said.

Abe swivelled slowly to look at her. His features softened a tad. "We got your message yesterday, Karen. That's the only reason I'm here. I wouldn't trust him an inch otherwise."

"Doesn't matter to me one way or another, Abe," I said. "Just listen for a change. Your father can drop the lawsuit against Jenny. Sheila herself brought the food that killed her at dinner. This is not about negligence. It's about murder."

Dugan broke into laughter. Abe didn't.

"We thought so," Abe said. "What are these facts you've got?"

"MC124 was fatal to a lab mouse. Sheila was investigating how it killed the mouse. The reason appears to be that it puts the immune system of certain mammals on a hair trigger."

"A dead mouse and a dead woman are quite different things," Dugan said.

"We believe Sheila herself injected MC124," I said evenly.

"She'd already knocked her own genes into the mouse," Karen added. "It came over from Salzmann's lab with her."

Dugan and Abe simultaneously leaned forward. "You have proof?" Abe demanded.

"We can back it up, Abe," Karen said. She avoided Dugan's scowl. "The shellfish protein that set her anaphylaxis in motion had been engineered into a tomato line by Tomagen, which is now part of LifeScience's agri division. Sheila brought those tomatoes to the dinner party, tomatoes someone at LifeScience had given her that day. She suffered an allergic response. She might have had only a mild reaction to the protein in the tomato if that was the whole story. But MC124 had primed Sheila's immune system. It went after the allergen with a fury. That's what killed her."

Abe was bent forward now, elbows on his knees. "This is incredible, Karen. If it wasn't you telling me . . ." He glanced at Marion.

"It's plausible," Marion agreed. "The shellfish protein protects the fish from cold. People have been trying to put antifreeze proteins to use in tomatoes, strawberries, and so on for some time. You find the proteins in fish, bugs, bacteria, and certain plants. I don't know why Tomagen chose the shellfish one. Pretty stupid idea, if you ask me."

"I'm sure they thought they could neutralize its allergenic properties," Karen said.

"What I'm saying is that neither the protein nor MC124 alone would have killed Sheila," I went on. "The two were put together on purpose by someone at LifeScience. Someone who knew how MC124 worked. Someone who also had access to the tomato."

Abe's gaze travelled across the table from me to the man sitting next to him. Dugan's rock of a head remained steady on his shoulders, his expression surprisingly chipper. He took his time with a sip of wine, just for effect. "Not bad," he said, swirling it. "This has been a productive visit. I've heard some useful information tonight." He looked at me. "I thank you for it. And I'll thank you to turn over documentation of your claims. If there's a problem with MC124, we need to know about it before ten o'clock Monday morning. Our lawyers will get a court order if necessary."

"We'll give the documents to the right people at LifeScience," I responded. "As soon as we know who they are. I'd like to know why you were so persistent and aggressive about getting your hands on Sheila's diary. You had Pratt following her the day she died. I've got it on tape. You were willing to do anything to stop her from exposing the flaws in MC124."

A broad smile, which for all the world looked genuine, sliced across Dugan's face. "Your theory's got one problem. You pointed it out yourself. Access to the tomato. We don't grow it at LifeScience."

"But you know that Carl Steiner still grows it at home. You got him to bring in a bagful to give to Sheila."

Dugan drained his glass. "How very helpful you are, *Bill*. We'll be speaking to Carl about this."

I touched Karen's shoulder. "Call Carl. Warn him."

"In the kitchen," Marion said.

Karen went. Dugan rose halfway to his feet. "If he destroys evidence, he's as good as proven his guilt," he called after her.

"Your board of directors will be fascinated to hear all of this," I said.

Dugan snorted, then bumped into the stack of magazines as he sat down again. They spread like a deck of cards. He glanced over them idly. "Oh, they'll be fully briefed. I have nothing to hide."

"I want to know what's going on, Neil," Marion demanded. "Why were you after Sheila?"

"We had reasons." He raised the corner of a magazine gingerly. "Just how active in Greenpeace are you, Marion? They're not exactly biotech's best friend."

"It all depends, Neil," she said coolly, "on what we use the technology for. We had a good bioremediation program going, before you came along."

"Maybe *you're* not LifeScience's best friend either," Dugan replied. "Maybe your goals and ours have diverged."

Marion was flustered. "You weren't invited, and you have no right to poke into my private business. It's time for you to leave."

Dugan stood. He moved surprisingly quickly around the coffee table to block the path to the front door. "I'm not going anywhere without those documents."

"You are too."

Marion's sharp intake of breath matched my own. Karen had emerged from the kitchen, behind Dugan. In her hand was a large knife.

"Put that down before you get hurt," Dugan commanded.

I moved in Karen's direction. So did Dugan. When I stopped, he did.

Karen bit her lip. She was upset, but she wasn't shaking. "You killed my friend."

She gripped the knife a little tighter. When she didn't retreat, Dugan realized she was serious. He forced a laugh and sidled toward the front door. "The least you can do is call me a cab," he said to Marion.

"How about an ambulance?" she replied.

Dugan's arms hung ready at his sides. Now that he was a few steps out of Karen's range, his alpha bearing returned. I went quickly over to Karen before the situation got out of control again. I was more concerned about him hurting her than vice versa, but avoiding bloodshed seemed wise all around.

Abe joined me. "Don't get excited, everyone. I'll take Mr. Dugan home."

I looked Dugan up and down for the bulge of a weapon. If he had one, he wasn't going for it. Not yet.

Abe made his way cautiously to the door. "We're leaving. I'll talk to you later, Karen. Right now, there are some things I'd like to ask you about, Neil."

"There are some things I'd like to tell you about," Dugan answered smoothly, opening the door.

"We don't have the documents on us," I called after him. "In case Pratt is waiting outside."

Abe looked at Dugan. "Don't worry," Dugan said. "He's not."

The three of us watched from the doorway as Abe's car drove away. Karen nonchalantly replaced the knife in the kitchen and picked up her coat. "I'm tired. I'm ready to go," she said.

Marion stood hugging herself. "That man . . ."

"I'm sorry," I said. "I had no idea Abe would bring him."

Marion seemed to accept my apology, so I went on. "I'd like to go into LifeScience tomorrow to talk to Doug Englehart and Frederick McKinnon. Can you get me inside?"

Marion didn't hesitate. "Shall we say noon?"

"Fine," I said. "I'll meet you at the entrance to the parking lot. I don't want to take my jeep in there."

"You're on. God would it feel good to nail Dugan."

"What's happening to us, Marion?" I said. "We agree on more and more every day." I decided not to add my lurking fear that we could end up nailing McKinnon instead. There was always the chance he and Dugan had perceived Sheila as a common enemy and collaborated on her murder. Now that she was out of the way, their alliance was done and they'd reverted to their original rivalry. Except that each held a trump card that could destroy them both.

Karen and I said little on the drive back to Redwood City. I half expected her to break down, but she remained collected. My impression was that she really would have used that knife on Dugan, if he'd come at her.

When we exited the San Mateo Bridge, I made a few U-turns and dashed through a few yellow lights, in case Dugan had lied about Pratt. No one followed us.

Back at Karen's hideout in Redwood City, a note said her friend was staying with her lover that night. Karen had the place to herself. Though her features still seemed composed, I noticed that her knees were going weak. The emotions of the night were catching up with us both.

"I'll stay here with you," I offered. "You shouldn't be alone."

She let herself fall onto the couch. "That's all right," she sighed, lying down. When she noticed me standing awkwardly in the middle of the living room, she patted the couch. "I don't mean to hog the whole thing."

She sat up partially so I could sit, then put her head right back where it had been. Except now it was in my lap. Her hand found mine and squeezed. For reassurance, I was sure, nothing more.

"We've been through a lot, haven't we?" she murmured.

"I think I'm your bad luck charm."

She laughed, then pulled my legs up to the couch. "Lie down."

I took off my shoes and scrunched into the couch on my back. She slid alongside me and put her head on my right shoulder. Her hand tucked under my left shoulder. I held the back of her head. We lay like that for quite a while as the tension drained from our bodies.

My eyes closed and I drifted into a half sleep. I awoke to the sensation of lips on my cheek. Karen's lips. Her mouth slid over to mine, and soon we were engulfed in each other. I liked her taste. She wore no scent or makeup. No flower or spice or store-bought musk. Just skin and tongue. Very pure. Very simple. Very human.

I don't know how long we went on like that. It could have been twenty minutes, it could have been hours. Our hands moved slowly up and down each other, outside our clothes, brushing a more sensitive zone now and again. We stopped for periods of time and simply rested with one another, drifting.

At some point, I found my hand sliding under her shirt. I felt the strap of her bra, and then, under the material, her breast. Her breath quickened. I nudged the nipple with the tip of my finger, and felt her hand moving up along my thigh. We let the moment linger on the edge of something more. Somehow it was more erotic and delicious than the most avid sex. I felt close to Karen, disconcertingly so in just two days.

I kissed her neck once and put my arms around her, tightly. My head came to rest on the pillow of her hair. She returned the embrace, and we were still.

I awoke to find a blanket over me and a pillow
under my head. Light streamed in through windows unknown
to me, but it was hard to tell what time it was. Nor could I fathom
what was I doing on a plaid sofa.

A faucet turned on in the kitchen and it all came back.
Marion's house last night. Abe. Dugan. Karen.

She poked her head out of the kitchen. I blinked at her. She
smiled. "Just checking."

I was still in my clothes. That was good. I shuffled into the
bathroom, splashed myself with some cold water, and shuffled
into the kitchen. The kettle was humming over a burner.

"Did you sleep all right?" she asked.

"Like a wall. I didn't know where I was for a minute."

She folded her arms and leaned against the sink. Her form
was hidden under a long flannel nightshirt decorated with blue-
bells. I stood by the refrigerator with my hands in my pockets.
The patina of morning brightness fell from her face. She looked
at me from under lidded eyes. I remembered why it had been so
nice to kiss her.

"I'm sorry Bill. Last night, I—"

I stepped forward and took her hands. "Same for me." I was sorry, too, though I wasn't sure whether it was for what happened or what didn't happen. Not that I would have cheated on Jenny—more out of principle, I had to admit, than direct feeling at the moment. The little pang of guilt I'd felt when I awoke did not center on Jenny, but on Sheila. As if somehow we'd taken advantage of her death.

Karen touched a finger to my lips. "You have the nicest little fold at the corners of your mouth. And eyes."

I kissed her forehead. She gave me a slap on the hip. And we got on with our morning. She fitted a filter into a coffee cone. I hunted up some food in the cupboards and refrigerator. We moved past each other easily in the kitchen, as if it were a familiar choreography.

We ate quietly, looking through the Sunday paper. Karen did the crossword. It was a pleasant fiction to eat the little smorgasbord we'd rustled up—toast, apples, cheese, tomatoes, olives, jam—as if we had nothing much else to do today.

At eleven-thirty I folded the paper and said it was time for me to go to LifeScience.

"Do you want me to come with you?" Karen asked.

"I better go alone. Marion is taking me inside. You never know, Dugan might be hunting for you."

"Nah, he's scared of me now." The hint of bravado in her smile told me she didn't mind staying in.

I tucked in my shirt and put on my jacket. The DAT and mini-DV were still in the pockets. I changed the DAT cassette and cued it up. Karen gave me a peck on the cheek and asked at what point she should start to worry about me. I waved it off, but she fixed me with one of those direct looks.

"I'll check in around three. Call Wes if you don't hear from me." I borrowed her pen and wrote Wes's number on the crossword.

"Fine. What do you plan to do when you get inside?"

I'd started thinking about it last night on the way back to the condo. "I'll see what else I can get out of Doug Englehart and Frederick McKinnon. New information tends to make people talkative. Marion's going to look for more on MC124. I'll try to find other senior people in the company, too. With the big Curaris deal happening tomorrow, I expect they'll all be working. I'll tell them I know how Sheila died. I won't accuse anyone; I'll act like I think someone else is to blame. Then I'll watch how they react. See what I see on their faces, listen to what they say, and decide on my next move."

"What if you run into Dugan?"

"I'll hope I don't. But if I do—same as the others."

Karen nodded and sent me off. The sky was an immense plate of scalloped ridges, puckered with billows and whorls. The first big rain front of the season was approaching from the Gulf of Alaska. The barometric pressure had dropped, and there was an expectancy in the air.

Marion was waiting for me about a hundred yards down the street from the turn to the LifeScience parking lot. I motioned for her to follow me, then I drove another quarter mile to an empty industrial street. I parked the Scout and got into her car.

The first thing I did was explain why I'd invited Abe Harros to her house the night before. I wanted to make sure she wasn't sore about Dugan showing up. "I was trying to bring Abe over to our side," I said.

"Are you kidding? I wouldn't have missed it. If you ask me, Dugan practically convicted himself. All we need to do is gather a little proof, and we've got him." Her elbows flapped with excitement as she took the turn into the parking lot. She disliked Dugan more than I did, if that was possible.

We parked in the back. Marion used her card to get in through an electronically controlled door to the agri division. She was wearing a slim pair of black jeans, a sweater, and a scarf. I asked if I could put the scarf over my head just long enough to get through the door. "For the video cameras," I explained.

The halls of the agri division were empty. We had to pass through the central tower of executive offices to get to Doug's lab. We crossed over on the second floor to avoid running into anyone before we were ready: Dugan's office was on the fifth floor, McKinnon's on the fourth.

In the next wing, we took stairs up to the lab on the third floor. I waited in the stairwell while Marion checked out the lab. "Doug Englehart is working by himself. I can't poke around with him there."

"I'll draw him into his office."

She nodded. I unpaused the DAT recorder and went in. Doug gave me a glare, but it was a hard-at-work glare. He had a deadline tomorrow and didn't want to be interrupted.

"Give me just ten minutes," I said. "I have new information about Sheila."

"What is this, social hour?" he growled. But he went with me into his office. I made a point of closing the door.

"We—Karen Harper and I—know how Sheila died," I said.

This brought only a disappointingly small lift of his brows. "You were going to bring the notes."

I ignored the request and went on. "It was a combination of MC124 and a shellfish protein genetically engineered into a tomato. The protein wasn't pure enough to induce anaphylactic shock on its own. But it was enough to stimulate MC124 into triggering a severe immune reaction."

Doug's fingers were spread on his desk. He was startled now, but not stunned. A flash of respect crossed his face before a mask of denial descended.

"Any connection to MC124 is coincidental. Where did this tomato come from?"

"Carl Steiner's garden, by way of LifeScience's agri division."

Doug shook his head. "I knew that guy was trouble. Bothering Sheila the way he did. You know, I think he actually tried to prevent her from going to your party that night."

"Why do you say that?"

"Well, Carl was up here, badgering her about what she was doing, who she was having dinner with."

"He said she didn't return his call."

"That's why he came up. He was agitated, I'm telling you."

"Yet he said it was someone else who requested that he give the tomatoes to Sheila."

Doug tilted his head back. "Who?"

"Who do you think?"

"I'm not a psychic—*who?!*"

"Frederick McKinnon."

"No . . ." Doug bit his thumb. "Frederick wouldn't . . ."

"Tell me what's really going on, Doug. You knew about the problems with MC124, didn't you? Sheila injected it, didn't she?"

He dug a finger into his ear. A whole range of possibilities seemed to run through his mind, until he lashed out: "Who the fuck are you, anyway? I'll talk to the proper authorities about this. If they've got a case against Frederick, well . . . It would be very sad, if he went and did such a thing to protect the program. But you're not part of this. I have nothing more to say to you."

"You've been very helpful already," I replied calmly.

"Get out of here! Now!"

I gathered my jacket around me and made as much noise as I could opening the door to give Marion notice. The lab was empty. I passed by it quickly, but not before I heard Doug yelling after me, "Wait a minute! How'd you get in?!"

I turned the corner and raced back to the stairwell. Marion was gone. I wondered if Doug had seen which way I went. He might be calling security. I descended a flight, hurried through the corridors back to the central tower, and ascended to the fourth floor.

The lanky frame of Frederick McKinnon was bent at his door. I called to him from down the hall. He swung around in alarm.

"Sorry to surprise you, Dr. McKinnon. Can we talk?"

"I was on my way to lunch. What are you doing here?"

"I've got new information about Sheila." I was getting good at sidestepping questions I didn't want to answer. "I'll go to lunch with you."

"No, you won't." He turned the key in the lock, opened his office door, and waited for me to enter. "Make it quick."

We stood on the rug between the two sofas. "We know what killed Sheila," I began, and went on to repeat what I'd just said to Doug.

McKinnon's first question was about the tomato. I told him where it came from. He began to pace in front of the door. "We never should have acquired Tomagen. It was a bad deal. We're losing our focus as a company. It's just ruining—"

He stopped and glared at me. "Wait a minute, what did you say about MC124? It had nothing to do with Sheila's death."

"She injected it. It caused her immune system to overreact. Just like the knockout mouse. We've got the documentation. We've got the pathologist's report."

"No. That can't be." His face showed genuine fear and anguish.

"I'm sorry, Dr. McKinnon." I actually felt bad for him, until I remembered what he might have done.

"This will not prove out," he declared. "Who are you in league with? Dugan?"

I laughed. "No. In fact, I suspect he's the one behind all of this. I was hoping you'd help me find out how. Carl Steiner said you were the one who requested the tomatoes for Sheila."

McKinnon's eyes widened with incredulity. But before he could speak, his phone buzzed. He went to pick it up. His voice became irritated. "Yes, he is . . . No . . . Really, what business is it of yours?" He slammed the receiver down and strode back to the door.

"Neil's trying to set me up," he said. "He must be stopped. We can't allow this to destroy LifeScience. But I'm late for lunch with my wife. Keep this under your hat for another forty-eight hours. Then I'll give you all the assistance you want. But only, *only* if you keep out of sight until then."

He jerked the door open and waited for me to exit. I stepped into the hall and was about to slip in one last question. Then I saw the two security guards moving rapidly down the corridor. McKinnon had already shut his office door behind us. I was cornered.

"Walk me out," I said to the doctor.

One of the guards grabbed my right arm. "There's no need for that," McKinnon said to the guard. "He's with me."

"Orders of Mr. Dugan," the other guard said.

"He's mine, Frederick." The commanding voice echoed down the hallway. It was Neil Dugan, briefcase in hand, striding confidently toward us. Behind him were Pratt and his partner. My time was up.

The other guard took my left arm. "I said to let him go!" McKinnon bellowed. "What is this, Neil? He's my visitor."

Dugan's lips stretched into a grin. He didn't bother to answer the question. He and Pratt inserted themselves between me and McKinnon. Then Dugan turned and walked away. The guards pulled me along behind him.

"Start counting, Frederick," Dugan said over his shoulder, not bothering to look. "Your days here are numbered."

31

As we rode down the elevator to the lobby, I could have sworn I smelled salami. Mustard, vinegar, onions— I looked at Pratt. His mouth opened in a smile of triumph, and I saw specks of the remnant sandwich in his teeth.

As the guards jostled me out of the elevator, one knocked his hand against the camera in my right pocket. He let go of my arm to reach into the pocket. "Mr. Dugan, he's got something—"

I gave the other guard a swift heel stomp on his foot and yanked my arm away. Using this split-second opening, I bolted across the marble floor to the exit in the rear of the atrium. The guards ran after me, but neither was in very good shape. Their lumbering forms blocked Pratt. Dugan was last, with his brief-case. I made it out the door before any of them could lay another hand on me.

"Go that way!" I heard Dugan yell to the guards. "Find his car!"

I vaulted the planter enclosing the patio and sprinted to the rear of the building, again passing between the agri division and the garden. I had a thirty-yard head start on Dugan, Pratt, and the other PI. The guards were headed to the front lot.

A tall wire fence defined the outer perimeter of LifeScience. On the other side lay an industrial culvert. I hit the fence at full speed, scaled it with three quick toeholds, and dropped down the other side. The shallow water was a sick green. I didn't want to think about what chemicals turned it that color. As I splashed through the culvert, Dugan and Pratt reached the fence. Dugan was as athletic as he looked, but Pratt was also surprisingly agile for a man with his figure. I kept moving.

A wood fence ran along the bank on the far side of the culvert. It was too high to climb without hand- or footholds. I ran alongside it, looking for a way through. At last I found a rotten board, turned my back, and gave it a few well-placed heel kicks. The wood splintered. I broke open the hole wide enough to wriggle through. A loose shard gashed my cheek, but the pain didn't register.

I found myself in a derelict yard of twisted rebar, old railroad ties, and random truck trailers. Gasping for breath, I moved as fast as I could across the yard to a locked gate along another wire fence, this one fifteen feet high. I scrambled up the fence, the wire cutting into my fingers. Balancing precariously at the top, I swung my leg over, and then lost my footing on the other side. For a long moment I hung by my fingers, legs pedalling for purchase. Finally I found new toeholds and finished my descent.

Now I was on the street where my jeep was parked. I dug into my jeans for the keys. I fumbled the key into the lock and got the door open as Dugan and Pratt began their assault on the locked gate, then on the fence. The other PI was lagging behind them.

This was going much better than last time, I thought. I wouldn't even have to body slam one of them with my door.

I cranked the engine. It turned, and turned, and turned, but wouldn't start. I pumped the gas twice and cranked again. Again it whinnied, as if on the verge of catching. Then it groaned to a stop. Maybe I'd flooded the engine. I pressed the pedal to the floor and cranked savagely. It gave one more whine, and then expired.

I slammed the palm of my hand against the steering wheel. I'd be having a long talk with the Scout when this was all over.

Dugan and Pratt flanked the car. I jammed down the door locks. Pratt took up a position at my window. Dugan was at the passenger door, banging on the glass.

The first few sprinkles of rain splashed on the windshield. Of course the Scout wouldn't start. It had listened to the weather report and I hadn't. Dugan continued to pound as my view became pocked with drops. I considered just sitting here until the men went away—if they did go away. The third one had arrived and had positioned himself in front of the jeep. He looked watery from behind the windshield. I thought about blowing the horn just to make him jump.

Dugan pounded harder on the window. "Listen to what I have to say," he shouted.

How many people had gone to their doom by accepting such seemingly reasonable requests? But realistically, Dugan was going to get in one way or another. I might as well not have broken glass all over my interior. I reached over and lifted the lock.

Dugan opened the door and slid in. His lips drew back in that canine way he had.

"Now what?" I said.

A chuckling snort escaped through his nose. He placed the briefcase in his lap. The report of the locks opening sounded like shots in the small space.

He opened the lid, and I braced myself. Instead of a weapon, Dugan pulled out a sheet of white paper. He handed it to me. It was a memo.

> To: DE
> From: FM
> Re: MC124
>
> I know you are telling the truth about MC124. I've triple checked the results. What I am telling you is we must keep this completely confidential, at least until after Phase I. And yes, effective the start of the month, you shall have your new program and the rest. Let's hear no more about it until then.

The time and date stamp indicated the memo was written two and a half weeks ago and sent by email.

"Frederick is a scientist, a good one, but he's not a technologist," Dugan said as I read. "He didn't know that just because you delete an email, it's not gone. We've recovered this and a few more. I have to thank you for pointing us in the right direction."

I was still absorbing the memo. "Englehart identified the problems with MC124 first. McKinnon is acknowledging them and telling him to keep it quiet. There's some sort of quid pro quo."

"The program has a fatal flaw, as I have suspected for some time," he announced.

"You left one thing out. You're the instigator of the cover-up."

"Incorrect." Dugan pressed his thin lips together. He plucked the memo away with one hand and with the other dropped a small sheaf of papers in my lap. "Go ahead, read them. I suspected the defect, but didn't have access to the data that would prove it. That was why I pursued Sheila, then you."

"Come on, you don't expect me to believe that." My words were losing their fire, though. The papers, more transcripts of email between McKinnon and Englehart, bore him out.

"I'll be frank with you," Dugan said, reaching for the sheaf. He snapped the memos shut inside the briefcase. "Originally, I suspected none of this. My initial hunch was that Sheila was stealing company IP. I tracked her document flow and hired Pratt to track her movements. I had reason to think she was selling information to BioVerge. An insider deal, perhaps. When I discovered the real subject of her activities, my suspicions took a new direction."

"You ought to pay more attention to your company's science."

Dugan just smiled. He was proud of his detective work and wasn't going to let me spoil it. "That's not my job. This is my job," he said, tapping his briefcase. "When you outlined her conclusions for me, I had cause to look into McKinnon's files."

"You could have faked the memos."

"I could have. But you know I didn't. You've observed enough yourself to know they're authentic. When the investigation is complete, it will show that McKinnon induced Doug Englehart to suppress data adverse to MC124. McKinnon is the mastermind. Englehart did the dirty work of falsifying results."

"I wonder . . ." I stopped. What I wondered was why Doug would do McKinnon any favors, given what I'd witnessed between them. "What was in it for Doug?"

"Mr. Englehart is about to be promoted. Frederick recommended he be put in charge of his own program. We approved the request. Doug had earned it. If he cooperates with us, he'll get to keep it."

"He's also gotten McKinnon to agree to giving him top billing when they publish their paper on MC124," I said.

Dugan's teeth shifted as if he was chewing on some bit of food. A look passed between us. I was willing to bet we had the same thought: Doug had virtually blackmailed McKinnon into giving him his new position. Apparently this did not disqualify him.

"Dr. McKinnon murdered your friend, Bill. He had the motive, the scientific knowledge, the opportunity."

"You really want to get him, don't you?"

Dugan's pinpoint eyes took on a certain shine. "I want to do my job. Think what's at stake for the company. For our reputation. For our investors. Not to mention punishing the guilty."

I slumped into my seat. All the air had gone out of me. Rain streaked the windshield, blurring the world outside. Everything fit and nothing made sense. McKinnon had killed Sheila. A man I'd taken to be a good man was as self-serving as the rest, and in the end more ruthless.

A knock came at the passenger window. It was Pratt, soaked, hugging himself. He pointed to the offending sky.

Dugan held up a finger. "One more thing, Bill. Thanks to you, we can't locate Carl Steiner. Please share with me what he said, if you don't mind."

I did mind, but shared anyway.

"Carl sent the tomatoes to Sheila spontaneously?" Dugan asked.

I let out a deep sigh. "No. Dr. McKinnon asked him to. He said she'd like them."

"Thank you. That seals it, wouldn't you say?" He yanked the door handle. The door popped open.

"You can't leave yet," I said. "I've got a dead car here."

Dugan instructed Pratt to bring his car around to give me a jump. I'd have to do the whole hair dryer routine before that, but there was plenty of time.

Dugan stretched his hand across the passenger seat. "I'm glad we had this chance to talk."

I stared at the hand. "Dugan, this doesn't mean were friends."

He showed me the canines one more time, withdrew the hand, and prepared to slam the door. "I didn't intend it to."

32

"What happened to you?" Karen asked.

I was at the front door of her temporary home in Redwood City, dripping like a soggy mutt wanting in from the rain. She grabbed my hand and pulled me inside. When she touched the gash on my face, her fingers came away red.

"No big deal," I said. I'd completely forgotten about it.

Karen ran to get some hydrogen peroxide. "Take off your shoes. And your jacket," she ordered.

I sat in a chair and let her clean the wound. The sting penetrated deep into my head. It felt good. I wished it would wipe away the taste of Dugan's triumph.

"Now your hands."

The creases in my fingers were sticky with blood. When Karen was done, I trooped off to the shower. The hot water helped, at least with how my body felt. I threw on someone's terrycloth robe and sank into the couch in the living room. Karen sat next to me. I recounted what had happened at LifeScience. We drew closer and closer until my head was on her shoulder.

Karen's voice was somber. "This is not how I thought it would turn out. Frederick McKinnon. Of all people."

I straightened. "The worst part was having to admit to Dugan that was he right. And that he wasn't the murderer himself. But

McKinnon knows the molecule, and he was in a position to know about the tomato. He couldn't bear to fail again. If MC124 flopped, McKinnon was finished."

"He had a lot to lose. And I can see how he'd want to reclaim control of the company from Dugan. But I still can't believe he would hurt Sheila."

"I keep trying to imagine a scenario in which it could be someone else. Doug. Marion. Carl. Or Dugan, in league with McKinnon. Dugan was not the man whose side I wanted to end up on. He and Pratt were not the ones at all."

"Sheila thought she was in heaven when she went to work for Frederick," Karen mused. "Yes, he was single-minded, but he really did inspire people. He cared about the work. He was a true scientist."

"I have to admit, I admired him, too," I said. "I hate the idea of seeing him brought down, leaving Dugan in charge."

"It's the old story all over. A good idea ruined by money."

We were silent. The rain tapped on the roof.

"So where was Marion during all this?"

"Good question." I went to the phone. Marion's voicemail answered. I left a message saying that I was all right, thank you very much, and I hoped she was, too. I called Wes and got his voicemail as well. I wondered if he and Marion were unavailable for the same reason.

"So what do we do now?" Karen wondered.

"It's probably safe for you to go back to your apartment."

She gave a sly smile. "I kind of like our secret hideout."

I returned to the couch. Karen pretended to sway unsteadily, then toppled over into my lap. I stroked her eyebrows. Karen let them grow, which I found sexy after Jenny's plucked commas. I tried to put the comparison out of my mind.

"Case closed," she murmured.

I looked down at her for a sign as to which case she meant. Her eyes remained serenely shut. I decided to take her words literally. "It's closed unless we come up with an improved set of facts before tomorrow. That's when Dugan will take his evidence to the police."

Karen's eyes opened. "Results can be tweaked, but don't make the mistake of trying to force them to the conclusion you want. Accept what the results tell you."

"I'd like to have one more look at Sheila's apartment," I said. "Maybe I can talk Abe Harros into it this afternoon."

"Good idea." Karen sat up slowly, stretched her arms, and yawned. Her hand came to rest on my knee. She searched my eyes. Her mouth resolved into a bittersweet smile. "Accept the results," she repeated, more to herself than to me.

I went into the kitchen and picked up the phone. Having the receiver in my hand reminded me I hadn't called Jenny today. She'd want to know what happened, to know I was safe. My finger hesitated over the keypad. I punched in Abe's number. He, of course, wanted to hear the whole story on the phone. I made a deal: he could hear it inside Sheila's apartment. He told me to be there in half an hour.

In the living room, Karen was holding the large brown leather bag I'd seen Sheila carrying in the parking lot. Karen hefted it with one hand, mutely asking what to do with it.

"Hold on to it a little longer. The police can have it, if they want it. I don't want to give it to Dugan. Right now I'm going to meet Abe."

"I'd come, but I think it's better if I stay here and clean up this place."

"I'll be back soon. I'll help you move back to your apartment."

I opened the door. The rain was coming down steadily now. The Scout started right up—it usually did, once it overcame its initial obstinacy about dampness.

Abe was waiting for me by the back gate to the complex. The lounges around the pool looked wet and forlorn. Raindrops pattered in the blue water.

He said nothing as he led the way to the apartment. We sat at Sheila's dining table. It was still stacked with books and journals.

Abe demanded to know all. I told him, leaving out no details. The further into it I went, the more his features tightened into objection. He didn't believe McKinnon was the one. I said I didn't want to believe it either, but everything pointed toward him.

"I'm a doctor, Bill," Abe declared. "I've worked in Africa and the Balkans. I've seen killers and I've seen healers. Dr. McKinnon is ambitious, like most of us, but he's not a killer."

He was a couple of years younger than me, but his somber eyes had soaked up plenty of illness and death. They were the same almond shape and rich brown color of Sheila's eyes, but showed less openness, more authority. The kind of authority a doctor expected to command. I stared into them for a long moment before saying, "You thought I was."

"I thought you were covering up for your girlfriend. I thought you were sneaky. I thought you were in the way."

"Your father saw what he wanted to see, and you followed suit. You wanted someone to blame—fast. But you never put your theories to the test."

"We tested what Pratt got out of your kitchen. It was clean."

"You could have let me know. We could have worked together on this. Face it, you were late on the scene, Abe. You resented that there were people who knew more about your sister's life here than you did."

"Proximity is not knowledge."

I paused. He wasn't going to budge. "Did you ever wonder why Sheila moved so far away?"

Abe froze, then drew up as if he was going to hit me. I held my ground. His eyes fixed on the gash on my cheek. Then his shoulders collapsed and his hands covered his face for several seconds. I felt like a cad. But when he spoke, his voice had softened.

"I thought we had plenty of time."

I nodded. "I'm sorry, Abe. I shouldn't have said that."

He shook his head, then looked away. "No. I can handle it. I've read the diary. What you said about my father was also true. We were unfair to you."

I let that sit for a minute. "To be honest, I'm hoping this thing isn't settled yet, either. That's why I wanted to meet you here. I want to look for the pages Sheila tore out of her diary. With your permission."

He regarded me, perhaps recalling his accusation that I had taken them. Or maybe he was considering how it would feel to search his sister's apartment. I assumed he'd already gone through her effects and found the obvious things. We'd be searching the nooks and crannies.

He stood. "Let's look."

We started with her shelves, reasoning that she might have folded the pages and inserted them into a book. Abe kept expressing delight at the volumes he found. Novels, poetry, history of science. He was getting to know his sister anew.

As we worked, I said, "If you don't think McKinnon did it, then who did?"

Abe paused. "Last night, I would have said Neil Dugan. But the fact is, Dugan didn't know the science. If he engineered the murder, he succeeded through sheer luck."

"He wouldn't do it in such an elaborate way anyhow. If he wanted to kill Sheila, he'd just have killed her."

Abe let out a bitter laugh. "True. Whoever planned this thought they had everything figured. It has the intricacy of science."

"What about Doug Englehart? His stake in MC124 is almost as big as McKinnon's. And his resentment of McKinnon is strong enough to blackmail him."

Abe nodded. "Possible. Or Marion. I still haven't deciphered her motives."

"Marion becomes more mysterious every day." I was as baffled by her disappearance yesterday as by her recent call to Wes.

Abe and I looked at each other. I saw a new receptivity in his face, and a humility. "Let's not drop this yet, Abe. Let's go down to LifeScience tomorrow morning. Dugan will see us if we ask him to."

"Some big meeting tomorrow, isn't there?"

"McKinnon is supposed to be signing the Curaris deal," I answered. "If, that is, he's not in jail."

33

Neil Dugan's office was in an uproar. By coming at eight in the morning, I had thought we'd beat the crowd. I was wrong. The secretary, who was as orderly and methodical as a Dugan secretary ought to be, showed us in. "The *Mercury News* is on line one," she told him.

"Bastards! Someone at the police leaked." He punched the button and grabbed the receiver. "Who is this? All right, listen. You leave us alone for twenty-four hours, and I'll give you the exclusive tomorrow morning. Got it? Good."

The office was slightly bigger than McKinnon's and had better views. The furnishings were all sharp edges, black metal, mahogany. The desk was so polished I could see cloud reflections moving across it. Few books were on the shelves; instead an elaborate media center was in the back corner of the room, faced by two sofas in tight leather. Dugan himself sat in a high-back leather chair. He was outfitted in double-breasted pinstripes. It was probably the suit he saved for really big days, when he planned to squash someone.

Dugan slammed the phone down. He gave us barely a glance, then started punching furiously at a keyboard on one of the many gadgets on his desk. We retreated to the sofas. For the first time

I noticed the figure pressed into the corner of one sofa, looking small and frightened. It was Carl Steiner. I introduced Abe, and asked Carl if he'd been treated all right. He nodded.

"Quiet!" Dugan shouted at everyone.

The door burst open. I heard the secretary's protesting voice outside. Frederick McKinnon strode in. He went straight to Dugan's desk and slammed it with his palm. "You can't do this, Neil!"

Dugan leaped to his feet. "What are you—"

The two men began a shouting match. McKinnon raised his voice another notch. His face was red. "I demand an explanation!"

"You demand nothing! You can't—"

"You spilled to Curaris!"

"I spilled nothing. You're no longer—"

"Curaris cancelled!"

"Bullshit they cancelled!"

"They called off the deal!"

Dugan stared at him with wide eyes, fists pressed to his desk. Echoes of the shouts still rang in the room. "What do you mean called it off?"

McKinnon turned down the volume. "Someone told them about MC124. Told them everything. They're out. Gone."

"It wasn't me, Frederick. I had every intention of proceeding with the deal—with or without you."

"Oh, stuff your absurd accusations. We've got real problems to handle, not delusions of murder."

Dugan's mouth went into a little pucker. "The police are reviewing the evidence. They will arrive later today."

"This is outrageous, Neil. It's a scheme to unseat me. The board will see right through it." McKinnon's voice had reached a new calmness and resolve. He realized it was going to be a battle to the end with Dugan.

Dugan finally acknowledged my presence with a demand. "Bill, I hope you brought the materials you promised."

"They're safe." Abe and I had failed to turn up anything new in our search of Sheila's apartment. I had my DAT recorder, but everything else was with Karen. "If the police request them, we'll turn them over. But only to the police."

McKinnon slowly turned to me. His look of betrayal made my stomach go queasy. I stood up. "We're not sure who actually—" I started to say.

I was interrupted by the arrival of Doug Englehart. Abe stood up with me. Doug marched straight past us to the desk, across which McKinnon and Dugan faced each other. Carl was still sitting in his corner, staring at the door.

"What's going on?" Doug said. "I heard Curaris—"

"Were you the one?" McKinnon demanded. "You told them about the problems with the antibody?"

"Why in hell would I do that?" Doug looked at McKinnon as if he were an imbecile.

"Come on, Doug." McKinnon's face had gone red again. "You've been trying to undermine me for months now. Are you in on this with Neil?"

"Get off it, Frederick. I found the antibody! It's mine, and you virtually stole it!"

"What happened to your loyalty, Doug? Where would you be without me?"

"Where *you* are!" he cried, his mouth twisted in spite.

Dugan raised his hands. "Enough. Enough! I'm going to find out who's responsible for this breach of confidentiality. In the meantime, the program will continue. Contrary to what either of you might think, we do not want to kill it. We simply want to know whether MC124 is what the two of you say it is. We have information now that it's not. But under the right leadership, the program can be salvaged."

Doug wrinkled his forehead. "What *are* you talking about, Neil?"

"Forget it, Doug," McKinnon said. "They know about Sheila and the problems with MC124."

"I don't care what they know. One little knockout mouse does not destroy a brilliant antibody. Yes, we know now not to use it on people with food allergies. We know to be careful with dosage. So what? Add a caution. Aside from that, Phase I will prove it's safe."

"That's not right," McKinnon said. "We have to ascertain whether it stimulates immune hyperreactivity in other groups. There will be no Phase I, not until we've done more animal tests and we understand better how it works. We may have to rethink the molecule."

"Bullshit!" The veins in Doug's neck were bulging. He directed his words at Dugan. "It's safe, and it will be proven safe in trials. How do I know this? Because I injected it. I put myself on the front line. What kind of reaction did I get?" He jabbed a finger at his neck. "This little rash. Nothing more."

Dugan returned his attention to McKinnon. "So you were lying at the funeral, Frederick, when you told me you were planning to inject it—you and Doug had, in fact, already done so without authorization."

"Sheila did, too," I put in. "She mentions a rash in her diary."

"Oh, stop with that," Doug scoffed.

"Doug, *enough!*" McKinnon commanded. He looked at me, eyes flashing with a mixture of anger and contrition. "It's true that Sheila injected it. The whole team did, to test its safety. We hoped the mouse was an anomaly. I genuinely thought it was. I didn't know that Doug had cooked the data. I didn't know he'd use that fact to blackmail me—"

"That's a ridiculous—"

"Don't waste your breath, Doug," Dugan cut in. "I've got documentation. Your new position is safe. You may, in fact, have more responsibilities than you thought."

McKinnon glared at Dugan. But Abe fixed on McKinnon. "You allowed her to inject it," Abe said in a measured, indicting voice.

"She volunteered," Doug snapped.

"Reluctantly," McKinnon admitted to Abe. "It was a hard decision for her. I could see that. She cared so much about the work. She was afraid not to test it. Afraid of what we would say. I can't really forgive myself."

"That's the least of your problems, doctor," Dugan suggested.

"If you're referring to this murder charge—"

"Who's charged with murder?" Doug demanded.

"Your superior," Dugan said. His look was triumphant. "And I'm more convinced of it than ever, Frederick."

Doug focused a full load of hate and reproach on his mentor. I could take it no longer. I cleared my throat, loudly enough to break through the vicious triangle around Dugan's desk, and said, "You may be wrong about Dr. McKinnon, Mr. Dugan. I'd like to ask Carl a question."

The room fell silent. I prayed that my hunch was right.

"Get on with it," Dugan ordered.

I turned to Carl. He stood as if to take an oath. "Carl, you said that Dr. McKinnon wanted to give the tomatoes to Sheila for the party last week. Think carefully. How did you know he did?"

Carl scratched his head. "Well, he just did."

"But how did you know that, Carl?" I pressed.

Carl's eyes grew wide as the realization dawned on him. "It was Doug who told me so, the day before."

Doug burst on Carl like a pit bull. "That's a lie! You did it, Carl! You were in love with her!"

Carl was on the verge of tears. "Yes, I was. So why ever would I kill her?"

"Carl," I said, "did you come up to Doug's lab before the party and try to make Sheila tell you where she was going that night?"

He cringed. "No. I told you, I respect her. I admire her. I'd never do something like that."

"Doug said you did."

"No, see, I was up in Davis all day Wednesday, at our farm facility. Anyone there will tell you."

"I never said Carl did that," Doug declared. "You're inventing things."

I pulled a DAT cassette from the inside pocket of my jacket. "This was recorded yesterday. It'll be fuzzy, but we'll all recognize your voice."

I started to load it into my player. Neil Dugan grabbed the cassette away from me, muttering something about my rinky-dink machine, and put it into the DAT player in his media center. After a few fast-forwards, I found the segment. The voices were muffled, but as I cranked up the volume, they could be made out.

"*. . . Carl was up here, badgering her about what she was doing, who she was having dinner with,*" came Doug's words.

"*He said she didn't return his call.*" My voice.

"*That's why he came up. He was agitated, I'm telling you.*"

I stopped the tape. Carl looked unbearably hurt. "You're trying to lay it on me, Dr. Englehart?"

Doug's teeth were clenched. "This is crap." He turned on his heel and started for the door. I got there first and blocked his way.

"Have a seat, Doug," Dugan ordered. He went to his desk and picked up the phone.

Doug made a lunge for the door handle. He got it open a few inches before I rammed it shut with my shoulder. He flailed at my face. I hit him in the stomach, and when he doubled over, I grabbed the back of his collar. Forcing his head down, I swung him around and drove him back to the sofa. Abe was with me now. Together we pushed Doug facedown into the leather cushions.

"Stop!" Doug's scream was smothered in the sofa.

Once he stopped resisting, we allowed him to turn over. He lay on his back, shirt twisted, the top two buttons torn off. Abe loomed over him. Seeing just how much Abe would like to hurt him, Doug said, "Take it easy. I'll stay here."

Dugan was on the phone, summoning security. McKinnon came over to look down on Doug. He shook his head, searching for the right words. "A perversion of science," he said.

Then he became aware that Abe's eyes were boring into him. Abe appeared to be calculating something. When he spoke, his voice was slow and even. "How many other mice were there?"

"There were a handful," McKinnon admitted. "Doug destroyed them. I should have caught it. In the back of my mind, I knew Sheila was on to something. I didn't want to believe it." His gaze fell to the floor. "I simply didn't want to believe it. By the time Doug told me he'd falsified the results, it was too late. The financing was in place, the deals were rolling. I assumed we could finesse any problems in clinical trials."

"At whose risk?" Abe said.

McKinnon's eyes rose. But they had nowhere to go—Abe, Dugan, Doug, me. Finally they rested on Carl Steiner. "It was unprofessional. It was unethical. But I still believe MC124 can save lives. I don't know if I'll be the one to move it forward. I suppose the review board will decide that."

Carl looked as though he felt it was his duty to come up with the right words to console McKinnon. I knew it was the last thing Carl wanted to do. A sharp knock at the door saved him.

The security men bustled in. As they pulled Doug to his feet, I said, "I've got one more question, Doug."

He glared at me.

"Sheila's Epi-Pen," I went on. "She wouldn't have let the solution go bad. Did you replace it with spoiled epinephrine?"

His look turned disdainful.

"The injector is sealed," Abe said. "The solution can't be replaced. But it could be heated. Thirty minutes in a toaster oven would do it."

The disdain left Doug's face. Abe had hit the target.

"Hold him downstairs for the police," Dugan instructed the men. "Then seal his office and lab."

I stood near the sofa. A silence hung in the room. For the first time, none of us had anything to say to one another. McKinnon rocked on his feet, hands in his pockets. Abe watched him, appearing to understand that further words of blame were pointless. Carl stared at the speakers through which the tape had been played.

Dugan had turned in his chair and was looking out the window. His moment of victory over McKinnon had been spoiled. Their battle would go on to the next round. Mine was over.

34

The air was fresh and sharp as we ascended into the Berkeley hills. The windows of the Scout were open. Karen was next to me in the passenger seat, and Abe was in the back.

After LifeScience, Abe and I had gone to Karen's apartment. In reviewing the course of events with her, we'd come to the conclusion that Marion had the answers to our remaining questions. The receptionist at LifeScience said she was out of the office, and I got an answering machine at her house. So I tried the next most likely source. It took three attempts to get Wes to answer his cell phone, but finally he picked up.

"Wes," he said, his voice thick and dreamy.

"Get dressed. We're coming over."

"We who? You're doing nothing of the sort, Bill. I'm not home anyway."

"That's all I need to know."

I hung up and we headed for Berkeley. Wes's Jeep was parked in the space next to Marion's Volvo above the bungalow. It took a minute for Marion to answer the door. She was wrapped in a silk robe. Her hair was tangled, and she didn't look happy to see us.

"You missed the fireworks at LifeScience this morning," I said.

Her face brightened. "Come in. Tell me all about them."

The three of us walked into the living room. An open bottle of white wine was sitting on the coffee table. Karen took the rocking chair, and I sat in a straight back chair next to her. Abe sat on one side of the sofa, Marion on the other.

"We found out who killed Sheila," I said to her. "Doug Englehart. But I think you already knew that."

Marion cocked her head. "You're sure Doug's the one?"

"You wanted it to be Neil Dugan, didn't you?"

She avoided the question. Nodding at the bottle of wine, she said, "This calls for a toast."

It was three in the afternoon, but I didn't object. "Have Wes join us," I said.

Marion went to the kitchen. "Wes!" she called into the bedroom. She came back out with five glasses. Wes followed, barefoot, rubbing his head. His sweatshirt was inside out. He curled up next to Marion on the sofa. Abe shifted to the far edge.

Marion filled the glasses and passed them out. She raised hers and said, "Here's to getting your man."

She clinked Wes's glass first. Judging by the heaviness of his lids and the hang of his jaw, the love, or at least lust, hormones were flowing again.

"So it was Doug Englehart," Marion said. "I suppose he was driven enough to do something like this, if his molecule was threatened."

"For a long time I thought it was Dugan, too," I said. With Abe's help, I rehearsed the scene that had taken place in Dugan's office this morning. Marion nodded. She said she wished she'd been there, but she didn't appear shocked by our revelations.

"Do you have the day off?" Karen asked.

"I have a lot of days off," Marion replied. "I quit."

"You're the one who spilled the beans to Curaris, aren't you?" I asked. "Yesterday, while I was being chased down by Dugan."

She smiled benevolently. "Oh now, you can't prove that. But they ought to have known the truth before signing the deal."

Abe folded his hands and peered at Marion. "Was it just Dugan you wanted to discredit, or the entire company?"

She grimaced. "You just put your finger on the problem. They're becoming one and the same."

"That's still not a good enough reason to withhold information that pointed to Doug," I said.

"What information?"

"The missing pages from Sheila's diary."

To Marion's *moi?* gesture, I replied, "You were the last one in Sheila's apartment before the manager shut it down. You figured out where she'd hidden the pages. Where are they?"

Wes's eyes opened a little wider. He stared at Marion. She sighed. Using Wes's leg to boost herself up, she went to the bedroom. She returned with a handful of folded, crumpled pages, which she handed to Abe. "Sorry, Abe. I would have given them to you eventually."

"What do they say?" Karen asked.

"That Doug was forbidding her to continue research on the mouse. That he tried to force her out of the group. That she thought he'd cooked the results. That his resentment of Frederick was turning pathological."

"You're so irresponsible, Marion," Abe said. "Those pages would have saved us a lot of conflict." He turned to me. "But you hadn't read them either, Bill. How, up there in Dugan's office, did you suspect Doug was the one?"

"It started when he told me Carl Steiner had come looking for Sheila. That didn't square with what I'd seen of Steiner.

Doug was the one with the temper. As I thought about it, I realized Doug was in a similar position to McKinnon in terms of knowledge, motive, and opportunity. When Doug ranted about MC124 being his creation, and shifted the blame to Carl, I began to think he was the one."

"It seems so logical now. What amazes me is that he didn't try to cover his tracks better than he did," Karen said.

"You know how some scientists can be," Marion said, trying to recover some credibility. "They grow up being first in their class, first in their school, smarter than anyone for miles. Supremely confident in their own mental powers. Doug saw his scheme as foolproof. He was so sure of his genius, it didn't occur to him anyone could unravel it."

"I know the kind," Karen said. "But don't paint us all with that brush."

"I'm not. McKinnon has an ego this big," she responded, spreading her arms, "but he's sensitive enough to know he can be wrong, too. That's what makes him more of a leader than Doug. There was a reason Doug was never put in charge of his own program."

"And Sheila was another kind of scientist altogether. The truest kind, I think," Karen added.

"I don't understand why she tore those diary pages out," Abe said.

"Because they implicated Doug," Karen answered. "She began to suspect he was out of control. She didn't know how far he would go. What if he found her journal?"

We all took a drink of wine, contemplating how far Doug did go. His inability to control his emotions was clear. Sheila must have seen it, too.

"Marion," I said, "if LifeScience was doing something illegal or unethical, I would have been glad to help you stop it. Why didn't you come forward with these pages and work with me?"

"I was afraid you'd come up with the wrong answer," she replied. There was no indecision in her voice.

"Meaning the right answer."

"Right for you, wrong for me. Our objectives were different. That was why I couldn't trust you."

Wes had edged away from Marion. He was sitting up straight now. "But this was a murder," he said.

A quick series of emotions flashed across her face: indignation, betrayal, and finally resolve. She sat erect and said, "There's a lot more to this than one scientist doing wrong, Wes. I had my sights on bigger issues. What Doug did to one woman was reprehensible, but what Dugan is doing is, in the long run, far worse for far more people."

"McKinnon could have gone down for the crime," I said.

"I wasn't worried about Frederick. He'd have beaten the charge." She took a sip of wine, then realized we were waiting for more. "I would have helped you get Doug *eventually*, Bill. Other priorities came first."

"I don't like Dugan either, but—"

"You saw what he was doing to the company. Undermining its original purpose. Twisting it away from genuinely useful science and toward straight short-term profit. It's bad enough when an old-economy business operates that way, but in a field like this . . . We're appropriating more and more cosmic powers for ourselves. How do you feel about a man like Dugan holding the keys to the code of life in his hand?"

Marion shuddered. Karen did too, and that gave me pause. "I love my work," Karen said. "But it's true, a lot depends on who's in charge of this technology. And what their motives are."

Abe had been quiet, absorbed in thought. "Marion," he said at last, "I'm going to think about what you're saying. I may even find that I agree with some of your ideas. But I'll never agree with your methods."

"You're a doctor, Abe. You save one life at a time. I admire that. I couldn't do it. I couldn't have a life depend on me. What happened to Sheila was terrible, inexcusable, and people should be punished for it. I just have a wider view of which people are responsible."

Abe's hands and eyes remained steady. He did not look at Marion. "Your perceptions may be valid," he said. "Perhaps they would remain so even if it was your own sister's life in question. I hope you never have to find out."

Marion drained her glass and looked away. Wes stared straight ahead, avoiding her eyes.

"LifeScience will be investigated, you can count on that," I said. "When this murder comes out, the company will draw all kinds of attention—but not the kind they were expecting from the Curaris deal."

"And I'll be helping every inch of the way," Marion said.

"You're leaving the bench?" Karen asked.

Marion shook her head vehemently. "No, I'll keep working in the field somewhere. It's up to us, Karen, the ones on the inside. We know what's really going on."

"I don't know that anyone knows what's really going on," Karen said. "Every degree closer we come to the control of nature—to what we tell ourselves is the control of nature—convinces me that we're not in charge. I'm not saying anyone else is. All I can tell you is that the more I know, the more it becomes clear how little I know."

"You know what you choose to know," Marion replied.

"And you see what you choose to see," Karen said. "McKinnon wanted to see MC124 as saving the world and his own career. He couldn't bear the idea that it was flawed, and that made him quite willing to be fooled by Doug. Dugan was trained to see breaches in company security, and that's what he saw when he looked at Sheila. You saw Dugan's guilt, Marion, and you keep on seeing it. I don't mean to single you out—we all do it. I don't know what the solution is, except to look at the results. Just take an honest look at the results."

>> >> >> >> >>

I dropped Karen off at her apartment and we said our good-byes, at least for the time being. I had a feeling I was going to miss her honesty and her clear-eyed readiness.

I thought about what she had said at Marion's house. Earlier in the day, I'd picked up a message from Jenny on my answering machine. Her voice was back to its old chirpy self. She told me not to worry about the mess in her apartment: it gave her a chance to get new curtains and new lamps. She hoped I was safe and that Sheila's murder had been resolved.

Jenny sounded back in charge of her life. I was glad for that, even though things had become difficult between us. I didn't want her to feel bad. But the congeniality of her voice masked something else. She'd taken some kind of decision, and I had a good idea what it was. She'd decided to break off our relationship. It wouldn't surprise me. I wasn't who she thought I was, she'd tell me. And I would agree, without rancor.

The time had come for us to separate what we wanted to see in each other from who we actually were. I wasn't who *I* thought I was just two weeks ago, when I'd been in search of bearings. As awful as Sheila's death and all that came after it had been, they had propelled me into a new state. The compass needle was vibrating. I was getting a reading.

I pointed the Scout west across the valley. The sun was setting and it shot straight into my eyes. The turn to Jenny's apartment came and went on my left. I felt no urge to hit my blinker. The ramp for 280, the freeway to San Francisco, came along soon after. I flipped up the blinker handle, turned right onto the ramp, and headed north.